Travis let
"Sir, I'm going
vo

"You've turned on your own kind! Sellout!" He pulled his arm back, and Mayweather tried to size up whether he had room to dodge the coming swing or would be forced to block it and escalate.

To his surprise, Kivei Tizahr shot out of her seat, caught the man's arm, and twisted it a certain way. The Boomer was half again her size, but he yelled out in pain and fell to his knees, ending up with Tizahr's slim left hand pushing his face into the tabletop while her right kept his arm wrenched back. The smaller drunk stumbled back in panic, fell on his rear, and scrambled away.

"That's enough, Kivei," Mayweather advised as the big drunk continued to moan.

"Oh, he's just being a crybaby. Don't worry, sir, I'm an engineer. I know how to apply just the right amount of force to get the job done." She let the drunk go, then leaned closer to speak loudly into his ear. "Wouldn't you agree?" Nodding meekly, he shuffled away on his knees, then rose to his feet and ran after his friend.

"There," Tizahr said, brushing her hands as she resumed her seat. "Problem solved."

Sangupta was grinning at her with something strongly resembling lust. "Commander," he said to Mayweather, "would I be out of line to say I think that was awesome?"

a bit of steel into his voice.

going to have to ask you to lower your

er and step back."

— STAR TREK —
ENTERPRISE®

RISE OF THE FEDERATION
PATTERNS OF INTERFERENCE

CHRISTOPHER L. BENNETT

Based upon *Star Trek*®
created by Gene Roddenberry
and
Star Trek: Enterprise®
created by Rick Berman & Brannon Braga

POCKET BOOKS

New York   London   Toronto   Sydney   New Delhi

Pocket Books
An Imprint of Simon & Schuster, Inc.
1230 Avenue of the Americas
New York, NY 10020

This book is a work of fiction. Any references to historical events, real people, or real places are used fictitiously. Other names, characters, places, and events are products of the author's imagination, and any resemblance to actual events or places or persons, living or dead, is entirely coincidental.

First Pocket Books paperback edition September 2017

POCKET and colophon are registered trademarks of Simon & Schuster, Inc.

For information about special discounts for bulk purchases, please contact Simon & Schuster Special Sales at 1-866-506-1949 or business@simonandschuster.com.

The Simon & Schuster Speakers Bureau can bring authors to your live event. For more information or to book an event, contact the Simon & Schuster Speakers Bureau at 1-866-248-3049 or visit our website at www.simonspeakers.com.

Manufactured in the United States of America

10 9 8 7 6 5 4 3 2 1

ISBN 978-1-5011-6570-2
ISBN 978-1-5011-6577-1 (ebook)

For the defenders of truth

"It is our highest law that we shall not interfere with other cultures."

—Jean-Luc Picard, 2366

"There can be no justice so long as laws are absolute."

—Jean-Luc Picard, 2364

2165

Prologue

December 9, 2165
San Francisco

THIS TIME, there had been no parades.

Twice before in his life, Malcolm Reed had come home from lengthy deep-space missions to be met with celebrations of the successful work he and his *Enterprise* crewmates had performed in defense of humanity: first at the end of the Xindi mission in 2154, then again six years later after the Battle of Cheron brought victory in the war against the Romulans. Both times, his vessel had been crippled in the final battle and lives had been nobly sacrificed, but Reed and his crewmates had been able to set foot back on Earth with a palpable sense that their ordeal had been worth the cost—for the very fact that there was still an Earth to stand on and a free humanity to share it with meant that their quest had succeeded.

This time, though, when Captain Reed and the crew of the *U.S.S. Pioneer* had returned to Earth alongside Captain T'Pol and the crew of *Endeavour*, there had been no cheering crowds or throngs of reporters to greet them. There had only been questions and recriminations—days of debriefings at Starfleet Headquarters as every action of the task force Reed had led against the rapacious, autonomous technology known as the Ware had been questioned and deconstructed in an attempt to understand how the mission had gone so wrong.

"It isn't as though I wanted a celebration, of course," Reed said now to the ginger-haired woman sitting next to him at the 602 Club's bar. "All I ever wanted was to do my duty to Starfleet." He took a sip of his latest ale, leaving foam on his graying goatee.

The tall, striking woman nodded in understanding, and Reed was still sober enough to remember that she had introduced herself as a Starfleet commander, though he was blanking on the name that had come after the rank. "You just didn't like being reminded that it didn't turn out so well this time," she said.

"The task force did help many people," he insisted. "We saved dozens of worlds from exploitation by the Ware. The Menaik, the Vanotli, the Balduk, more. They can live free now, not at the mercy of mindless machines using their brains for spare parts."

"And now the Ware is gone. It'll never endanger anyone again." The ginger shrugged. "Okay, so it was at Klingon hands, and they weren't gentle about it. And now they've conquered a whole sector that the Ware controlled. But that's hardly your fault. When they came in, you had no choice but to pull out."

Reed shook his head. "No, you don't understand. It was so much more complicated than that. We made mistakes. Well intentioned, to be sure, but we meddled in something we didn't understand and set off the whole chain of events." He wanted to say more, but even through the haze of mild—all right, more than mild—intoxication, he still remembered his duty. He always remembered his duty. There were many details of the incident that should not be discussed in a public place, even the preferred hangout of Starfleet's finest.

To her credit, the woman seemed to get the idea. "I see. That's why Admiral Archer's suddenly pushing for this Vulcan-style noninterference policy. Saying we need to keep our noses out of other people's problems so we don't make them worse."

Reed studied her face—something that he found quite pleasant to do. "You don't sound convinced."

"Not so much. But my captain's never been a fan of Archer's hands-off philosophy. He thinks we have a responsibility to help where we can."

"And what do you think?"

"I think we've helped a lot of worlds that way. But I won't deny there have been a couple of cases where things didn't turn out as well as we'd hoped. Sauria, for example." She glanced skyward. "When my crew helped open diplomatic relations, we had no idea that two-bit dictator Maltuvis would leverage our trade deal into a planetary conquest barely three years later."

"Oh, of course," Reed said, remembering. "You're from *Essex*. Bryce Shumar's ship."

"You were listening, weren't you?"

"Certainly I was, Cath—Caroline." Remembering *Essex* had led him to the memory that the ship's first officer was named Caroline Paris. "Although I don't think you told me what you're doing on Earth. Didn't I hear that your ship was reassigned near the Klingon front?"

Paris grinned. "That's right—Starbase 12. But we got pretty banged up evacuating Ardan IV. The repairs are taking a while, so Admiral Narsu gave us leave for the holiday season."

"Ardan," Reed repeated, shaking his head. "I thought my task force had seen its share of devastation in Ware space, but . . ."

"Yeah. Seeing a whole planet blasted like that . . ." She shuddered. "I still have nightmares. We got the people off in time, but, you know, animals can suffer too. A whole ecosystem, extinct just like that." She was quiet for a moment, then braced herself with a sip of her drink. "Thank God the Klingons backed down, or they might be trying to do that to Earth or Alpha Centauri."

Reed concealed his reaction. He was one of the few who knew that the Klingons had only suspended their invasion plans due to an underhanded backroom deal made by a certain secretive group of ex-Starfleet personnel without official sanction—and without regard for the terrible cost that another civilization would pay for the Federation's safety.

Paris reached out and touched his hand. "I'm sorry— I didn't mean to get you even more depressed. Tell you what, let's talk about something more cheerful."

He smiled. The warmth of her hand against his

was doing wonders for his mood. "All right, let's see. Hmm. Have you seen any good movies lately?"

"As a matter of fact, I'm a huge movie buff. But I haven't been on Earth in a while, so I haven't had a chance to catch up yet."

"Neither have I," Reed replied. "But I've been dying to see *The Singing Swords of S'harien.*"

Paris's grip on his hand tightened appealingly. "That new Bollywood epic about pre-Reformation Vulcan?"

"That's the one."

She laughed. "Ancient Vulcan warriors having huge song and dance numbers. I hear Commissioner Soval absolutely hates it."

"That sounds like a fine recommendation to me."

"Think we can catch a late showing?"

"Let's find out!"

Reed followed Caroline out of the club, their hands still brushing together. He hadn't expected anything like this to happen tonight, or anytime in the foreseeable future. But here it was, and he was happy to make the most of the moment.

December 12, 2165
U.S.S. Pioneer NCC-63

Samuel Kirk entered Valeria Williams's quarters to find her packing a midsized travel case. "Hey," he said in greeting. "Not bringing much, are you?"

"Starfleet brat. I travel light." The wiry armory

officer pulled him into an embrace with the strength that intimidated and excited him so much, and he was lost to her kiss within seconds. "Besides," she said when she let him surface for air, "I thought you'd like us to wear as little as possible while we're on leave."

"I don't object in principle," the blond historian said with a grin, "but it's likely to be a long leave, what with the refit coming up. We can't spend all of it naked."

"We can certainly try," she said, pulling him in for another kiss. She was rather surprised when he interrupted it several moments later with a massive yawn. "Hey!"

"Sorry. Not a commentary on your technique," he said, ruffling the curl of auburn hair that arced across her forehead. "These debriefings are just so tiring. They kept me talking for so long. All the worlds we found out there, how the Ware affected them, what I learned about their histories before and after . . ." He trailed off.

"Not pleasant to be forced to remember, is it?"

"And we haven't even gotten to the Partnership yet. That will be rough."

"I know." Val held him tighter. Sam relaxed into her embrace, amazed at his good fortune. He'd fantasized about being with Val Williams ever since they'd met two and a half years before. She was gorgeous and strong, bold and heroic and devastatingly sexy—and, he'd thought, completely out of his league. It was miracle enough that she'd somehow come to return his affections, and that was every bit as athletic, exciting, and exhausting as he'd dreamed. But it was these quiet moments, when he felt her gentle strength sheltering and nurturing him, that had come to have the most profound meaning for him. For all her raw passion and aggression, all her fighting prowess, it was Val's bottomless well of empathy and kindness that defined her as a security officer and as a person.

For a while, Val simply held him, respecting his fatigue. But then she started to get playful, asking for his help packing her lingerie for the trip. Which then turned into Val modeling various lingerie items for him, which then turned into Sam helping her change into and out of them, and then just out of them, and then it was athletic, exciting, and exhausting for the next hour or so. Finally, they snuggled together on top of a hopelessly rumpled pile of her clothes. "This is not an efficient way to pack," she observed at length, and they laughed for a while.

"So who do you want to visit first?" he asked. "Your folks or mine?"

She hesitated. "Are we up to the meeting-folks stage already?"

Sam stared at her, concerned. "Is there some reason you don't want to introduce me to Captain Williams?"

"Oh! No, it's not . . . Sorry, Sam, that came out wrong. I'm just surprised at how fast this has gone."

"You were the one who said you were tired of waiting for me," he said with a smile. "And I'm very glad you pushed me."

"I know. I am too. I just . . . I'm used to more casual romances. Brief flings, or friendships with benefits." She chuckled. "Most of the men I've dated in the past have been . . . well, their strengths haven't been in the emotional arena. So this is just kind of new to me." That evoked a faint chuckle from Sam, and she stared. "What?"

"I'm just surprised that I'm not the only one who feels overwhelmed by this. Or maybe not surprised . . . more like reassured. It puts us on more of an even footing."

Val snuggled closer. "We're in this together, aren't we?"

"Yeah. For as far as you want it to go."

She gave a nervous laugh, then playfully pushed him off the bed. "In that case, you'd better start helping me pack again."

December 15, 2165
Starfleet Headquarters

". . . in your judgment, Captain T'Pol, had the Partnership of Civilizations truly achieved a functional coexistence with the Ware?"

The question came from Soval, the Federation Commissioner for Diplomatic Affairs—one of several senior officials who flanked Admiral Jonathan Archer at the wide table in the front of the hearing room. Normally this debriefing process would be conducted by Starfleet brass—and by lower-ranking officers, rather than chiefs of staff like Archer and Admiral Thy'lek Shran, who also held a seat at the table. But the ramifications of the Ware debacle had the potential to transform Starfleet and Federation policy, so this review was being conducted at the highest levels. Archer's own superior, Defense Commissioner Vinithnel sh'Mirrin, was also on the panel.

Unfazed by the brass ensemble before her, T'Pol sat calmly in her command-green dress uniform and answered with her usual calm precision. "Our opportunity to observe the Partnership was inadequately brief to make a firm determination on that point, Commissioner. On the surface, it appeared they had a stable symbiosis with the technology, providing volunteers to function as adjunct processors for the Ware and swapping them out after several months to minimize the neurological damage thus sustained. However, in our time among the Partnership, some Partners did question whether they had mastered the Ware or simply appeased its appetites. Once we offered the prospect of an alternative, a means of modifying the Ware so that it would no longer require live brains to sustain its functions, a number of Partners expressed the opinion that this could liberate them from a burden they had endured since the beginning of their civilization."

"And yet we have heard testimony that other Partners considered this a compromise of their civilization's core principles," Soval countered. "That they considered the act of voluntary submission and service to be the essence of their cultural unity. Indeed, none of the member species would likely have been capable of technological civilization or space travel without the assistance of the Ware."

"That is correct. As with any civilization, there was a multiplicity of opinions."

"Yet when the Klingons obtained the Ware self-destruct protocol and unleashed it upon the Partnership, Captain sh'Prenni and the crew of *Vol'Rala* presented their offer to defend the Partnership as atonement for the damage they caused to Etrafso, the Partnership world whose Ware they had deactivated. So in their view, that uninvited intervention had been a mistake—even a crime."

Shran bristled. "I object to that characterization, Soval. We're not here to prosecute *Vol'Rala's* crew. They're no longer here to defend themselves. They gave their lives protecting the people of the Partnership!"

"Nobody denies that, Shran," Archer interceded in calming tones. "But the goal here is to understand what happened so we can prevent another tragedy like this from happening in the future."

The Andorian Guard chief of staff was not mollified. "Which still implies that sh'Prenni and her crew were in the wrong. What if they hadn't intervened? If we'd just left the Ware alone, kept our hands off because we were afraid of making mistakes, it'd still be out there infecting and enslaving whole worlds. Eventually it would've reached us! Sometimes you have to intervene!"

"Admirals," sh'Mirrin said. "Need I remind you that we are here to get Captain T'Pol's account of events?"

Both admirals fell silent under the Andorian *shen's*

chastising gaze. As *Endeavour*'s captain resumed her testimony, Archer felt a renewed surge of regret at the strain that had arisen between himself and Shran in the wake of recent events. Theirs had always been a turbulent relationship—indeed, Shran had captured and tortured Archer when they had first met as starship captains at the P'Jem monastery nearly fifteen years earlier. But over time, as misunderstandings had been overcome and trust had been slowly earned, the two captains had developed a strong mutual respect and eventually a firm friendship—and Shran was extremely loyal to his friends.

But then, that was the root of the problem now. Reshthenar sh'Prenni had been a protégée and close friend of Shran's, and her death along with nearly the entire crew of *Vol'Rala* had hit him hard. Archer believed that she and her crew would have welcomed his proposal for an official Starfleet directive of noninterference. As Soval had just said, it had been sh'Prenni's own judgment that she had acted recklessly in deactivating Etrafso's Ware without the consent of its inhabitants, before she had learned enough to understand their symbiotic relationship with the Ware and their inability to sustain a civilization without it—or, in many cases, even to live without it. In Archer's view, sh'Prenni would have wanted Starfleet to learn from her mistake, and so he saw his proposed directive as a tribute to her memory, a legacy she could leave for future generations. But in Shran's view, it was a betrayal of that same memory, an indictment that would stain her reputation forever. Thus, he had not been inclined to give Archer's proposal a fair hearing. The human admiral hoped that, in time, his Andorian friend would calm down enough to listen to Archer's side. But he knew how long Shran could nurse a grudge.

Jonathan Archer was convinced that a noninterference policy was the right way to go. But to achieve it, he might have to sacrifice one of his closest friendships.

December 18, 2165
Sapporo, Japan

"Why don't we just . . . get married now?"

Hoshi Sato suppressed a wince as she huddled with Takashi Kimura under the narrow awning of a souvenir stall. They'd chosen this unseasonably warm night as their best opportunity to come out to Odori Park to enjoy the White Illumination festival and the annual Munich Christmas Market honoring Sapporo's sister city. Both were traditions that Hokkaido's capital had observed every winter for more than a century and a half, and Kimura had been eager to show them off to his fiancée now that they finally had the opportunity. But their plan had backfired; the warm air had provoked an intense rainstorm that had opened up on their heads while they'd been enjoying the panoply of multicolored holiday lights that festooned block after block of the long, narrow strip of parkland at the center of the city. They hadn't thought to bring umbrellas, they were four blocks away from the Ekimae-dori underground walkway, and Takashi's mobility issues limited his running speed, so they'd huddled under the nearest stall awning to await a break in the storm. But the chilly wind and the minimal awning ensured that they continued to get drenched.

"You know we can't, Takashi," she replied over the rain. "I still have duties aboard *Endeavour*."

"Oh, right. I could come with you there . . . oh. No, because . . . need able bodies. Minds."

The hitch in Kimura's voice that would once have been bitter frustration was now worn down to a mix of weariness and resignation. It had been nearly seven months since the battle with V'Las's insurrectionists on Vulcan had taken his left arm, lung, and kidney and damaged the frontal and parietal lobes of his brain. That had been long enough for Kimura to adjust to his physical and mental impairments and be able to function relatively well, but also long enough for him to realize that his recovery might have gone as far as it ever would. The nerve damage and scarring to his left shoulder made it unlikely that his arm could ever be replaced with a biograft or a fully responsive prosthetic, his fine coordination was shot, and he struggled with problem solving and advance planning, as well as with verbal expression—which was why he hadn't thought to check the weather forecast before dragging her out here. Hoshi knew that Takashi was still the warm, wise, strong, and gentle man she'd fallen in love with, but his career as a Starfleet armory officer had ended that day on Vulcan. Leaving *Endeavour* had given him the freedom to propose to her without any question of conflict with their shipboard duties—but her acceptance had come with the understanding that marriage would have to wait until the time was right. And that kind of longterm planning was one of the hardest things for Takashi to keep in mind anymore. They'd had some version of this conversation more than a dozen times now.

A gust of wind blew the biting rain into their faces, and Takashi moved to shelter her with his burly frame, his lone arm cradling her shoulders. "Sorry," he said. "My fault we're out here in this."

She chuckled. "I was on Denobula during the monsoon season not that long ago. This is nothing."

Her reassurance didn't cheer him. She belatedly realized that it had been a poor example; she'd been on Denobula for the wedding of Doctor Phlox's daughter, and Takashi had needed to decline the doctor's invitation due to his ongoing physical and cognitive therapy. It was a reminder he could have done without. "Shouldn't coddle me," he said. "I'm not fragile. You can get mad."

"But I'm not," she said. "If you actually do something to make me mad, I promise you'll know it." She laid a hand on his chest. "This is fine. It's beautiful out here, even with the rain. And this is a good excuse to hold each other close." She matched action to word, though she didn't kiss him, mindful of the presence of the souvenir seller and the others sheltering from the rain along with them. "Trust me—I'm having a good time."

After a moment, he nodded. "Yes. We should . . . make most of every moment. Until you go out again. And then once you're back." His brow furrowed as he contemplated. Plans came slowly to him now, but there was still a keen mind in there. "There's a hotel with an *onsen*. Just two blocks. Half as far as the . . . walkway. If we brave the rain for two blocks . . . we can warm up. Wait out the storm in comfort. Yes?"

She smiled and nodded. A nice hot soak in a public bath sounded wonderful right now. "Yes."

As they ran for the hotel, Hoshi resisted the urge to race ahead—in part because his larger frame made a good windbreak for her. Still, at his peak, with his longer legs and armory training, Takashi could have left her in the dust. Impaired as he was now, he was only marginally slower than her best running speed in these conditions. And the slower pace gave them more time to admire the gorgeous lights; if anything, the halos they formed in the surrounding rain made them even more beautiful.

Fortunately, the hotel offered a *konyoku* bath, so Hoshi and Takashi were able to bathe together— though not alone, since a number of other tourists visiting the festival had had the same idea. Once she and Takashi had disrobed and cleaned themselves thoroughly in the adjacent washing area, Hoshi noted that the other occupants of the *furo* were trying not to stare at her fiancé as he lowered himself into the hot, mineral-infused water. Of course, staring would have been rude in any case, but the aversion of their gaze was more self-conscious than usual. Modern medical science had made it fairly rare to see an amputee on Earth, and the extensive scarring along the left side of Takashi's body had not yet been fully healed, as his treatments to date had prioritized health and functionality over cosmetic concerns.

Still, Takashi visibly chose not to let it get to him, instead immersing himself both literally and figuratively in the sensory experience of the artificial hot spring. Hoshi sighed loudly as she lowered herself in alongside him, the shock of the heat almost instantly driving any remaining chill from her bones. "Oh, this was a wonderful idea."

They just enjoyed the warmth for a while, but in time, once the pair of Zami Rigelian women sitting nearest them had left, Kimura spoke again. "I know you go out again soon . . . but we could still marry. Just a small ceremony. Quick. Before you go."

She laughed. "It's sweet that you want to, Taka-*kun*. But our parents would never forgive us! Not to mention my little sister. Mitsuki would never speak to me again if I got married while she was off-planet!"

"Mitsuki would never stop speaking. To anyone. For any reason."

"Then I'd never hear the end of her complaining. You know this."

"All right. All right. Idle thought."

She leaned against his right side. "Sweet thought. Always. Don't worry—we'll find the right time."

He didn't say "I hope so." But she heard it in his silence.

2166

1

CAROLINE PARIS craned her neck upward to gaze through the pair of portholes on the curving hull above. "Amazing," she said. "I've never seen a Bussard collector this close when I wasn't in an inspection pod." The reddish-brown cabochon dome at the fore of *Pioneer*'s starboard warp nacelle loomed darkly outside the port, powered down but still impressive to see looming just a few meters above her head.

"It is striking," Malcolm Reed said. "And with the improved cooling and vibration damping Commander Tizahr has promised, it should remain relatively comfortable in here even during warp operations." The room in question was a small common area and observation bay on C deck, overlooking the starboard cargo bay.

"I'm not sure why they even put viewports here," Paris remarked. "There's nothing to see *but* the nacelle cap."

"I admit, the *Intrepid* class is a bit of a kludge," Reed confessed. "It was an offshoot of the NX class, putting its pieces together more compactly for more efficient warp dynamics, in case the warp-five engine didn't perform as hoped."

"Never apologize for your ship, Captain," Paris said. "Compared to the antique I've been serving on for the past five years, this is a regular hot rod."

Reed chuckled. "It occurs to me that much of our conversation would be incomprehensible to people who aren't fans of old movies."

She patted his cheek, leaning in for a conspiratorial whisper. "So much the better. Helps us keep our secrets."

Paris had never expected her dalliance with Malcolm Reed to last more than a few nights. He wasn't her usual type; if anything, his formal, stiff-upper-lip English manner, facial hair, and military bearing reminded her of Captain Shumar, which should have been the opposite of a turn-on. But then, "usual" had gone out the window since her close call on Delta IV last April. It was only recently that she had felt ready to explore that side of herself again, and perhaps she had turned to Malcolm Reed because he seemed safe. Though he was clearly attracted to her, he had his own natural reserve—and some sort of inner hesitancy toward intimacy that reminded Paris of her own. They had not spoken of it, but perhaps their mutual recognition of each other's restraint had let them both feel that they could pursue a casual involvement without feeling pressured to go further.

Yet, as they had spent their time watching movies and playing tennis and talking about their careers,

Paris had discovered that there were other things she and Reed had in common. They both loved classic cinema, though Paris had been unable to get Reed to understand her fondness for ancient, youth-oriented adventure serials like *Flash Gordon* and *Captain Proton*. They had a similar love of antiques, though Paris's fancy was vintage toys and games while Reed's was military hardware and weaponry. They both came from service families with a strong sense of legacy and tradition—though Malcolm had defied his family custom to serve in Starfleet rather than the Royal Navy, while Paris had readily followed the starfaring example of her mother, Argonne, a United Earth Space Probe Agency veteran who had become one of the UE Starfleet's first flag officers upon its founding in the 2130s, and her older brother, James, who had commanded one of the old *Marshall*-class ships in the Earth-Romulan War.

Not that there weren't plenty of differences between them as well. Paris had always been the class clown, the little sister who'd acted out in defiance of her family's pressure to perform—and who had maintained her irreverent manner even after embracing her aptitude for the family business, as a way of announcing that it was something she did to please herself instead of anyone else. Reed's reserved, disciplined style couldn't have been more different, at least on the surface. But as she got to know him better—particularly today, as she saw him interact with the members of *Pioneer*'s crew who were on duty during the refits—she realized that he wasn't as much like Bryce Shumar as she'd initially believed. Shumar could be arrogant, prideful, and judgmental. He was a perfectionist who demanded no less than perfection from those around him. Paris had only earned the license to be informal on the bridge by proving to him that it did nothing to diminish her exemplary performance. But Reed's perfectionism was more self-directed. She got the sense that it came from a deep insecurity, a need to prove his worth to himself and to others. And so he was slow to judge others, as though he did not feel entitled to do so. He ran a looser ship than she expected and gave his crew plenty of rein—as Paris saw when Reed's tour led her to main engineering, their next stop after the nacelle cap.

"No, no, no!" a woman was shouting as they came into the engine room through the heavy forward hatch. "You have to polarize the magnetic field in *parallel* with the crystal impurities to reduce the unspent reactants! Calibrate each chamber individually, like this." The speaker, standing on the raised control platform before the warp reactor, elbowed a fellow engineer aside to enter the settings herself. She was a Jelna Rigelian, craggy-faced and parchment-skinned—an exofemale, if Paris remembered their four-gendered system correctly—but her streaked gray-white hair was cut short and lacked the elaborate beads commonly worn by her people. She wore a red-brown tunic with lieutenant commander's stripes and a *Pioneer* mission patch on the shoulder. Paris was still getting used to seeing those two-piece uniforms on *Pioneer*'s crew. They had been in use fleetwide for several years now, the Class A uniforms meant to stand for the entire Federation fleet—but the member fleets' individual uniforms had not been entirely phased out, and Shumar was one of a number of human captains who preferred his crew to wear the one-piece gray uniforms of the Earth division, as Paris did now. No doubt Reed favored the fleetwide uniform due to the greater species diversity of his crew.

Completing the recalibration, the Rigelian engineer ordered the ensign next to her to run a simulation of core performance. She frowned at the result. "No, didn't I say you need to adjust the injector pressure to compensate? Here, like this!" She clambered down off the platform and headed for the port injector frame, where the crewman tending to the injectors hastily stood aside to make room for her. "There. See?" she asked a few moments later. "Now try it."

"Commander Tizahr," Reed spoke up, drawing the exofemale's attention. "A word, if you please."

"Captain, I'm sure you think you have something important to contribute, but just let me get through with this—"

"*Now*, Commander." Tensing at the steel in his voice, Tizahr relented and came over to them, though her lean body practically trembled with impatience. Paris realized that, despite the impression created by her pale coloring and craggy features, she was unusually young for an officer of her rank.

"Lieutenant Commander Kivei Tizahr," Reed continued, "this is my guest, Commander Caroline Paris, first officer of *Essex*. Caroline, Commander Tizahr is *Pioneer*'s new chief engineer."

Paris extended a hand. "Pleased to meet you."

Tizahr took her hand with a wry smirk. "Which means that either you already know my work, or you know nothing about me personally. Stick around, you'll probably get less pleased by the moment. Now, Captain, is there anything of actual relevance you have to say? I'm trying to squeeze what efficiency I can out of these cobbled-together engines of yours, and explaining my techniques to your crew is only slowing me down. They've gotten slack, working under civilian temporary chiefs for so long."

"My engineers know how to do their jobs, Commander."

"They know how it *used* to be done, and if that were adequate, you wouldn't have called on me. Your Doctor Dax did come up with some effective workarounds for reconciling different species' technologies, but you're novices at that compared to the Rigelians."

"No doubt you do have the edge on technique, Kivei. But these people all have their own abilities and strengths, which you'll never discern if you keep doing all their work for them. Perhaps if you let them show you what they *can* do, it will help you better understand how to utilize them in achieving what you want them to do."

To her credit, Tizahr took only a couple of seconds to say, "You're right, Captain. If I'm to turn this crew into a smoothly functioning machine, I need to know the full specs and tolerances of its components. If I may, sir?"

"Go right ahead."

"All right, people, stop everything you're doing!" Tizahr shouted, clapping her hands over her head. "Time for some emergency drills! Show me what you've got!"

Reed and Paris wisely retreated before the chaos began. "She seems . . . intense," Caroline said once they were back in the corridor.

"She's very driven. She was one of Grennex Aerospace's top warp engineers by the equivalent age of twenty-two. The Rigelian Trade Commission made her a better offer at twenty-eight, so she became a chief engineer for their defense fleet, which means she got folded into Starfleet when Rigel joined. She's the best—but the best aren't always easy to like."

"Still, I'm impressed with how you handled her, Malcolm. Captain Shumar would've probably butted heads with her and loudly reminded her who was in charge, and I would've had to come in later as the good cop and finesse her into cooperating. But you had all the finesse you needed—even though you and Bryce come from similar backgrounds."

"All I know about finesse, I learned under Jonathan Archer. He understood that most Starfleet personnel are more scientists than soldiers. I had trouble understanding that for years, but I like to think I've gotten the hang of it."

"I'd say you have. You mesh well with your crew. And you've probably helped Tizahr mesh with them too."

He lowered his head. "I'm gratified to hear you say that. When I took this command, I was distant from them at first. I relied on Travis—Mister Mayweather—to be my bridge to them. But we've grown close . . . largely through sharing adversity."

Paris hesitated a few moments. "Speaking of growing close, Malcolm . . . when are we going to get to the most important part of the tour?"

"What would that be?"

She moved in closer—much closer. "Your quarters."

Reed flushed, surprised but far from unhappy. "You mean . . . you want to . . ."

"I want to."

"Are you sure?" he asked. "I mean—not that *I* don't want to, of course. But you've kept a certain distance . . ."

"Which has nothing to do with you. I just . . ." She sighed. "Can we discuss this in private? In your quarters?"

At once thrilled and confused, Reed led her there. Once they were alone, Paris paced the small room and gathered her thoughts. "About nine months ago, I led an *Essex* landing party making the first official Federation contact with the planet Delta IV."

Reed's eyes widened. "The Deltans. I've heard the stories about them from Travis—it was his family's ship that made the original contact."

"I know. Small galaxy."

"And I heard that there were some . . . difficulties . . . with *Essex*'s visit. That their sexual proclivities were more potent—more dangerous—than even the spacers' tales. Like the pheromones of Orion females." He gazed at her solicitously. "Did they . . . do something to you?"

"No, nothing like that. The Deltans are a remarkable, open, compassionate people. That's just the problem. The connections they form with their empathic powers are so deep, so profound . . . It's easy for a human to get lost in them. The Deltan man I had sex with . . . what he offered was a casual, friendly gesture among his people, and I was—" She laughed. "Well, I was just being a good diplomat and accepting the natives' hospitality. But . . ." She sobered quickly. "I almost lost my sense of myself as an individual. The other member of my crew who slept with them—with several of them at once—he's still in a catatonic state. He's not expected to recover, *ever*. I got lucky." She needed a moment before she could continue. "But it was a struggle. It's taken me months to get past the yearning for more, the depression, the withdrawal. I've been afraid to attempt normal human sex . . . though I'm not sure if it's because I'm afraid of losing myself again or if I'm afraid I'd just find it inadequate next to the memory of . . . *that*."

Reed cleared his throat. "No pressure, then."

She laughed. "No, it's all right. Because it's not just about the physical. What was so overpowering was the emotional connection. The way it made me feel like being part of another person. Maybe nothing human can match that intensity.

"But it doesn't need to. I feel really close to you, Malcolm. I let you in because you didn't push, because you respected my boundaries and gave us a chance to get to know each other first. So I know that the connection I feel for you isn't just some ghost of what I experienced on Delta. It's grown organically within us. And I think that wherever that leads us is somewhere I'm ready to go."

She pulled his head toward hers—slightly *up* toward hers, for she had three centimeters on him in height—and kissed him deeply. When it finally ended, she took a deep breath of satisfaction. "That said . . . there are some things I picked up on Delta that I'd be happy to teach you." Laughing, she pulled him toward the bed.

January 5, 2166
Oakland, California

"Your move."

"I'm thinking, I'm thinking."

Val Williams tried not to fidget while Sam Kirk studied the chessboard in her father's living room, stroking his chin as he contemplated his options. Normally she was more patient with his deliberations, but Captain Marcus Williams was watching over her shoulder, his burly arms crossed in a way indicating that Sam was not making as good an impression as Val had hoped.

For her own part, Val was playing an aggressive, risky game in the style her father had taught her, deliberately exposing her king to danger in order to lure Kirk into a trap. But he wasn't taking the bait; instead, he was playing it safe, passing up opportunities to capture her pieces and instead positioning his own with a longer strategy in mind. He was now a move away from checking her black king with his white king's pawn—a move she'd almost missed because it was so unassuming. But if she let it happen, she could then move her king into a position that would lure out the white queen. She had moved her queen's bishop to the second rank to position it for that strategy.

That was the situation Sam was now contemplating, and the senior Williams was growing more impatient as the time dragged on. "Maybe you should be using the timer," he suggested.

"It's just a friendly game, Dad," Val reminded him.

"Well, okay. I guess some people need a handicap."

Val glared up at her father, but fortunately, Sam was too immersed in contemplation to notice the dig. Finally, he went ahead with an unexpected maneuver, putting his king's knight one move away from checking her king again, from either of two black squares. As soon as she realized this, she moved a pawn to force him to choose the one that would let her move her king to threaten the knight in return.

"This is ridiculous," her father said while Sam considered his response. "Eight moves in and not one piece has been captured yet."

"But he's had me in check three times, Dad."

"Only because you're giving him too much time to think."

"I'm not as good at thinking on my feet as your daughter, Captain," Sam said to him. "And I don't want to make any mistakes, so if you don't mind . . ."

At another glare from Val, her father subsided. Sam eventually moved a pawn, leaving a clear path for his queen's bishop to protect his knight. "Okay," Val muttered, seeing where things were headed and how bad it looked for her king. She tried to distract his attention using a feint with her queen's knight, but he didn't fall for it. With careful consideration, he began to spring his trap, a series of moves that checked her king and left her only one response leading immediately to another check, three times in a row. Yet each time, he pondered and bided his time before making the obvious move.

Captain Williams could no longer keep his silence. "You're closing in! Don't you know what you want to do?"

"Just making sure, sir. Ah, yes." Moving his knight to e6 not only exposed her king to his other bishop, it put the knight one move away from capturing Val's queen.

But the only move she could make was to counter the check with the one available pawn, which would inevitably be captured to end the game. Instead, Val tipped over her king. "I resign. Well played, Sam!"

"I don't believe it," the captain said. "A whole game without one piece captured!"

"He would've taken my pawn for mate, Dad."

The elder Williams puffed air through his lips. "One measly pawn."

"Don't underestimate them. Sam checked me with a pawn three different times."

Kirk shrugged. "The triumph of the little guy."

"I'll say," Val replied. "You really had my king on the run there. Half my moves were of the king, most of them to get him out of check. I never even got to move my queen."

"I only moved mine once."

"Yeah, but you made her the anchor for the formation you assembled around my king." She shook her head as she examined the board. "Look at that. We only moved seven distinct pieces each. And you mated me in thirteen moves." She smirked. "In case you're wondering, Dad, his mating usually takes a lot longer than that."

Sam blushed, and her father winced. "More than I needed to know, hon."

"It's just a matter of focusing on the long-term goal instead of instant opportunities," Sam said—and then blushed harder. "In, in the game, I mean. The chess game."

Val was laughing now. "Among other things."

Her father cleared his throat. "I understand strategy," he said, trying to get back to a more comfortable topic. Predictably, the former wide receiver followed up with a sports metaphor. "There's no game without a game plan. But you can't always win by playing it safe. I mean, not only did you shy away from sacrificing your own pieces, you didn't even take any of hers!"

"I didn't see the need, sir. My real target was the king. And luckily, I was able to work around the other pieces this time. Taking hers would've cost me mine and reduced my options."

"And leaving her strength completely intact didn't bother you?"

Sam smiled, meeting Val's eyes. "Her strength is what I love about her, sir. And playing the long game until she gave me an opening has worked for me before."

Her father seemed unimpressed. Later, when he went out to the rear patio to heat up the barbecue for dinner, Val managed to get him alone while Sam chopped vegetables in the kitchen. "You don't approve of him, do you?" she asked bluntly.

Captain Williams was just as blunt, as had always been their way with each other. "He's sure not the kind of guy I ever thought I'd see you fall for. So timid and intellectual. No toughness in him."

"Why do I need someone tough? Don't you think I'm tough enough for two?"

Her father's eyes widened. "Of course you are, hon! But if we're talking . . . well, if you think this is serious . . . I'm your dad, Val. I can't help thinking about what my grandkids are gonna be like."

She rolled her eyes. "Oh, for—I'm not trying to pick out a stud horse here. And *if* and when I'm ready to think about that, it's my decision, not yours."

He held up his hands placatingly, though one still held a large pair of tongs. "That's not what I meant. I just don't think he'll be able to keep up with you in the long run, and I think you'll get tired of waiting for him."

"That's what I thought at first. That's why it took me so long to realize what he had to offer. But I was wrong. He's taught me the value of patience and quiet." She gently touched her father's muscular arm. "Which is why I believe he'll win you over too, if you just keep an open mind."

He lowered his head. "I'll try, hon. For you." But his tone was grudging.

Val could tell she would need patience. This was going to be a long game.

January 8, 2166
Smithsonian Orbital Annex,
Enterprise XCV-330 exhibit

"This seems to be my week for giving tours," Malcolm Reed said as he led T'Pol through the enviropod of the first UESPA ship named *Enterprise*. The cylindrical pod was the approximate size and shape of a midsized passenger shuttle, though with a cramped, submarine-like interior. Luckily, this was a private tour after the museum had closed for the evening, a perk of the captains' combined clout, so they did not have to contend with crowds of tourists squeezing their way through the cramped hatches. The pod sat at the front of a long, narrow boom, almost like the kind used in Klingon ship designs—but at the rear of the boom was a single vertical vane connecting it to a pair of wide, flat rings instead of the more familiar cylindrical nacelles. "You've really never been to see this exhibit before? I'd have thought it would be the sort of thing to interest you."

"Not particularly," the Vulcan captain answered. "Humans were not the first protégés of the Vulcans to attempt to emulate the annular warp drives of Vulcan starships. And the Experimental Coleopteric Vehicle program was discontinued twenty years before I came to Earth, in favor of Henry Archer's Warp Five Project. As you are aware," she went on as they entered the navigation and briefing area just aft of the bridge, "the latter was of much greater concern to then-Ambassador Soval when I was assigned to his staff."

"He sure made me plenty aware of it back then," came a new voice from the bridge. One of its acceleration seats rotated to reveal Charles Tucker III smiling back at them. As usual, their secret-agent friend had managed to slip into the vessel without being observed until he wanted to be. Reed had done his share of intelligence work, but he'd never mastered that particular trick. "But we've all come a long way since then, haven't we?"

The other two descended the short flight of steps to the deck of the bridge, which occupied the top half of the foremost section of the enviropod, giving it somewhat more headroom than the three decks of quarters and crew facilities farther back. At the front of the bridge was the upper half of the transparent aluminum dome that formed the nose of the pod, affording a view of the Orbital Annex hangar beyond. A portion of NX-01, the subsequent *Enterprise* on which Reed, T'Pol, and Tucker had once served, was visible beyond, giving Reed a rush of nostalgia.

The warmth with which T'Pol greeted the former engineer was subtle, recognizable to Reed only because of his fifteen years of friendship with them. "It is good to see you safely returned from your recent travels, Trip. We have been understandably concerned for your welfare."

"Oh, don't worry," Tucker assured her. "Phil Collier of Abramson Industries may be one of Starfleet's most wanted right now, but the Section did its usual thorough job of severing any data trails that could tie that identity back to me." He rubbed his clean-shaven chin. "And as you can see, their cosmetic surgeons put my lovable mug back to rights, or as close as it gets these days."

"I'm just surprised you went back to that nose," Reed teased. But it was said with fondness and relief. He and Tucker had been given a rare chance to renew their friendship during the lengthy Ware mission. They had seen each other infrequently over the preceding years since the former engineer of *Enterprise* (the one visible outside, not this abandoned prototype) had faked his death to become an operative of the secretive, extralegal intelligence cabal informally known as Section 31, after the clause in the Starfleet charter whose ambiguous wording about extraordinary measures in times of great crisis was regarded by its leaders as the authorization for its existence. Reed had only himself to blame for that separation, for it had been he who had proposed the idea, seeing it as a way to infiltrate the Romulan Star Empire and undermine their impending war plans. Reed believed that Tucker had done important work during the war, even playing a key role in preventing a Romulan victory.

Yet Tucker had remained dead in the eyes of the galaxy even after the need for that deception had passed, carrying on as an anonymous intelligence operative. Reed had come to fear that Tucker had gotten too deep into the spy game and begun to lose himself in the process.

The discovery of the widespread threat posed by the Ware, a technology that the two men had encountered and bested once before aboard NX-01, had allowed Reed to offer Tucker a chance to become an engineer again, even if it was under an assumed identity as the civilian consultant Philip Collier. It had worked out well, with Tucker's team discovering a means to deactivate the Ware and liberate its captives—and later, on behalf of the Partnership, attempting to develop a bioneural surrogate that would enable the Ware to be used safely without drawing on the brains of imprisoned sophonts. Things had gone wrong when their research had accidentally created a program that triggered the Ware to tear itself apart in an autoimmune reaction—an ideal weapon for its destruction, yet potentially devastating for the Partnership races that depended on it. Tucker and his colleagues had continued their search for a better option . . . but Section 31 had used another infiltrator to leak the destruct protocol to the Klingons as part of a secret deal to head off their invasion of the Federation. The Section had then arranged for "Collier" to be implicated as the source of the leak—both to tie off loose ends and to compel Tucker to abandon that identity and return to the shadows.

But they had not counted on Tucker's conscience. Saving the Federation from Klingon invasion had meant condemning the Partnership to the same fate and wiping a unique civilization from the galaxy. That had been the last straw for Tucker, and his former *Enterprise* crewmates had agreed to assist him in doing something about it. Something decisive—and hopefully survivable.

"In any case," T'Pol told Tucker, "your propensity for secret meetings aboard museum vessels named *Enterprise* is growing predictable. It might be best to choose a different type of venue in the future."

"She's right," Reed said. "If you're serious about bringing Section Thirty-One down from the inside, we'll need rendezvous protocols you haven't used while on assignments from them."

Tucker held his gaze. "Believe me, Malcolm, I've never been more serious. I've already set certain things in motion. I have . . . a very resourceful ally now. I've just gotten back from making arrangements with him.

He's not willing to get his hands dirty directly, since he has good reason to protect his secrets. But he's been around a *long* time and he's learned a lot of tricks. He's given me some leads that have helped fill in some of the bigger picture that Harris has kept me from seeing." Harris, Reed knew, was the name of Tucker's supervisor in the clandestine organization—the same senior officer who had recruited and handled Reed as an intelligence asset early in the latter's Starfleet career. "And he's given me the means, when the time comes, to disappear in a way the Section won't be able to track."

T'Pol frowned. "But your hope is to expose and neutralize the organization."

"Yeah, but we humans can be the vengeful type. I can't be sure they don't have some failsafe set up to retaliate against whoever brings them down. Better safe than sorry."

"That will only become an issue *if* we succeed in bringing them down," Reed said. "I presume that's why you requested I bring my own dossier on Thirty-one."

"That's right. Between what you've pieced together, what I've learned from eleven years on the inside, and what my new silent partner's been able to add, I'm hoping we can finally build a complete enough picture of the Section's structure that we can tie all its players together—and hopefully link them to tangible proof of a crime." Tucker sighed. "There's no shortage of things I could come out and confess to, but that wouldn't implicate anyone else without hard evidence."

"Of course," Reed said. "They've always been careful to compartmentalize that way. That's why we need enough to bring it all down at once."

"Not to mention," T'Pol added, "that if Trip were to reveal himself to the authorities, it would raise many questions about why he falsified his death and what actions he has taken in the interim. This would risk exposing certain facts that could be damaging to many—for instance, facts pertaining to the Romulans' true nature."

"Believe me, I'm well aware of that, T'Pol," Trip said. "That's why I'd prefer to leave that as a last resort. Better to just disappear again—make Harris and his cronies think I'm dead. That way, they won't come after me *or* any of my friends."

"Then we'd better get started," Reed replied.

Tucker led them back into the navigation and briefing area, where he'd attached a more up-to-date interface to its small situation table. "This archaic tech should be harder to tap into or decrypt later," he explained. "Most of the folks who'd know how are retired or dead."

Reed loaded his dossier of collected intelligence on Section 31 into the interface, and the two captains and the engineer began to look it over. "To summarize," Reed said, "I'm fairly certain by now that the 'Section' is essentially one man's rogue operation." He highlighted the name and image of a gray-haired man he and Tucker both knew well, bringing up a sparse informational inset. "Matthew Harris. When I first met him more than twenty years ago, he was a captain in Starfleet Security, assigned as its liaison with

Starfleet Intelligence. SI was a fledgling organization then, and it needed to draw heavily on Security assets for its operations—which is how I became involved." That was a story all three knew well by now. "I eventually became aware that some of the missions Harris assigned me to were not officially sanctioned by either Security or Intelligence. Since his division was operating in an administrative gray area, he'd taken advantage of that ambiguity to turn it into his own black-ops unit, in the belief that it was sometimes necessary to do the wrong things for the right reasons."

"The 'extraordinary measures' supposedly authorized by Article Fourteen, Section Thirty-one of the charter," T'Pol interpreted.

"As a matter of fact, I don't remember Harris ever mentioning that clause at the time. I suppose he saw his formal Starfleet authority as enough of a justification—at least until he ran up against its limits. Harris's superiors began asking too many questions, so he made himself scarce and went freelance. He vanished from the official record in December 2149, and over the next year, several other current or former members of his division began to disappear, retire, or be listed as dead, along with various personnel in SI and the Earth Security Agency. I can't prove their connections to Thirty-one, but these are my top suspects."

Tucker studied the list of personnel Reed had brought up. "I can confirm most of these from my own data." The two men worked to correlate their data sets, with Tucker's information firming up the web of connections between Harris and most of his other suspects—and eliminating a few suspects as red herrings or even victims of the cabal. Several more remained inconclusive, such as Harris's former Starfleet Intelligence liaison, Admiral Parvati Rao. Some of her ex-subordinates were among the suspected founding members, suggesting her possible involvement or support, but proof was elusive. The data trails surrounding her activities had been expertly erased, and she had spent the two years since her retirement in deep, virtually unreachable seclusion on Mars.

"Okay," Tucker said as he looked over the revised timeline. "For most of 2150, Harris is quiet, and just a couple of his top Security people show signs of suspicious activity. He must've spent those months building his infrastructure and gathering resources, paving the way for the rest of his core team and trusted allies to follow once he was ready. The whole thing seems to reach critical mass in October or November. People from his and Rao's inner circles, a couple from ESA, and a few others start dropping off the grid in various ways, and by the end of the year, we're already starting to see signs of Section activity."

T'Pol's eyes roved over the various data insets on the situation table's screen. "Although neither of your data sets appears to contain any specific evidence of that formative process. It will be challenging to make a case against Harris without it—and Harris is the nexus of the case against the entire Section. Unless he can be implicated, none of this can be proven."

"That's our main problem," Trip conceded. "However he covered his tracks, he did it flawlessly."

"In any case, the timeline makes sense," said Reed. "Early in 2151, Harris contacted me and invited me to participate in a 'new project' of his—something that was continuing the 'good work' we'd done together, but with fewer restrictions. He believed that having an asset embedded aboard *Enterprise* would be of use. I said no, of course—though we know how that turned out. And judging from how rapidly the Section came together, he didn't waste time recruiting other assets."

Tucker shook his head and whistled. "So the Section was only, what, a little over four years old when I joined up? Everyone acted like it was older, like it had been around since before the ink dried on the Starfleet Charter."

"The pretense of age is often used to convey a sense of authority and tradition," T'Pol observed.

"My first handler, Phuong, said he'd gone off the grid three years before. He must've been one of the earliest recruits." Tucker smiled slightly. "And he called it 'the bureau.' Sure, officially it has no name, but its members hadn't even settled on a nickname. Makes sense if the group was still young."

"I appreciate the effort to let me off the hook," Reed said. "But as far as I'm concerned, Thirty-one is a direct continuation of the rogue security operation that I was part of for years."

"Nonetheless, this is encouraging," T'Pol said. "If Section Thirty-one is only fifteen years old as an independent entity, its degree of entrenchment and influence must be limited. This makes it a more manageable opponent."

"You may be right," Reed conceded. He worked the display controls to assemble an organizational chart from the combined data. "As I expected, it appears that the core membership of Section Thirty-one is still fairly small even today. There are still a few gaps here, but I'd say there are no more than ten central decision-makers and perhaps two dozen full-time field agents, not counting collaborators and informants. As it would have to be in order to avoid detection, contrary to the clichés of so many spy movies."

"Logical," T'Pol said. "Any successful conspiracy relies on maintaining secrecy, and the probability that its secrecy will be compromised, either by accident, external discovery, or willful betrayal, increases linearly as more conspirators become involved. The larger the conspiracy, the sooner its exposure becomes inevitable. Extending the duration of secrecy would require the conspiracy becoming dormant and the number of individuals aware of the secret diminishing over time as they age and die off. This is, of course, a simplified best-case scenario for the conspirators; the likelihood may vary based on the loyalty and commitment of the conspirators, the efficacy of external investigators, and so forth."

Reed frowned. "It's the 'dying off' part that concerns me. The easiest way to keep conspirators from talking is to arrange for their deaths."

"Except that the act of murder requires another conspiracy that must be kept secret, and thus it can actually increase the likelihood of discovery."

"I wouldn't put assassination past Harris if he thought it was necessary," Tucker said. "After all, he didn't have a problem condemning millions to death on Sauria or in the Partnership if he thought it helped the Federation." They shared a solemn silence. "But I think he'd rather go for staying dormant. He likes to say that Section Thirty-one needs to keep its head down, to be a last resort when all else fails. 'The first rule of not being seen is not to stand up.'"

"And yet," T'Pol replied, "Harris has had you intervene in three major situations that I know of in as many years. First the Vertian affair, then Sauria, then the Ware. As we discussed following the fall of the Partnership, the Section has begun to move beyond taking extralegal action in defense of the Federation to using the defense of the Federation as an excuse to take extralegal action."

"And Harris doesn't see it happening," Tucker added. "I tried to suggest that we were overreaching, and he just rationalized it away. He's convinced he's making the right decisions for the right reasons, and he's too much of a true believer to see otherwise." He lowered his gaze. "Maybe he couldn't live with himself if he had to face the possibility that the mass deaths he's caused weren't absolutely necessary and justified."

"So Harris is the weak spot," Reed said. "We can use his increased recklessness to our advantage. We may not be able to implicate him in the Section's founding, but if we can catch him in a mistake, tie him to action-able proof of a criminal act in the here and now, then we can turn over the rest of our evidence and expose the entire conspiracy."

"The proof is the hard part, though," the lanky agent replied. "The Section has an uncanny ability to manipulate digital information to cover its tracks. I've spent years trying to figure out how they do it, but it still eludes me."

"I am a former science officer," T'Pol pointed out. "I have skills of my own at unearthing information. If you can tie Harris overtly to a criminal or treasonous act, I can help you to ensure that the proof reaches Starfleet and Federation authorities."

"So what we need is a smoking gun," Tucker sum-marized. "All we have to do is figure out how to get Harris to fire it."

January 9, 2166
San Francisco

"There's something I think you should see," Harris said.

Charles Tucker schooled himself to calm. This was his first face-to-face meeting with the spymaster since his decision to turn against the Section. He had years of training in concealing his true plans and emotions—but much of that training had come from the silver-haired, pale-complexioned man before him.

What if Harris could tell that he was hiding something?

But even thinking about that risked giving something away. So he cleared his mind and simply asked, "What's that?"

Harris turned to activate his desk display, and for a moment, Tucker feared he would see surveillance video of his meeting with T'Pol and Reed—or perhaps even of his earlier visit to Centauri VII, where he had solicited assistance and information from the immortal Akharin, whose acquaintance he had made during the Ware affair. The 5,999-year-old man (his six-millennial birthday was sometime this year, by coincidence, though changing calendars had obscured the exact date) had many lifetimes of experience at faking his death and disappearing—a skill that Trip expected to draw upon in the near future—and he had sources of intelligence rivaling the Section's. But what if Tucker had overestimated Akharin's talents, or underestimated the Section's? Some of Harris's abilities to gather information, communicate without a data trail, and alter digital records seemed to border on the supernatural.

But instead, what came on the screen was an interview between Jonathan Archer and Gannet Brooks, the Sol System Information Network journalist. Brooks had been an outspoken critic of Starfleet during the Earth-Romulan War, a saber-rattler who had insisted that Starfleet's defensive strategies were too timid. The journalist was taking a similar tack now as she grilled Archer on his noninterference campaign.

"Just look at how many civilizations Captain Reed's task force liberated from the Ware. Would you really advocate just standing by and doing nothing to help people in such dire need? We have the power to do so much good. We have done good, in defeating the Romulans, in ending the Vertian raids, in combatting organized crime beyond our borders. Should we renounce all that and declare that, from now on, the only beneficiaries of Federation strength will be ourselves?"

The admiral gave a patient smile. "I'm not proposing isolationism, Gannet. Of course we should be a good neighbor, be there to help when we're asked. But good neighbors don't force their help on people who don't want it, or assume they're better qualified to make someone else's decisions for them."

"The victims of the Ware didn't want to be liberated from it because they didn't know it was a threat. We made them aware of that."

"And once they were aware, it should've been up to them to decide what to do about it. That's what the Partnership did. They're being painted as victims of the Ware, but the fact is, they'd achieved a workable symbiosis with it. Maybe they could've helped others do the same, given time and the chance to decide their own fate."

"That chance was taken away from them by the Klingons, not us."

"But the Empire only got involved because the Partnership sold Ware to their enemies—and the Partnership only did that because they thought we were invading them. It all started with a misunderstanding we could've avoided. The risks of intervention without understanding are too great."

"Let's not forget, Admiral, that it was a Starfleet consultant, Philip Collier, who sold the Ware destruct signal to the Empire. While some credit his action with preventing a war between us and *the Klingons, that is still an act of treason. Isn't this campaign for nonintervention just a distraction from where our focus should be? What is Starfleet doing to find Philip Collier and bring him to justice? Or give him a medal, as the case may be?"*

Harris paused the playback and smiled. "Justice or a medal. Which one would you prefer?"

Tucker withheld his anger. Harris knew full well that Tucker, under the Collier alias, had not been the one to provide the destruct protocol to the Klingons. Instead, Harris had suborned Olivia Akomo, a civilian engineer whom Tucker had recruited to the task force, by playing on her concern for her family in the path of the imminent Klingon invasion. Akomo had traded the destruct protocol to the Empire in exchange for peace, and now she had to live with the destruction of the Partnership on her conscience. She had done it, she had explained, so that Tucker would remain sufficiently untainted to continue serving as Section 31's conscience. Despite that, it was largely on her behalf that Tucker had decided that the only action his conscience would allow was the destruction of Section 31.

Which meant that this meeting was edging close to dangerous terrain after all. "Is there a reason you wanted me to see this?" he asked.

"Just curious to hear your thoughts on this nonintervention push of the admiral's."

Tucker took his time answering. "I understand where he's coming from. Back on *Enterprise*, T'Pol always advised against interfering in other cultures. We saw examples of the harm we could do if we weren't careful. Not every world is ready for contact."

"The admiral's position seems to be that *we* aren't ready to decide whom we should contact or intervene with."

"That seems fair. He doesn't want us to get arrogant—to assume our technology makes us smarter or better than other species."

The older, black-suited human peered at him. "I seem to recall you *wanting* us to get more involved on Sauria a while back."

"Only to mitigate the damage we did by getting involved in the first place." He studied Harris. "Look, if you're suggesting I should try to talk Archer out of it, or—"

The spymaster held up his hands in a mollifying gesture. "Not to worry, Mister Tucker. As a matter of fact, I think an official Starfleet policy of nonintervention would be an excellent idea."

Tucker blinked. "You do? I mean . . . isn't intervening basically our whole deal?"

Harris chuckled. "But we keep our interventions unseen. Meddling openly creates enemies. It invites retaliation. The more foreign affairs the Federation gets itself involved in, the more security risks it creates. So if Archer can convince the public and his superiors that we should stay out of matters where we aren't invited, I say more power to him." He went on with a sly smile. "It just gives us cover for whatever clandestine interventions do become necessary."

"So . . . you actually want to help Archer succeed."

"Let's not get ahead of ourselves. We don't know yet if our involvement will be required. Archer can be a persuasive fellow."

"That he can," Tucker agreed.

Still, Harris's words had gotten him wondering. In order to entrap the spymaster into exposing himself, Tucker needed to know what Harris wanted. Traps needed bait, after all. If Harris wanted the non-intervention policy to succeed, was there a way to use that?

And if there was . . . could Tucker pull it off without jeopardizing Archer's agenda—or Archer himself?

2

"You look like you had a rewarding day," Danica Erickson said after welcoming Jonathan Archer back aboard his houseboat with a hug and kiss.

"I did," he replied as he moved into the living area. But he spotted Porthos lying on the couch and headed over to greet him. Once, the little beagle would have been there to meet him at the door every evening, but Porthos rarely had the energy for that anymore, so now it was the mountain's turn to come to Muhammad. Archer greeted the dog warmly, cradling his head and skritching his ears, before settling down on the couch to pet him.

After allowing Archer and his old friend a few moments for each other, Dani took the chair opposite and asked, "Did you finally make some progress on the noninterference front?"

He shook his head. "Still working on that, I'm afraid. Shran won't budge, and he's got Flar and Zenohr firmly on his side," he went on, naming the Tellarite and Rigelian members of Starfleet's joint chiefs of staff. "They both see too many benefits from trade with new civilizations to be comfortable with restrictions on first contacts. So far I've only got T'Viri solidly in my corner, though Osman's wavering."

"I thought Alexis understood your arguments."

"She does, but the public back on Alpha Centauri? Not so much. Or here on Earth, for that matter. It's hard getting the complexities of the Partnership situation across to them. They see the Ware as a threat, plain and simple. The idea that the Partnership could've been better off with it than without it, and that we should've been more careful to understand that before we took action, is a hard nuance to get across."

"Especially without making it sound like you're insulting the memory of *Vol'Rala*'s crew."

"Exactly. I know this is for the best, but it's hard to find a way to articulate *why* in a way the public will understand."

"Then why do you look like you won a victory?"

"Because President al-Rashid and the Council have finally agreed to issue a resolution condemning Maltuvis's sentient-rights violations on Sauria. Soval's been given the go-ahead to bring all our diplomatic pressure to bear on Maltuvis to comply with interstellar ethical standards or risk facing sanctions."

The bright smile on Dani's dark bronze face was as beautiful as ever. "That's a welcome surprise! What about the trade deal? The risk of losing Sauria's dilithium and rare earths?"

"With the threat of war with the Klingons subsided,

we don't have as much need for those minerals." He sighed. "Plus, admittedly, with new worlds not so eager to join us lately, it doesn't look like we'll need as many resources for growth. Not great news, but at least it reduces Maltuvis's economic leverage over us."

In the wake of the Partnership debacle and the resultant hit to the Federation's reputation, a number of worlds that had been in negotiations for membership had quietly or not-so-quietly backed down over the past few weeks. The Tesnians, who had lost an entire colony to the Vertians several years ago, had been close to forgiving the Federation for negotiating peace with that mysterious culture, but now their mistrust of Federation motives had returned with a vengeance. The Xyrillians, whose exotic environmental needs and traditional isolationism had been a challenge for Commissioner Soval's diplomatic teams, had now not only retreated from their tentative flirtation with membership, but had become formal signatories of the Vissians' embargo on technology transfers to less advanced civilizations such as the Federation. Perhaps the biggest loss had been the Lorillians. They had been considered a cinch for membership due to their close relationship with the Rigelian trading community, but the fall of the Partnership had come just before a planetary election on Lorillia, bringing about the narrow victory of a xenophobic nationalist party whose opposition to Federation membership had been the heart of their campaign. At least the Ithenites had joined back in October, bringing the number of Federation member states just barely into double digits before the slowdown, for what little that was worth as a milestone.

But Dani's thoughts remained focused on Maltuvis. "And what about the risk of him breaking the trade deal and selling his minerals to the Klingons or Romulans instead?"

"I'll tell you what I told the president. It was Chancellor Khorkal's rivals who were behind the push for war on the Federation, so it's in his best political interests to leave us alone—to focus on dealing with the aftermath of their civil war and solidifying their grip on Ware space." He kept quiet about the fact that Section 31 had provided the Ware destruct protocol to Khorkal's faction, thus enabling his conquest of Ware space and his rise to the chancellorship and giving Khorkal a reason to feel indebted to the Federation. Not only were those matters of the utmost secrecy, but Archer doubted he could speak of them without losing his temper. Instead, he simply said, "As long as we leave the Klingons alone, we can expect them to leave us alone. And there hasn't been a peep out of the Romulans since the treaty. That still leaves the Orion Syndicate, but we're all but certain they're already secretly in cahoots with Maltuvis."

Dani smirked. "Cahoots. Why do only bad guys ever get to be in cahoots? I mean, it sounds like fun, doesn't it?"

Archer furrowed his brow. "Sounds kinda noisy."

"Anyway . . . I'm more worried about who else might be out there. It's a big galaxy and there's a lot of it we don't know yet, even close to home. Who else might Maltuvis want to deal with if he breaks ties with us?"

Porthos managed to gather the strength to roll over slightly and lean against Archer's thigh, bringing a wistful smile to the admiral's face. "Well, at least the Federation will no longer be helping to bankroll a dictator's conquest of his planet," he said as he scratched the beagle's neck. "Maybe it's too little, too late, but we're finally washing our hands of a bad deal. And maybe, just maybe, it'll weaken Maltuvis's position and reduce the damage he can do to his people."

January 24, 2166
Imperial Palace Grounds, M'Tezir, Sauria
(Psi Serpentis IV)

"This latest insult by the Federation is the final affront! For years, they have drunk in the generosity of Maltuvis, depending on the endless riches of our M'Tezir lands for their very survival as an interstellar state. Now they believe the strength they have gained through my indulgence entitles them to meddle in N'Ragolar's affairs! To demand that the mighty Maltuvian Empire hobble itself with their weak offworlder values or lose the *privilege* of their custom! Well, I say they are the ones who shall lose! From this day forth, they will not receive a single gram of this planet's mineral wealth. Let them starve on their own ingratitude. So says Maltuvis!"

Emperor Maltuvis basked in the roar of sound as the crowd before him chanted his name with religious fervor. He always made sure his speeches and rallies were well attended. Over the years of his rule—first in his native M'Tezir, and now across the rest of N'Ragolar—his enforcers had aggressively cultivated the crowds, weeding out any voices of protest and beating them, arresting them, or killing them outright, depending on the severity of their protest, the mood of the crowd, the level of media scrutiny, and the whims of the enforcers. So all who now remained in his audience were true, fervent loyalists—or at least had been well trained to give proper obeisance lest they suffer the fate of those who failed to do so. Maltuvis reveled in praise, *deserved* praise, and he would not tolerate any dissenters who would sour the experience for him and his loving followers.

He spoke again, and the roaring crowd swiftly fell silent, keen to hear his every word, as they rightly should be. "Indeed, my subjects, we of M'Tezir have always known of the pernicious threat these outsiders posed. Only my forebears in the Basilic lineage, and the strong M'Tezir people whom they led, stood against the enfeebling values of the Lyaksti Empire and the other founders of the so-called Global League. Because we have always suspected what I am now able to prove to you: that the Lyaksti have been the puppets of offworld influence for centuries!" The crowd gasped, and after a moment, many began chanting anti-alien slogans. Maltuvis gave them rein for a few moments, then spoke once again. "Yes—now that the last pockets of Lyaksti resistance have fallen, my investigators have uncovered damning proof that their leaders have long been complicit in an alien plot to weaken N'Ragolar and slowly, insidiously take it over from within. We are still sifting through a large trove of evidence, so it would be premature to release it now. But rest assured, when the time is right, you will see this proof."

Of course, there was no proof. The first offworlders, a crew of human traders, had made a brief visit to N'Ragolar only a few years before. The confirmation that life existed beyond this world had inspired the Lyaksti and most of the other nations of the planet—already infected by their weakling ideology of inclusive democracy—to formalize their alliances under the Global League and work together to develop spaceflight. They had barely managed to loft a single station into orbit by the time the humans had returned, now representing a league of their own called the Federation. But Maltuvis, then going by the hereditary title of Basileus, had recognized the threat this posed to M'Tezir's sovereignty and mobilized his nation to join in the space race. The efficiency of his industrial spies and forced labor had allowed him to place his own station in orbit in time to meet the Federation ship, proving that not all of N'Ragolar's people ("Saurians," as the humans ridiculously called them) were united under the League's weakling values.

Like all offworlders, the Federation had soon proven weak themselves, not only in stamina and senses but in resources and character. Once they had learned of M'Tezir's vast wealth in the minerals they craved for their space fleets, Maltuvis had them where he wanted them. He had used the wealth and leverage of the trade deal to undermine the Global League and expand his empire, spreading a plague in areas frequented by offworlders and offering a cure, then requiring infected nations to renounce League membership, expel the offworlders he blamed for the disease, and allow his armies in to deal with the medical emergency. Once his forces had been in place, of course, they had never left. And in time, he had gained enough territory and sufficiently weakened the enemy that he could strike openly and conquer the rest of the world. And the Federation had been able to do nothing, for they depended too much on the resources Maltuvis controlled.

Yet the facts were as irrelevant now as they had been during the plague. All he had to do was dangle the promise of proof to be revealed later, then distract the public with some other shiny object until they forgot. Any journalists who attempted to dig deeper and hold him to his promised disclosure could simply be charged as partisans working on behalf of the aliens to undermine his rule, giving him an excuse to have them executed, as he had already done with many of their kind. By now, the entire profession of journalism had been so discredited in the people's eyes that there had been little protest when he had abolished freedom of the press and made criticism or investigation of his regime a capital crime—and without the press, there was no one to expose his further abolitions of the people's freedoms. The public knew only what he wanted them to know.

"But do not worry, my people," Maltuvis assured his audience now. "For M'Tezir ingenuity protects the whole of N'Ragolar now. Over the last few months, our mighty fleet of orbital ships has ferreted out the last pockets of insurrection. Now the treason of the Lyaksti race is a memory. All their kind are registered and closely tracked, and any acts of disloyalty are swiftly punished. Offworlders are being deported at an ever-increasing pace, and soon our great world will be free of their contamination once again. But even then, the mighty ships of the Maltuvian Armada will remain, patrolling the heavens above N'Ragolar, forming an impenetrable wall against all aliens, against their disease and their pernicious ideas. I have made N'Ragolar strong again! I have united us and restored the martial greatness of our past! None of this would have been possible without my vision, my courage, my refusal to bow to my inferiors as so many 'Saurians' have done! And as long as you all stand behind me, you have the promise of Maltuvis that I will make our world even stronger, even richer! All remaining weakness will be purged! All threats to our greatness will be ferreted out and destroyed! N'Ragolar will be pure!

N'Ragolar will be united! N'Ragolar will be mighty! You have the promise of Maltuvis!"

Of course the only suitable climax was his name. It echoed through the crowd, and they echoed it back to him exponentially, chanting *"MALTUVIS! MALTUVIS! MALTUVIS!"* with the ecstatic fervor and blind love that the name naturally deserved. Maltuvis knew that this was just the beginning—that his name was destined to echo through history for all time to come.

Maltuvis rode the high of the crowd's adulation back to his private chambers within the palace, where he would have several young females delivered to him in a short while; it was only thanks to the energy these rallies gave him that he was able to perform reliably in the intimate arena. But first, he had to contend with the individual who oversaw the procurement of those females, as well as providing other services. "Excellent speech," Harrad-Sar said once he emerged from his concealed chambers abutting Maltuvis's own. The shaven-headed mammalian crossed his muscular green arms over his leather-attired chest. "I'm trying not to take the lines about alien weakness personally."

"You know I value your contribution to my conquests, Orion. The minerals I provide to your Syndicate should prove that. Indeed, you shall receive more than ever now that I have cut off the Federation." In truth, Maltuvis hated relying on offworlders for anything—especially ones that looked like green-skinned humans. Harrad-Sar's over-muscled body and the numerous metal adornments that pierced the skin of his face and scalp were absurd to look at—desperate attempts of a naturally weaker species to appear powerful and unafraid of pain. But the one benefit of offworlders' inherent weakness was that it had driven them to develop more advanced technologies to compensate, and Maltuvis had possessed the vision to recognize what those technologies could achieve if wielded by a truly strong hand such as his own. Thus, the Orion Syndicate was useful to him, and he had no more trouble telling their representative whatever lies were necessary to control him than he had doing the same with the people of N'Ragolar.

"My mistresses appreciate your generosity as always, great Maltuvis," Harrad-Sar boomed. "Yet they are concerned that the Federation will not simply roll over and accept the change. They are do-gooders, concerned for the so-called 'freedom' and 'rights' of your subjects. They may attempt to foment resistance."

"They lack the strength. Even now, their *great* Admiral Archer urges them to retreat into passivity rather than interfere in other worlds."

"But there are others who argue for more aggressive intervention. Who feel the Federation is responsible for your rise to power and thus has a duty to intervene."

Maltuvis scoffed. "Let them try! My fleet is strong and growing. My armaments are unsurpassed."

"Thanks to the technology and weapons that *we* supplied to you," Harrad-Sar reminded him.

"As far as the world and the galaxy know, those

ships are the sole creation of M'Tezir ingenuity. That is the truth that serves us, so let it be the only truth."

The Orion sighed. "Very well. *Your* fleet and armaments are unsurpassed. But the Federation does not recognize the advancement of *your* technology. They need a demonstration."

"Let them come, and I will give it to them. Their bodies will rain from the sky."

"Why wait? Why not demonstrate your power so decisively that they will not dare to come at all?"

"What do you have in mind?"

"There are still pockets of active resistance in Lyaksti and other recently conquered states. Your assertions that all such resistance has been wiped out are not yet entirely true. But with the ships you now have in orbit, you can make them true. A forceful demonstration of the power you command should make it clear to every state on N'Ragolar that any who allow resistance to thrive in their midst will be punished for it."

Maltuvis felt a thrill at the thought, on a par with the thrill he felt when he held a chanting crowd in the palm of his hand. "I have wanted to see the full power of my fleet's weapons unleashed upon my enemies," he said. "To vaporize a hundred lives, or a thousand, with the press of a single control—to make so many die in an instant, with no hope of survival or escape—to have such power is intoxicating. And it is the least that those who stand against me deserve. But against my own subjects? Might that not create anger and further resistance? Might that not goad the Federation to intervene?"

"Ah, but you have not seen the sheer power of the ships, nor have they. You know the Federation is weak and cowardly. They can bully worlds that they consider weaker, but they back down against a real threat, as they just did with the Klingons. When they see the full magnitude of your strength, your relentlessness, it will send them the message they need to hear."

The Orion was as much a fool as any offworlder, but he did hit upon good ideas sometimes—no doubt inspired by his proximity to Maltuvis's greatness. His proposal would surely have occurred to Maltuvis himself soon enough. Yes, now that he thought about it, he had no doubt already conceived of it, had telegraphed it in his words and actions, and Harrad-Sar had simply picked up on those signals and put the idea into words. Maltuvis's brilliance was so great that he sometimes needed it reflected back from others to see it clearly.

Maltuvis was so captivated by Harrad-Sar's idea— by *his own* idea—that he sent away the females when they arrived. The power he could wield over his harem slaves was satisfying, but it paled next to the exercise of power he now began to plan.

January 25, 2166
Orion homeworld (Pi-3 Orionis III)

Navaar entered the main chamber of the Three Sisters' estate to find D'Nesh and Maras lounging on adjacent couches to view an entertainment. On the cushioned floor before them, about a dozen nude male Orion slaves were entangled in an orgy with one another—mostly burly green males, plus a few from the more gracile blue-skinned minority, the kind who were useful for infiltrating the Andorians since one only needed to stick a wig and antennae on them. All the males were committed to their performance, compelled to obedience by the Sisters' potent pheromones—and yet at the same time, those pheromones were heightening their aggression and mental instability, with the slaves' tempers visibly growing frayed even as they cavorted together. It was only a matter of time before one of them erupted into violence against the others, and then . . . well, Navaar would probably need to buy a few replacement slaves tomorrow. But that was what slaves were for, after all. Navaar could hardly disapprove; her two junior sisters may not have gotten along with each other in most respects, but they did share excellent taste in recreational activities.

Predictably, Maras was watching the orgy so raptly that she barely noticed her sister's return. The youngest Sister had a libido that dwarfed that of her elders, and she would have been a serious threat to their dominance had she not been so charmingly dimwitted as well. Her only ambitions, mercifully, involved the gratification of her whims of the moment. But D'Nesh noted Navaar's entry and rose to greet her, moving away from the noise and aroma of the orgy. A short, diaphanous robe fluttered against her otherwise bare flesh as she approached. "Did you get the report from Harrad-Sar?"

Navaar grinned in satisfaction, twirling a lock of her long, curly black hair around her index finger. "Yes, and it's just what I'd hoped. Narcissists like Maltuvis are so easy to manipulate. A little flattery, a show of obeisance, and they'll do whatever you want and pretend it was their idea."

"I don't need a lesson in seduction, Navaar," D'Nesh replied crossly. "Tell me specifics."

Navaar resisted chiding her sister for her thin skin; she knew that would just get them sidetracked into a fruitless argument. "Maltuvis will use the orbital ships to strike a civilian population. Reprisals for harboring traitors, or some such pretense."

D'Nesh's eyes widened, and she grinned a little. "That should kill thousands!"

"Ohhh, at least. We'll have to make sure to get it recorded for Maras's benefit. You know how she loves her pretty explosions, especially when there are bodies in them."

D'Nesh sobered in the wake of her initial sadistic thrill. "But I don't get it. As fun as it will be to see those bug-eyed lizards fry, won't that just inflame the Federation? They already feel responsible for helping to fund Maltuvis's rise to power. The greater the atrocities he commits, the more the Federation's do-gooders will push to intervene, even to overthrow him."

"Exactly," Navaar replied, her grin widening.

"Are you insane? We don't want the Federation to

be *more* interventionist! I thought you agreed, we need to support Archer's push for nonintervention."

"Of course. But not just nonintervention—we need to push them all the way into isolationism. We may not have succeeded in tearing them apart, but that won't matter if we persuade them to retreat within themselves. Either way, it will free us to act unencumbered."

"Yes, but you're doing the opposite!"

"Am I?" She twirled her hair again. Things were getting louder; Maras, having grown impatient waiting for violence to break out, had leaped naked into the fray to overload the men with her pheromones, and now they were starting to roar, swing, and bite at one another. Eager to watch the bloodshed, Navaar moved forward, beginning to shed her own minimal garments. "Have patience, sister," she said before it became too noisy to speak. "This is only step one of my plan. After all—it's not just Maltuvis whose actions we can manipulate."

3

January 28, 2166
Lyaksti, Sauria

ANTONIO RUIZ HAD KNOWN from the moment he decided to stay on Sauria that things would get ugly. He had grown up on Earth in an era when oppression and revolution had been a thing of the past, but he had studied his history, and the history of his native Cuba and its Norteamericano neighbors was not lacking in illustrations of the atrocities that could be perpetrated by dictators—both the ones rebelled against and the ones installed by rebellion. When Maltuvis had solidified martial law in the nations he'd occupied during the "alien" plague he himself had spread, when the Saurian Global League and the Federation had been too paralyzed by political cowardice and economic self-interest to expose his crimes and take a stand against his rise, Ruiz had seen what was coming and resolved to stay and fight it, no matter the risk. He knew that it would be dangerous for him, as an off-worlder on a planet whose populace had been increasingly fired up with xenophobic paranoia by Maltuvis's deft propaganda. He had anticipated how things would progress when the Global League had refused to condemn that xenophobia for fear of losing the support of the electorate. He had known that aliens would first be ostracized, then required to submit to registration and tracking, then forcibly expelled, then even worse. And once the people had become inured to hate against aliens, it would open the door for Maltuvis's hate of Saurians not belonging to the M'Tezir race and culture, and they would be the ones getting registered, tracked, and worse. And they would not act to head it off until it was too late for them, because they had not thought it would matter to them when it was just the aliens who were affected.

But that was exactly why Ruiz had to remain, to try to get the message out. He may have been just a mining engineer before all this, but he had come to care about the Saurians as if they were his own people, and he had felt an obligation to help them in any way he could. He had been shown the way by another human, a man who called himself Albert Sims—though Ruiz was convinced that had been a cover identity for a Federation agent, an operative for some group so hush-hush that he couldn't even name it. Sims, or whoever, had worked with Ruiz to infiltrate M'Tezir facilities, retrieve the plague cure for mass distribution, and obtain the proof of Maltuvis's culpability for the plague and the oppression his forces imposed in the lands they had occupied. But when Maltuvis had gotten ahead of the publicity, releasing the cure himself and calling it a M'Tezir innovation, the Saurian people's fear had made them gullible, and they had praised Maltuvis as their savior, making the Global League and the remaining free journalistic outlets on Sauria too afraid to denounce him. After that, Sims's superiors had pulled him out and washed their hands of the whole affair, and Sims—a man Ruiz had thought he admired—had lacked the courage to defy them. He'd even come this close to threatening Ruiz with consequences if he stayed to fight Maltuvis, since the Federation relied on M'Tezir for much of their mineral reserves.

But Ruiz still loved Sauria, so he had chosen to follow the example of the man he had wanted Sims to be rather than the man he had truly been. Ruiz had stayed in Lyaksti, cultivating allies who had helped him stay ahead of the registries and the roundups and the purges. He had made clandestine sorties into occupied territories to gather evidence of Maltuvis's atrocities and broadcast it to Sauria and to the galaxy beyond—though Maltuvis had conditioned the masses to mistrust any news that came from offworld sources, or indeed from any source but his own propaganda engines. Ruiz had worked with those seeking to expose how Maltuvis had manipulated elections in several key Global League nations by undermining progressive candidates with trumped-up scandals and making sure his own puppets were put in power—but their efforts to expose the truth had been insufficient to overcome the voters' loss of faith in the League and their deep-rooted mistrust of aliens. Saurians were a robust, adaptable people who could withstand the harshest conditions and who rarely grew ill; in their eyes, most aliens were weak and handicapped, and Maltuvis's use of a plague allegedly caused by aliens had been an inspired way to tap into their fear that such weakness was contagious. Governments that welcomed offworlders were defeated in election after election, and the resultant crackdowns on aliens and those who harbored them had laid the groundwork for further subjugation of Saurian rights. Protests against such oppression had given Maltuvis's puppets a pretext to request military aid from the M'Tezir Empire and thereby surrender their countries to his conquest without a shot being fired.

Ruiz, like many other enlightened observers, had seen every step of Maltuvis's conquest coming in advance. Sauria had its own history of fascist states, just as Earth did, and the lessons were there for any who would listen—yet they had been unable to stop what they had known was coming. They could only watch helplessly as it happened, as in a nightmare.

But none of Ruiz's expectations could have prepared him for how bad things became when Maltuvis had finally launched his global conquest four months ago. He had been here in Lyaksti, the core nation of the Global League and the largest of the holdouts against Maltuvis, when the M'Tezir tyrant had launched a fleet of ships into the skies. In one terrible morning (for Saurians were nocturnal and at their most vulnerable when the sun came up), his fleet had swept across the planet and blasted every rival nation's military forces into slag, killing hundreds of thousands. The war fleet had been more advanced than anything ever built on Sauria before, attacking from low orbit and staying far above the range of enemy aircraft and missiles. Their weapons had been tactical atomics and high-energy plasma beams able to burn through any defenses the Saurians had devised. The leaders of Lyaksti and several other nations had gone underground before the invading forces had landed and destroyed or occupied the government headquarters, but a number of other progressive leaders had been either killed in combat or arrested and held for later execution. By noon that day, the entire planet had fallen, and the M'Tezir tyrant had announced the birth of the Maltuvian Empire.

Since then, it had become increasingly difficult to survive as an offworlder on Sauria. Ruiz had been sheltered by his allies in the Lyaksti resistance, but many other offworlders had been rounded up for imprisonment or deportation—though Ruiz had heard very credible rumors that the "deportations" were a cover for mass executions. In the adjoining nation of Chonaksti, one of the lands whose citizens were most willing to harbor and shelter aliens, there had been a suspicious release of volcanic gases that had swept over much of the land, causing merely discomfort and coughing fits for the hardy Saurians but killing any offworlders who hadn't found shelter in time. Ruiz and his fellow offworlders in the resistance had made sure to set up airtight bolt holes and carry oxygen masks with them, in case a similar "natural disaster" befell Lyaksti.

But now that the attack had come, it was far worse than Ruiz had expected. This time, there was no attempt to target only aliens or opposition forces. This time, there was no pretense of a natural disaster. This time, Maltuvis's ships soared over Lyaksti's capital and blasted it with plasma beams and X-ray lasers, targeting its inhabitants indiscriminately. Ultritium bombs were dropped on some of the larger buildings, blowing them apart or collapsing them to kill everyone inside, while also causing heavy damage to adjacent structures. Offworlders and Saurians, rebels and obedient subjects, adults and children, the bombardment felled them all. Ruiz, by a fluke of fortune, had been off in the hills, using his geological knowledge to find new hiding places for the resistance. It had given him an all-too-perfect vantage point to witness the horror of the attack—and to capture it on the imager he always carried with him.

"This is Maltuvis's idea of a stronger, richer Sauria," he choked out through his sobs as he recorded the atrocity for posterity. He did not know if his broadcasting facility would survive the attack, or if he could find another way to get the message out if it did not—but he had to document it anyway. Someone had to witness it. "Civilians, children . . . hospitals, schools, museums . . . He could've just dropped a nuclear warhead, but he wants it slow. He wants the Lyaksti to suffer, to feel terror at his wrath. This is not about protecting his people or making his world better. This is pure sadism—the brutality of a petty, bullying coward. This is what comes of the Federation turning a blind eye for the sake of their precious minerals. This is what comes of us failing to do something while we had the chance! We made Maltuvis wealthy, we started him on this path, and this is the end result that anyone could've seen coming!

"I don't know if I can get this message out to the galaxy. But if any of you ever see this, look closely. Look at all the people dying down there, and remember." Another volley of rays blasted into the city, another barrage of bombs fell, and the roar of dozens of collapsing buildings, explosions, and screaming crowds silenced his narrative. By the time he could be clearly heard again, he had reconsidered his words.

"No, don't just remember. If you see this . . . do something. God damn you, *do something!*"

January 31, 2166
Palais de la Concorde, Paris, European Alliance

The audiovisual recording of the atrocity in Lyaksti had spread swiftly across known space, bringing outrage and calls for action from multiple quarters. Countless voices, both inside and outside the Federation, called the young union to account for its role in funding Maltuvis's rise to power, and demanded that it follow the impassioned plea of the broadcast's narrator to "do something."

The tricky part, of course, was deciding what that "something" should be—if anything. That was the question that Vinithnel sh'Mirrin had called Admirals Archer and Shran to her office in the UFP's newly completed executive building to discuss. The office sat on the tenth floor of the Palais de la Concorde's cylindrical tower, its broad, curved window affording a spectacular view of the Champs-Élysées, the *Axe historique* of monuments along its length, and the Arc de Triomphe at its far end. Jonathan Archer supposed it was a fitting view for the Federation's defense commissioner to have while making decisions regarding the use of force—a view that invited a contemplation of history and a commemoration of the great cost inflicted by wars even in the midst of victory. So far, in the four years and change of its existence, the Federation had managed to avoid becoming embroiled in open war, though at times only by the narrowest of margins. Archer fervently hoped that was not about to change.

Shran, however, did not appear to have the same concerns. "We have to take Maltuvis down before he does this again!" he implored sh'Mirrin. "Our self-interest let this happen—we can't let our timidity stop us from correcting it!"

"We can't be sure what we're getting into, Shran," Archer cautioned. "Don't you find it suspicious that Maltuvis's censors somehow let this video slip through their net, when we've had to rely on scraps of intelligence about less extreme atrocities?"

"Why would he let it out on purpose?" Shran

demanded. "To dare us to come after him? Well, I'll take that dare. The Saurians on the ground may be helpless before those orbital ships, but an interstellar battle fleet would make short work of them."

"And then what? You know your history, Shran! If we go in there as an occupying force, we'll only turn the Saurians against us. Remember, that was V'Las's end-game in the Vulcan civil war. Maybe it's Maltuvis's too."

"You give that tin-pot tyrant too much credit for intelligence."

"We have good reason to believe the Orion Syndicate is backing him."

"Petty criminals and smugglers. We've put them in their place more than once."

"We can't underestimate them *or* Maltuvis! This is what I've been saying. It's easy to get overconfident, to assume our technological advantage makes us smarter than other species. But nobody's as smart about an alien species as its own people. The assumptions we make from the outside can be dangerous. That's how Maltuvis got to this point in the first place. We over-estimated how unified the Saurians were. We didn't realize how easy it'd be for a demagogue to stir up their xenophobia."

"Then, maybe, but this is now! This isn't another Partnership, Jon. We've had years to get to know the Saurians. Even if you're right that it was a mistake to rush into that trade deal, we can't change that now. Not unless you have a time-traveling friend you haven't mentioned." Archer remained studiously quiet.

"We made the deal," Shran went on, "and what's happened since is our responsibility. We can't just turn away from it."

Commissioner sh'Mirrin had been standing before the window, gazing out at Paris while the admirals argued. Now she turned and spoke. "Shran is right, Jon. You both make good points, in fact. Yes, we do bear a responsibility for what's happening on Sauria, and it would be wrong to walk away because we're too afraid of making further mistakes. If we let our policies be governed by fear, we might as well dissolve Starfleet and go home." Shran puffed out his chest, his antennae taking on a curl of smug satisfaction. "But it is also true that no one is better qualified to judge the Saurian situation than the Saurians. The decisions should be theirs, yes. But that does not mean they have to be left to make them alone."

The lanky Andorian *shen* resumed her seat behind the desk. "What I propose we do, for now, is to send in military advisors. A small contingent will be landed in secret to make contact with the resistance forces and any surviving leaders of the Global League. They will work with the resistance to provide logistical support and training, and depending on what the Saurians decide they need from us, Starfleet will provide additional materiel, intelligence, and further support as warranted. It's their world to liberate on their own terms, but we will help them do it. Agreed?"

Shran appeared guardedly satisfied. It was less than he had wanted, but at least it was something. "Agreed."

Archer was more uneasy, aware that any intervention had unseen pitfalls. But he couldn't dismiss the widespread consensus that the Federation bore some responsibility for Maltuvis's rise. Archer had spent years pushing the UFP's leaders to sever the trade deal with Maltuvis before it made the dictator too powerful. By the time he had finally convinced them to act, it had been too little and too late. Now that Archer's fears about Maltuvis's tyranny had been realized, how could he advocate just walking away?

This was the whole reason Archer felt that nonintervention was the best policy for Starfleet. The surest way to avoid the kind of disasters reckless contact had brought to the Partnership and on Sauria was to avoid contact altogether, at least until a civilization was mature enough to meet the Federation on an equal footing. But when contact had already been made and damage already done, surely that entailed a responsibility to stay involved, at least until the damage was dealt with. He would continue to push for a hands-off policy regarding new contacts, but Sauria had to be a different matter.

"Agreed," Archer conceded. "Who do you recommend we send in, Commissioner? It should probably be someone who's had prior experience with the Saurians, who understands their society and how they think."

"My thinking as well. I propose Captain Shumar and the *Essex* crew. Who better than the ones who first opened relations?"

Shran's antennae folded back in displeasure. "They were reassigned last year to Starbase Twelve, on the far side of the Federation from Sauria. It would take them more than two weeks to get there."

"I know it's not ideal, but it gives us more time to gather intelligence and formulate plans. As Admiral Archer has persuasively argued, it's better to learn all we can before intervening." She turned her gaze to the human chief of staff. "Please apprise Captain Shumar and Admiral Narsu of *Essex*'s new mission. I want them under way for Sauria at their earliest convenience."

"Yes, Commissioner." Archer thought it over. He was aware that *Essex*'s first officer, Caroline Paris, was still here on Earth, taking an extended leave. This new mission for *Essex* would not allow time for a stop-off at Earth, so the *Daedalus*-class vessel would need a new first officer, along with replacements for other crew members still on leave.

But that need not be a bad thing for Commander Paris, he decided. The commander's exploits as part of Shumar's crew had come to his attention before, and he had found her record most impressive. Her sudden lack of a posting would simply create an opportunity for Archer to do something he'd already been contemplating.

Starfleet Headquarters, San Francisco

". . . And so, in view of her achievements and her demonstrated potential to serve in the higher grade,

Commander Caroline Cecile Paris is promoted to the permanent grade of captain, United Federation Starfleet, effective this date, the thirty-first of January, 2166. By order of the Commissioner of Defense and the Joint Chiefs of Starfleet."

Captains Malcolm Reed and Marcus Williams applauded as Admiral Archer pinned a rank sigil to Caroline Paris's dress uniform, officially granting her equal rank to themselves. On the wall screen in Archer's office, Captain Bryce Shumar and the command crew of *Essex* applauded as well, with a slight delay over their subspace link from Starbase 12. Once the applause subsided, Paris cleared her throat and restated her Starfleet oath:

"I, Caroline Cecile Paris, having been appointed an officer in the United Federation of Planets as indicated in the grade of captain, do solemnly swear to uphold the regulations of the United Federation Starfleet as well as the laws of the United Federation of Planets: to represent the highest ideals for which they stand, to become an ambassador of peace and goodwill, to protect the security of the Federation and its member worlds, and to offer aid to any and all beings that request it."

"Congratulations, Captain *Paris,"* Shumar boomed over the screen after the second round of applause. *"It's a shame to have to lose you, but this honor is well deserved. Vesta's crew will be just as lucky to have you as we have been."*

"Aw, I was getting tired of you guys anyway," Paris teased. "But seriously—I wish we didn't have to part so suddenly. I wanted my own ship, but not like this. I thought we'd have more time."

"Don't worry about it, Caroline. I've no doubt we'll have plenty of opportunities to reconnect over the years ahead. And I'm certain that Mister Mullen will be more than capable of rising to the responsibilities of Essex's first officer—isn't that right, Steven?"

The younger, darker-skinned man beside Shumar tugged on the collar of his gray jumpsuit—its epaulets and trim still in sciences blue, for Mullen would need to double up as XO and science officer until a permanent replacement for the latter post could be found. That was a lot to ask of a new-fledged exec, and Paris felt a twinge of guilt at leaving Mullen in that position, even though she'd had no part in the decision. "I'll do my best to live up to your example, Comm— Captain Paris."

She laughed. "I know, it sounds weird as hell to me too. You know, if you need any advice, Steven, I'm a subspace call away. Not that I don't trust you to do the job, but, you know, any outstanding projects or procedural quirks I haven't had time to brief you on—"

"Understood and appreciated, Captain. But I'll have plenty of time to catch up on the way back to Sauria." He shook his head. "Under other circumstances, I would've been eager to go back. I really hope we can help the Saurians rebuild that lovely, inviting world we found three years ago."

Admiral Archer spoke up. "We're all counting on you for that, Mister Mullen. The Federation's supply of Saurian brandy has gotten dangerously low since the embargo, so you can appreciate our urgency." Everyone on both sides of the screen laughed, though there was a solemn undercurrent to it.

Once Shumar and the others had exchanged their farewells with Paris and signed off, she moved over to Malcolm Reed and blinked away a few tears, though she maintained the formal distance and decorum that befitted the setting. "I always thought I hated long goodbyes, but the abrupt, unexpected ones are even worse."

"The nature of the service, I'm afraid," Reed replied, though not without sympathy. "I had plenty of advance notice of my promotion to *Pioneer*, but it was still just as hard to say goodbye when the time came."

"At least you were able to bring Travis with you. I'm starting out with a blank slate. Hell, I hardly even have a crew. Or a complete ship, for that matter."

Archer moved closer, having overheard. "Sorry about that, Captain. But *Vesta* was the most suitable opening, given the timing. The *Ceres* class is meant to fill the *Daedalus*'s niche, so your experience with *Essex* makes you a good fit. But given the construction delays, I'm afraid you'll have to be a dry dock captain for the next month or so."

Paris nodded, understanding the challenges involved in the *Ceres* design, a joint project incorporating technologies from multiple Federation founder worlds. Outwardly, it looked like a more flattened version of *Essex*'s sphere-and-cylinder design—indeed, *Vesta*'s forward hull had a shape not unlike its namesake planetoid—but its internal systems were more fully hybridized than even those of *Pioneer*, which had been one of the early test-beds for the technological integration of the fleet. *Ceres* itself had been undergoing shakedowns for the past couple of years, with the lessons learned from its mistakes being incorporated into the systems design of its successors *Vesta* and *Pallas*, but even the refinements were proving challenging to achieve in practice. "That's okay, Admiral," she said. "I don't mind starting off slow. I'm not as prone to rush into things as I used to be. I've learned that too much haste can lead to unintended consequences."

Archer nodded solemnly. "That's a principle we could all learn to live by."

4

It would be fitting, thought Charles Tucker, if Sauria became the key to bringing Section 31 down.

It had been Harris's refusal to let Tucker organize a resistance against Maltuvis that had planted the seed of the ex-engineer's disaffection with the Section. Harris's willingness to let another civilization suffer tyranny for the profit and convenience of the Federation had been a harbinger of his decision to condemn the Partnership to destruction for the same end. The shocking video of Maltuvis's latest, greatest atrocity had only intensified Tucker's conviction that the Section must fall—particularly since he recognized the narrator as Antonio Ruiz, the passionate young mining engineer whom Tucker had befriended and harnessed as a resource in his time on Sauria, only to let him down when Ruiz had most needed his support. The young Cuban had pledged to stay behind and organize a resistance against Maltuvis, the very thing that Tucker's orders from Harris had prevented him from supporting—and it looked as though he had succeeded. It would be poetic justice, then, if his heroic act in documenting the atrocity for the galaxy gave Tucker the leverage he needed to expose and dismantle Section 31 for good.

"I've been thinking over what you said about the noninterference policy," he told Harris now, by way of setting his stratagem in motion. "You're right that the Federation would be better off if we avoided meddling in other worlds' affairs—at least openly. Our foreign entanglements in the past few years have made us some enemies."

"I'm glad you agree," Harris replied.

"But Archer's having a hard time selling the idea. It's mainly about the Partnership mess for him, but that's too ambiguous a situation for the public to come to a consensus on. It's too easy to blame the Ware or the Klingons instead of admitting Starfleet's responsibility."

"Yes, that is a conundrum. It would be handier to have some clear-cut example where Starfleet interference went disastrously wrong, due to our insufficient understanding of a native culture."

"What Maltuvis did on Sauria is sure clear-cut," Tucker said.

"The brutality of it, yes. The culpability less so. Maltuvis is undeniably a monster, and it was our ill fortune that the minerals we found most valuable were concentrated in his lands. Too many people see it as him taking advantage of our need."

Tucker nodded, as if he were letting Harris lead him to the idea instead of the other way around.

"So what you're saying is that the best way to make Archer's case would be a different kind of disaster. One where the blame was undeniably on Starfleet. Like, say, if the mission to assist the rebels went horribly wrong somehow."

Harris peered at him. "Are you suggesting a specific kind of horrible wrongness?"

"Well . . . look at the way similar things on Earth went wrong. Like when the United States went into the Middle East to train resistance groups against the Soviet bloc, except those resistance groups included religious fanatics who ended up using the tactics and organization they got with American help to launch terrorist movements against their own people, and occasionally against the Americans as well. Say maybe the Starfleet advisors hook up with a resistance group without realizing they're extremists, as bad as Maltuvis. Say those extremists get their hands on Starfleet weapons and use them to pursue their own agenda, maybe make a terrorist strike." He shrugged. "Or at least it looks that way to the galaxy."

The silver-haired spymaster folded his hands on the desk in front of him. "Just so we're clear . . . are you proposing that we intervene on Sauria to engineer just such a catastrophe? See that Starfleet gets the blame, and thereby tilt public opinion in favor of Archer's new directive?"

("Of course I don't plan on actually going through with it," Tucker had insisted to Malcolm Reed when he had suggested this plan to him the night before.

"The last thing I want is to see more Saurians slaugh-tered. But it's just the sort of plan Harris would go for. If we can get him involved in *planning* the disaster, then expose the plan before it gets carried out, then we have our smoking gun, right in Harris's hand. We bring him down, and the rest of Section Thirty-one comes with him.")

Now Tucker simply said, "Do you think it wouldn't work?"

"On the contrary—it very well could have the de-sired effect," Harris replied. "It's just unexpectedly ruthless, coming from you. I know you've objected to such exigencies in the past."

"And you've insisted they were necessary for the greater good of the Federation. I have to accept that." He sighed. "If I want to sleep at night, I have to."

"And what about the continued oppression of the Saurians if Starfleet intervention is sabotaged? What about the immediate death toll of such an engineered incident?"

"Look, I don't like it. But doing ugly things when necessary for the greater good is what we're here for. Starfleet intervention on Sauria could become a quag-mire, for all we know. These things hardly ever go smoothly. If we mess up once, pull out, and leave it up to the Saurians to save their own world, that might actually be better in the long run. They're a strong, de-termined people. I'll just have to hope they can pull through on their own."

"Still, I know it would weigh on your conscience

to be responsible for the immediate casualties." Harris gave him a sympathetic look. "There's no shame in admitting that. We aren't the bad guys, you know."

Right, Tucker thought. *Hence the black suits and shadowy meetings.* "You're right," he said. "It's not an easy thing to suggest."

Harris smiled. "Then you'll be relieved to know that the answer is no. I have no interest in engineering such a mishap on Sauria."

Tucker tried to mask his surprise. "May I ask why not?"

"For one thing, it's too soon. With the investigation still under way on the Partnership affair, the last thing we want is to get embroiled in another heavily publicized, scrutinized galactic event. At this point, we're better off keeping our heads down. If an existential threat on the level of a looming Klingon invasion rears its head, then we will certainly intervene. But for anything less than that, we're better off biding our time and trusting the conventional authorities to do their jobs." He chuckled. "I suppose it's my own version of a noninterference directive."

Tucker let a feigned chuckle mask his disgust at the comparison. Archer's cause was about respecting others' right to self-determination. Harris's only concern was not getting caught. And that was a problem for Tucker, who needed to maneuver him into a position where he could be caught.

"You said 'for one thing.' Is there another reason?"

Harris steepled his fingers. "Why, yes, there is.

The reason we don't need to sabotage Starfleet's advisory efforts on Sauria . . . is because someone else already is."

He worked his console, bringing up an image feed on the desk screen. Tucker instantly recognized the lovely green face of Navaar, not only from years' worth of intelligence reports on the current head of the Orion Syndicate, but from his own firsthand encounter with her and her sisters aboard *Enterprise* eleven years back, when the trio and their nominal "master," Harrad-Sar, had attempted to collect a Syndicate bounty by capturing the starship and its crew. Tucker and T'Pol had been instrumental in foiling their plans, since their mating bond had somehow allowed Tucker to share in T'Pol's Vulcan immunity to the effect of the Sisters' overpowering pheromones. Tucker remembered it vividly, for it had been the incident that had made him and T'Pol aware of that bond in the first place.

Navaar stood in the foreground of a lavishly appointed suite; according to the metadata readout below the image, it was in the Sisters' estate on the Orion homeworld. Her junior sister D'Nesh watched from behind her, smiling maliciously as Navaar said, *"Yes, be sure to thank Harrad-Sar for giving us a sneak preview of the big show. The destruction was quite spectacular. Maras particularly enjoyed it when the hospital blew up."* Tucker noted that the youngest Sister lounged idly in the background, watching a lissome nude female slave dance erotically for her and seeming uninterested in the discussion. The time code marked it as soon after Maltuvis's bombing of the Lyaksti capital, and a day before Antonio Ruiz's recording had gone public.

"*You're sure the resistance documented the attack as well?*" Navaar went on.

"*No question, my lady,*" came the anonymous male voice at the other end, presumably one of the Sisters' enslaved agents. "*One of their cells has already begun making attempts to transmit a report.*"

"*Make sure Harrad-Sar impresses upon Maltuvis's censors how important it is that they allow this broadcast to pass. The Federation needs an irresistible incentive to intervene.*"

"*Not to doubt your wisdom, my lady, but can you be sure Maltuvis will cooperate? Even if the Federation does take the blame, the level of devastation will—*"

"*Maltuvis has one thing in common with us,*" D'Nesh interrupted. "*He doesn't care how many of those ridiculous-looking lizards get roasted as long as it benefits him. And destroying the Federation's reputation, making them too afraid and too hated to ever butt into anyone else's business again—that will benefit all of us.*"

Harris froze the image when he recognized that Tucker was about to speak. "My God," the younger man said. "The Sisters are already doing it."

"Devious minds think alike, it seems."

"But I wasn't thinking of anything on that scale. Enough to make the case for noninterference, not to damn the Federation in the eyes of the galaxy. Are you really all right with letting that happen?"

"I think the Sisters underestimate the goodwill

the Federation has earned among our neighbors. As well as underestimating our resolve. The Federation's peoples are not so timid as to retreat completely from galactic affairs, whatever Navaar and D'Nesh may fantasize.

"But if they think a nonintervention policy would mean complete isolationism, I'd say it's in our interests to let them believe that. If their actions on Sauria help sway public opinion in favor of Archer's directive, so be it. The Federation may come away with a black eye in public relations, but in the long run it will be safer, and the Orions will be overconfident about just how much of a free hand they'll gain. If necessary, we can arrange for the Orions' complicity in the disaster to come out after the directive is firmly in place.

"But in the short term, the Sisters are doing our work for us. We can just sit back and do nothing. Which should surely be a relief for your conscience, Mister Tucker."

Tucker offered a feeble nod of acceptance, cloaking his real concern as best he could. It did him no good if the engineered disaster could not be linked to Section 31—and it did the Saurians no good if Tucker was not controlling the situation enough to prevent the disaster before it happened.

But as he studied the frozen image of the Three Sisters on Harris's screen, he realized that he recognized the slender, pale-skinned female slave who was performing for Maras in the background. And the idea began to form that maybe there was a way he could make this situation work to his advantage after all.

February 2, 2166

"Her name is Devna," Tucker said as T'Pol studied the image he'd called up on the computer of her ground-side apartment. "I met her on Rigel during the Vertian incident. That's where this image came from—well, actually from the records of the ministerial conference leading up to it. But it's definitely the same woman. She's pretty hard to miss."

T'Pol threw him a look. "Really?"

"I-I mean because she's so pale for an Orion. Really contrasts with how black her hair is. Not as curvy as you'd expect, either." T'Pol continued to stare. "I just mean she's easy to pick out of a crowd of Orions."

"I see," she answered dryly. "And your meeting was significant?"

"She helped me crack the whole case. Tipped me off to how the Syndicate was stirring up the entire affair to distract Starfleet from their planned raid at Deneb Kaitos. She was the one who was manipulating Commissioner Noar to go on the warpath, but once I confronted her, she confessed everything."

"How did you persuade her to do so?"

Trip reflected back on the encounter—a brief, single incident, yet one that had stuck with him for the past three years. "By giving her something I don't think she'd ever known. Trust."

T'Pol examined him. "Go on."

"I had her cornered, and I was immune to her pheromones—thanks to you." T'Pol nodded in acknowledgment. "She expected me to try to torture her—said she'd been conditioned to enjoy pain." He winced. "I let her see how wrong I thought that was, that anyone would have to live like that. I offered her a better life. To get her away from slavery, take her someplace the Syndicate would never find her."

"Obviously she declined that offer."

"She said freedom was an illusion. Said I was just as trapped as she was." He gave a faint smile. "She realized it before I did. Maybe it was just that obvious to someone else in the game."

"Trip," T'Pol replied, "it has long been obvious to anyone close to you."

He stared at her for a moment. "I guess it has at that. You remember after that mission? How I finally told you what happened to me at the Battle of Cheron, and how it haunted me?" She nodded. "Well . . . I told her first. I didn't think anyone could understand, but she knew. She was the same as I was. So I just . . . I felt I could confide in her. No pheromones, no manipulation—she knew I was immune, she knew what I was, I knew what she was, so we dropped any pretense. It was the most honest either of us had been with anyone in who knows how long. It was weird, how easy it was. Maybe it was something we both needed."

After a moment, he gave a weak laugh, shaking it off. "Well, maybe it wasn't completely honest on her

end. I'm pretty sure she gave up the Deneb information because it was just a short-term goal, something
the Syndicate could withstand giving up if it diverted
us from their bigger goals. And she said she liked me
owing her a favor. I'm actually a bit surprised she
hasn't tried to collect."

"Yet now you hope to request another favor from
her."

"I don't see what choice I have. The Orions can't be
allowed to sabotage our relief mission on Sauria. The
loss of life could be catastrophic."

"Not to mention," T'Pol said, "that it would not
allow you to incriminate Harris in the attempt."

"That's why I need help from someone on the inside. Harris is happy to let the Orions do this themselves so he can keep his hands clean. But if I can
arrange not only to expose the plot before it goes off,
but to plant evidence implicating Harris in a conspiracy with the Orions, then I can still bring the Section
down, *and* save a lot of Saurians."

T'Pol frowned. "Predicating the case against the
Section on fabricated evidence is hardly a desirable
course."

"I know it's a risk, but it's all we've got. Maybe we
couldn't make it stick, but it'd be enough to get him
investigated by Starfleet and Federation Security, and
that would unearth the real evidence that would put
him and the Section away."

"And what if it comes down to a choice between
saving the Saurians and incriminating Harris?"

"Then I'll put the Saurians first, of course. Believe me, T'Pol, I know how this looks," he said, clasping her hand. "I'm not blind to the fact that I thought up almost exactly the same plan as the heads of the most ruthless criminal organization in known space. That's why I came here so early. I was lyin' awake all night, wondering if I could really bring Section Thirty-one down without becomin' just as bad."

Her arm went around his shoulders. "For what it's worth, Trip, I doubt Harris loses much sleep at night. Your insomnia is evidence that your conscience remains strong."

"I hope you're right. And that's part of why I want to recruit Devna for this. I want to offer her another chance at a way out of slavery. If she can help me save lives and expose the Section, then she'd earn a place in the Federation."

"What makes you confident that she would be willing to help? As you said, there was a tactical advantage to revealing information before. She did not act out of altruism."

"Maybe not. But I've been keepin' tabs on her. There are records showing her at Delta IV last year, as part of the Orion party that kidnapped a group of Deltans and tried to enslave them. *Essex* tracked them down and freed them, but the Deltans refused to press charges, so they had to let the Orions go. But *Essex*'s security chief interviewed the Deltans afterward, and it seems they felt Devna was more enlightened than the rest of the Orions—that they'd bonded with her during their time together, when she was supposed to be sizing them up as potential slaves.

"The thing is, *Essex* only found the slave ship by pure luck—or so it seemed. They had a huge volume of space to search, and the Orions had a big head start. But they picked up a stray signal from the slave ship's warp engines—the kind that would be produced by a very subtle misalignment that would be hard for its engineers to spot. What are the odds that their ship just happened to have the exact kind of malfunction that would give it the best chance of bein' detected in time to rescue those Deltans?"

"You believe that Devna caused the engine misalignment in order to save them?"

"I think it's possible."

"But far from certain."

"I'll just have to ask her when I see her."

T'Pol considered. "I will say one thing. Given her involvement in two failed Syndicate operations within two years, it is impressive that she is still alive. One wonders why the Three Sisters consider her valuable enough to offset those mishaps." She quirked a brow. "You did say that she was attending them personally. If she is in their inner circle, it may be premature to trust her."

Tucker chuckled. "Well, there are other kinds of value besides spy stuff. The way Maras and Devna were interacting in that signal I saw . . . I'd say they're lovers."

T'Pol's lips pursed. "Hardly an apposite word to use for a master-slave relationship."

"Okay, fair point. But Devna didn't exactly look reluctant, if you know what I mean."

Her gaze hardened. "And this is what captivated your attention?"

He pulled back defensively, opened his mouth—then laughed. "You know, it's really hard to tell when you're teasin' me."

She did that thing where she smiled without smiling. "Excellent."

"Look, are you gonna help me track down Devna or what?"

Endeavour's captain pondered. "Hoshi and Lieutenant Cutler did retrieve a considerable amount of data on the Orion Syndicate during our raid on Pheniot V last year. This included information on their organizational structure and contact protocols. The information was provided to Starfleet Intelligence, but we retained a copy aboard ship. You say you have kept tabs on Devna? I take it this includes some information concerning her activity or standing within the Syndicate."

"Some, yeah. Most of what I have is from when she's been offworld, but I've been able to extrapolate some things beyond what SI would know."

"Then if we review the Pheniot data together, we may be able to extrapolate still more."

Tucker smiled. "That's one thing I loved about our time in the Ware task force. You and me, workin' together to solve a problem. Felt like old times—back when I could be me."

"Then let us begin." She stroked his cheek and gave him a gentle kiss. "And if we succeed . . . perhaps you can be you once again."

February 4, 2166
Orion homeworld

Devna had hoped she would one day have the opportunity to encounter Charles Tucker again, in order to collect on the favor he owed her from Rigel—and perhaps for other reasons she hesitated to admit to herself. She had never expected him to take the brazen step of contacting her directly over the console in her private chamber—an indulgence she had only recently earned as a benefit of being Maras's favorite. He had assured her that his agency's technology allowed him to make contact with no record being preserved, even on the chamber's surveillance system—that, indeed, he had rigged his system to blind even his own agency to the contact. Still, what Tucker was asking her to do was startling.

"Perhaps humans have a different understanding of how favors work," Devna told the pink-complexioned, black-suited agent on the screen. "I'm the one entitled to ask you to do something for me."

"*I am doing something for you. I'm giving you another chance to do the right thing, to use your position to prevent an atrocity. Like you did with the Deltans last year.*" She tried to mask her surprise, but he caught it anyway. "*That's right, Devna. I know. Well—I suspected. Now I know.*"

"I see," she said when she'd recovered her poise. "Then you intend to blackmail me into cooperation."

He sighed. *"No, that's not it. What I mean is . . . you defied your masters to help the Deltans because you knew it was the right thing to do. Maybe you helped me on Rigel for the same reason, even though you got something out of it too."*

"'Got something out of it'?" Devna protested, her breathy voice growing chillier. "I spent a year demoted to the lowest tier of slavery as punishment for the indiscretion you pushed me into. I was an object, the property of anyone who wanted me at any time. I was used and humiliated in ways you'd be embarrassed to imagine. I had to earn my way back to a position of trust, and I only had that opportunity thanks to my mistress Maras's favor."

The sheer, unfeigned horror and guilt on Tucker's face defused her anger. *"My God . . . Devna, I had no idea. I never thought . . . You seemed to think you'd be okay."*

"I am 'okay,' Tucker. It was nothing I had not endured growing up. Nothing I had not earned my way out of before. I knew it would be the price for my action, and I chose to accept it."

He studied her. *"And what would the price have been if they'd found out what you did for the Deltans?"*

Devna hesitated. "I made sure they did not."

"They would've killed you, wouldn't they?"

"My life has always been their property, granted me at their indulgence. I have never expected to live longer than it amused them to permit it."

"Still, you didn't have to give them a reason. You chose to risk

yourself to help others—again. I believe in that impulse to do good. Even after all I've seen, all I've done . . . I know it when I see it. And it gives me hope.

"That's what I have to offer you, Devna. Hope. Come with me to Sauria, help me prevent the disaster your mistresses are trying to engineer, and I can get you out. I can offer you a better life in the Federation. Or on Delta, if you prefer. They'd be happy to have you back, I'm sure."

"I am comfortable where I am, as you can see. I have the favor of a Sister. There is no higher privilege for a slave."

"Slavery is never a privilege. I know you don't believe freedom is real, Devna, but there are much greater degrees of freedom than what you have now."

She studied him, gauging the intensity in his eyes and voice. "And that is what you seek, is it not? This is your play to win freedom from your own masters."

"Yes. For me and for a lot of people who could be at their mercy in the future. Not least of all the Saurians. They don't deserve to suffer for the Sisters' schemes any more than the Deltans did."

"People rarely get what they deserve."

"Not automatically. That's why other people have to take action to make it happen."

"Be honest with me if you want my trust. This *is* something you do for your own freedom, is it not?"

He took a moment before answering. "Yes. Yes, it is. But not just freedom from my employers. Freedom from . . . havin' to live with choices that condemn other people. I think you can understand that, Devna. If you're being honest with yourself."

She could find no answer to that.

Tucker took her very silence as an answer. *"If you decide to help me, then meet me at the coordinates I'm sending you."*

The coordinates appeared on the screen, and Devna committed them to memory rapidly, as she was trained to do. "What makes you think I can arrange to get away?"

"You're a resourceful lady, Devna. You'll figure something out." He smiled. *"See you soon."*

The screen went dark, and she marveled at his human arrogance. He was so sure he understood her. How could he, when she struggled to understand herself?

The curtains rustled, and Maras emerged from her own adjacent chambers. Tucker may have taken steps to shield their communication from electronic surveillance, but he had not reckoned on the junior Sister's gift for eavesdropping. Of course, hardly anyone was aware of that. Maras had carefully cultivated a reputation as an oblivious hedonist with the mind of a child. Her sexual allure and pheromonal potency were so intense that even her loving elder sister Navaar would have seen her as a threat had she not concealed her superior intellect and made herself appear harmless and unambitious. Devna was one of a privileged few slaves whom Maras had entrusted her secret to—and one of the only ones still alive. Maras's idiocy may have been an act, but her ruthlessness was real enough. Devna knew that her life depended on keeping Maras's secret. But the danger was worth it for the privilege of being Maras's confidante and the thrill of being her lover.

Devna rose and moved toward her mistress, shedding the filmy robe she had donned for her communication with Tucker. "You heard, mistress?" she asked, keeping her head deferentially lowered.

Smiling, Maras placed a long, sharp nail under Devna's chin and tilted her head upward. "I can never resist the sound of your voice."

"My lady, what should I do? Freeing the Deltans did nothing to undermine the Syndicate. They would have been poor slaves in any case. You assured me of that yourself." Devna had not even tried to keep the secret from her mistress, knowing that Maras would have seen through any attempt at deception and easily compelled her to speak the truth. She would have accepted death if that had been Maras's will. But her mistress had been pleased that her favored spy had shown the resourcefulness and cunning to defy the elder Sisters without detection, telling Devna that she might have a use for such skills in the future. "But this . . ."

Maras stroked her hair comfortingly and nuzzled her cheek. Her pheromones thrilled Devna at this range, even though Maras was keeping them restrained for now. "What do you want to do?"

She knew that Maras, unlike most owners, would not punish her for voicing a thought. "I want to help the human."

"Not the Saurians?"

Maras was a woman of few words, but there was much meaning in them when she wanted there to be. Devna nodded, acknowledging her insight. "I feel for him, mistress. He does not belong in this life. It brings him such sorrow. He set me free once . . . I would do the same for him, if I could."

The Sister tilted her head, pondering. "He appealed to your empathy. It is interesting. But you know it has little use to us." Devna nodded. She had told Maras everything Pelia and the other Deltans had taught her about empathy and the shared bond among all beings. Maras had opened her mind to the ideas, as she did with all ideas, but she had not been converted. She was a pragmatic woman, and practicality told her that cooperating with the sadism of Orion society, even appearing to rejoice in it, was better for her own survival. As she had explained to Devna, her current position could allow her some opportunity to mitigate the excesses of her elder siblings, by making subtle suggestions at the right moments to provoke ideas they believed to be their own. Yet any open attempt to change the Syndicate from within would merely lead to her death and that of accomplices such as Devna, and then nothing would be gained.

Devna accepted Maras's reasoning, but when she spoke to someone like Tucker, when she was reminded of the warmth and love she had shared with Pelia and her friends, some secret voice inside her found Maras's cold calculations unsatisfying. Self-interest was not all there was. She had tasted more, and sometimes she wished she could know it again.

Maras, perceptive as ever, read some of what she was feeling. She pulled Devna close and kissed her deeply. "I don't want you to be sad. If you want to help him, you can help him."

"Mistress!" Devna cried when she found some trace of breath. "But what of your sisters' plans?"

"Their plans," Maras echoed, rolling her eyes at her siblings' comparatively crude strategic abilities. "I have my own. Help your pet human tie his employers to my sisters' plot—but tie them only to D'Nesh."

Devna understood. Navaar doted on Maras, cherishing her so long as she maintained her façade of the innocent, silly child who needed her big sister to take care of her. But D'Nesh, the middle Sister, was jealous of Maras's privileged treatment and contemptuous of her apparent stupidity. Maras had explained that part of the reason she had cultivated Devna as an ally was that she expected D'Nesh's resentment to escalate to the point of betrayal. Now Maras was taking the opportunity to move on D'Nesh first. Evidence linking Tucker's employers to the middle Sister would create scandal not only in the Federation, but in the Syndicate as well. It could lead to D'Nesh's disgrace, even her death. After all, the Syndicate did not bother with the Federation notion of fair trials. Merely destroying Navaar's already tenuous trust in her sister would be enough to seal D'Nesh's fate.

Devna trembled as the danger of this move set in. "My lady . . . what you ask me to do . . ."

"I know," Maras replied, stroking her cheek. "Exposure will mean your death. But inaction could mean mine—and you would suffer without my favor." Devna nodded. The risk she took was only to herself; even if Maras didn't take steps to conceal her involvement, who would ever believe the idiot Sister was a secret mastermind? But it was her place to serve. At least Maras was an owner she was willing to die for.

Her mistress gave her another deep kiss. "I trust you, Devna. You learn. You grow. That's rare for us— our system doesn't reward it. It's your secret weapon, like mine. Our minds give us the edge. So you won't fail." Letting her own minimal garment fall to the floor, Maras pulled Devna down onto the bed. "You'll never fail me."

February 5, 2166
Sierra Nevada Mountains

"Are you out of your mind?" Jonathan Archer asked Charles Tucker. The two men stood together with Malcolm Reed on a broad ledge halfway up a mid-sized mountain. Archer and Reed had come up the hard way; this was not the ideal season for mountaineering, but Archer liked a challenge, and the fact that he made a habit of climbing in midwinter made it easier to conceal a clandestine meeting with a man who was supposed to be long dead. Reed had clearly not enjoyed the ascent, though he had made it stoically. Tucker, for his part, had arrived by transporter. He seemed unconcerned about the potential long-term hazards of using the technology, something that both Archer and Reed had experience with. The admiral's days of tackling challenges like Mount Whitney in winter were behind him due to the motor impairment that heavy transporter use had caused him, although Doctor Phlox's treatments had restored enough mobility to let him handle a more moderate slope like this one. Archer sometimes wondered if Tucker's casual transporter use meant that Section 31 had access to a more advanced, safer transporter technology that they were keeping from the rest of the Federation. But why would an organization supposedly dedicated to the safety of the Federation's citizens do something like that? Then again, the whole reason the three men were meeting was because they agreed that Section 31 had lost sight of that purpose.

But if Tucker knew of such an advance and kept it to himself, Archer had wondered, was he that much more trustworthy?

The proposal Tucker and Reed had just spelled out to him had made him wonder the same thing. "This is an incredibly risky plan you're proposing, Trip. Not just to yourself, but to the Saurians. If you know Maltuvis and the Orions are planning to stage a disaster and you don't tell anyone—"

"If I *did* tell anyone, it'd tip Harris off that I'm working against him. *And* it'd tip off the Syndicate that we've tapped their communications. And then either one, or both, could find some other way to hurt the Federation without us having a chance to stop it. And Maltuvis'd just go on slaughtering his people anyway."

"Still, you're playing with fire. If your plan doesn't go off just right, those deaths could still happen."

"Sir," Reed interposed, "it's not as if we haven't faced similar odds before. Trip knows what he's doing. He has an asset within the Syndicate and an in with the Saurian resistance."

"That's right." Tucker nodded. "Antonio Ruiz—the man who recorded that video of the capital attack. The fact that he's survived this long means he's even more resourceful than I knew."

"All right, all right," Archer said. "Even assuming you've got a realistic chance of pulling this off . . . have you thought about the effect it'll have in the Federation? I'm already struggling to convince the rest of Starfleet, the government, and the public that noninterference is the right policy. If it comes out that an illegal conspiracy *and* the Orion Syndicate are both trying to stack the deck *in favor* of noninterference, how do you think the public's going to react? Our efforts will be completely discredited!"

"That's a risk, I know," Tucker replied. "But maybe it won't be as bad as that. There are good arguments in support of noninterference. Those won't be erased by a single scandal. The people who really believe in the principle won't lose faith."

"They're not the ones we need to convince, Trip!"

"I know that, Jon. But there are bigger things at stake."

"Bigger than the whole future of how Starfleet interacts with other cultures?"

"That's exactly what this is about!" Tucker cried. "If Starfleet's gonna intervene in other worlds, let it be a Starfleet that does it openly, in the public eye, so it can be held accountable. Not a secret cabal that intervenes from the shadows and uses a nominal hands-off policy as a smokescreen. Jon, getting your directive passed won't do any good if Section Thirty-one is still there to pervert it. Let's cut the rot out of Starfleet first—then we can deal with how we treat other worlds."

Archer stared at his old friend, holding back an equally angry response. He could see how committed Trip was to his cause—probably even more than Archer was to his, for this was personal to Trip. And in all honesty, Archer couldn't think of a good counterargument. After a moment, he sighed. "I just . . . I'd prefer it if we could find a solution that didn't require choosing the lesser of two evils."

"We all would, sir," Reed replied. "But in Section Thirty-one's arena, there are rarely such clear-cut right choices—just one gray area after another. We're playing on their turf, after all."

Archer nodded. "All right. I'll sign off on your plan, Trip. I'll support you insofar as I can . . . and I'll start thinking of ways to do damage control on the noninterference front."

Tucker's shoulders relaxed. "Thanks, Jon. It means a lot."

"For me too, sir," Reed added.

"Just be careful," Archer advised, pointing at both of them. "Remember: if you're playing on Thirty-one's turf . . . that gives them the home field advantage."

5

February 9, 2166
GJ 1045 system

FARID NAJAFI stared through the viewport, watching eagerly for the first glimpse of the planet's surface as the shuttlepod descended through its dense cloud layer. Alongside him, the other members of the *E.C.S. Jules Verne*'s crew expressed similar anticipation. The yet-unnamed planet had been a font of surprises from the start. "This could be the find of a lifetime," Najafi heard Alec Castellano saying from the pilot's seat, for at least the sixth time since they'd left the *Verne*. The seventeen-year-old boy's enthusiasm was difficult to contain at the best of times.

Behind Alec, his mother, Maya, leaned forward and squeezed his shoulder. "And *we* made it, not those Starfleet know-it-alls," the raven-haired biologist said. "They wouldn't even have bothered taking a chance on a world like this."

Najafi wasn't sure that was true, but his fellow scientist was right that coming here had been a long shot. Dim red dwarfs like GJ 1045, an M4 star a parsec or so beyond Alpha Arietis, were by far the most abundant stars in the galaxy—yet finding habitable worlds around them was iffy at best. They had protracted, slow, and turbulent infancies, long enough for stellar flares and tidally induced volcanic activity to strip any habitable-zone planet of its water. Many a space pioneer had followed the siren lure of an oxygen signature to an M-dwarf system to find only a fossil layer of oxygen surrounding a barren, desiccated planet, a remnant of its original water supply after its hydrogen had been burned away by radiation. Sometimes a Neptune-like world would migrate into the habitable zone and lose its hydrogen atmosphere gradually enough to let its rocky, icy core become warm and livable once the star had settled down to a gentler phase, but the size and the timing had to be just right. And M dwarfs were prone to heavy flare activity throughout their lives, often enough to strip bare any remaining atmosphere and moisture unless the planet's orbit was sufficiently inclined to dodge most of the coronal mass ejections.

Even a planet that withstood all those challenges would still be close enough to the star to be tidally locked, with one side perpetually lit and the other forever dark. Without a dense enough atmosphere and large enough oceans to circulate the heat, such a world could end up with only a narrow habitable band around the day/night terminator, bracketed by fierce heat on one side and a hemisphere-smothering ice cap on the other. Any life that got a foothold might be snuffed out when plate tectonics carried it out of its comfort zone.

But this time, Captain Zang's gamble had paid off. This planet's evolution had proceeded just right to leave it with oceans and oxygen, survivable radiation levels, and a livable climate over the majority of its surface. The permanent cloud layer over most of its sunward half mitigated the excess heat and rendered the entire hemisphere habitable, although the substellar pole was engulfed in a vast, slow, perpetual hurricane. Orbital scans had confirmed an abundance of plant life, though it tended toward dark, purplish colors, its chlorophyll equivalents adapted to absorb the infrared light that was its star's primary output. Farid and Maya had spent hours debating the question of how plant life could thrive on a planet where the sun never moved in the sky, where any shade created by taller plants or geological features would be a constant. How would they compete to maximize their exposure to sunlight? How could smaller plants hope to survive at all? Were they like the dark-adapted floor-dwellers under a rainforest canopy? Could they simply draw on ambient infrared from the environment? And what animal or insect life might exist? Would any be able to survive the star's frequent flares—moderate enough to let an atmosphere survive, but intense enough to be problematical for nonbotanical life? But if there were no animals or insects, how did the plants distribute and fertilize themselves?

Thus it was an eager crew that gazed out the shuttlepod's ports as the clouds finally cleared. Soon, the pod approached a low rise near a river, covered with spongy, dark bluish growth. It was flanked on one side by a stand of stiff, bamboo-like grass and on the other by slender trees resembling asparagus stalks with their "scales" open wide and angled to catch the sunlight. Alec brought the pod in above the rise and activated the landing thrusters—and the planet delivered yet another surprise.

Below them, the spongy growth on the hillock was moving—not just trembling in the thrust from the shuttlepod, but actually migrating away from the disturbance. When the pod touched down, it did so on bare dirt.

As this happened, the asparagus trees folded up their scales before the survey team's eyes. "And look," called Maya Castellano as she pointed out a window. "The bamboo-like plants have folded down against the ground."

"Bent over by the wind," suggested Captain Zang.

"No, they're too stiff. Look!"

Young Alec had cut the engines and the wind had subsided. The stalks began to rise again, but not like bent reeds springing upright. Instead, they remained rigid, rising in a controlled, hesitant manner.

Farid grinned. "With plants like these, who needs animals?"

The wait for the final environment check felt interminable, though it was less than half a minute. Zang Liwei took the first steps onto the planet, as was his right as *Verne*'s captain, but Farid and Maya were close behind, followed by the rest of the team. They couldn't wait to sample the nearby flora—assuming they were flora and not some kind of strange animal life.

Maya had the honor of spotting the first flying creature, a wispy sylph that mainly drifted on the strong winds but occasionally flapped its wide, translucent membranes to maneuver and achieve extra lift. Spectroanalysis showed that it, too, was a plant. Farid and Maya followed it until it took in its sails and drifted down to alight on a small pond, where it began absorbing water through its "wings."

Moments later, a set of indigo tentacles breached the pond's surface and yanked the sylph into its murky depths. Here, it seemed, even the predators were plants.

"They are essentially plants, not animals," Maya Castellano was able to confirm once the party had finished setting up their camp. This planet may have had no day or night, but humans still needed sleep—as well as a place to shelter from stellar flares. "Their composition is plantlike, they photosynthesize, they have root systems or root analogues. Their contractile fibers are more like plant cells than animal, and their internal signals are more chemical than electrical; but these are the functional equivalents of muscles and nerves."

"I still can't wrap my head around it," Alec breathed, shaking his head. "Moving plants."

"Earth plants move," Maya reminded her son. "Flowers open their petals in the morning, close them at night, and turn to follow the sun as it moves across the sky."

"But . . . the sun never moves here."

"Exactly why the plants need to," Farid Najafi realized even as he said it. "How else would they get out of the shadow of a taller plant? This answers so many questions."

"Oh, but they lead to so many more interesting questions," Maya replied, her broad, olive-skinned face splitting into a grin. "The hybrid cell structures are remarkable, but they're nothing compared to what I'm seeing on the molecular scale. So many novel compounds—I can barely begin to imagine the commercial possibilities. New classes of pharmaceutical. New types of textile—imagine a material like cotton that could contract like muscle. New crops with the nutritional value of both plants and animals. Or—or imagine the value of crops that could move themselves to maximize solar exposure or dodge harmful weather."

"Now, there's a topsy-turvy idea," Farid said.

"What's that?" asked Alec.

"Corns with feet on them." The boy groaned.

Hoping to forestall further corny jokes, Zang asked, "Did you find anything at all that you'd call an animal?"

"Not yet," the biologist replied.

"Not even insects?"

"Not a one."

"So how do the plants fertilize each other?" Alec asked his mother.

"You're still thinking in conventional terms, kid," Farid said. "If the plants can move, insects are redundant. They can take care of their own fertilization."

The boy chortled. "You mean the plants have sex? Okay, now I'm interested."

"Hold it," Maya said.

"Aw, Mom, I'm not a kid anymore. I can talk about—"

"No, not that," Maya said, holding up a finger and listening. "What's that rumbling?"

Her hearing was very sharp, but the others picked it up soon enough. Seismic readings showed its origin several kilometers away and slowly approaching. *Verne* was in the wrong orbital position to observe, so Zang sent Alec up in the shuttlepod to investigate.

"What does it look like?" the captain asked over his wristcom once the youthful pilot had reached the site of the disturbance.

A pause. *"Like Birnam Wood coming to Dunsinane, sir."*

Zang frowned. "I'm glad to know you're keeping up with your Shakespeare studies, Alec. But I also appreciate clear reports."

"Yes, sir. Um, it's a group of treelike organisms—I don't know whether to call it a herd or a grove. I'd say about fifty of them, ranging from, oh, five to twenty meters tall."

"Twenty?" Maya exclaimed.

"I said they were treelike, Mom. They must be pretty heavy; they're really mangling the undergrowth."

"How fast are they moving?" the captain asked.

"Mmm, about walking speed, say five, six klicks. That'd bring

them to the campsite in about two hours. And, Captain, they're headed directly for the camp."

Farid turned to the captain. "Then the camp had better make like the local trees and—"

"Don't you dare finish that sentence," Zang said, irritated as always by Farid's puns. "Just start packing up. Alec, get back here now."

The timing was close; it took nearly two hours to break camp and get the shuttlepod back off the ground. The survey team watched from the hovering pod as the herd of tree-things shambled—or, as Farid was determined to think of it, lumbered—directly toward their former campsite.

And then changed course and missed it altogether.

Not by much, actually; they completely trampled the folding grasses east of the hill. The stalks had apparently evolved to bend flat as protection from the planet's high winds, but that naturally proved no defense against the walking trees. "But why did they bypass the campsite?" Zang asked.

Farid shrugged. "Hospitality?"

February 12, 2166
U.S.S. Pioneer NCC-63, Earth orbit

"There you go, Lieutenant Kirk," said Doctor Liao as she finished securing the osteogenic brace. "Just stay off this leg for the next few days, and your tibia should heal up nicely."

Sam Kirk sighed. "Thanks, Doc," he said with

little cheer but as much gratitude as he could manage. "I'll do my best."

The diminutive, gray-haired doctor smiled at him, then nodded at Val Williams and Bodor chim Grev, who bracketed the sickbay bed where Kirk lay, the former holding his hand and the latter clasping his shoulder. "Now, if you'll excuse me, I have to go bug Commander Tizahr about those power grid upgrades she's been promising for a week. If I'm not back in an hour, call security."

"I am security," Val reminded her.

"And I make the calls," Grev added.

"Fine," Liao said on her way out the door. "I wouldn't quit those day jobs if I were you."

Once she was gone, Grev turned to Kirk and shook his porcine-featured head. "Sam, Sam, Sam," the Tellarite ensign intoned. "I don't know what I find more unbelievable: that you finally let Val talk you into skydiving lessons, or that you broke your leg on your very first jump."

"I'm afraid I find the latter all too believable," Kirk replied. "What was I thinking?"

"Your problem was, you thought too much," Williams told him. "You hesitated instead of trusting your instincts. I warned you about that."

"I know, I know. But . . ." He sighed again. "I don't really *have* instincts. It's not that I have anything against being impulsive, I'm just really bad at it. Whenever I try to make a snap decision, it tends to be the wrong one." He winced. "Like deciding to surprise you with my newfound interest in spacewalking in an atmosphere."

"Sam, we've been in life-or-death situations together. You handled yourself pretty damn well back on Rastish."

"That's different. When it's an emergency, when I *have* to think fast for others' sake, then the adrenaline kicks in. Otherwise, I struggle to find the right choice. I hoped that skydiving would be intense enough to help me think fast, but I guess it didn't." He smiled up at her sheepishly. "Maybe because I was too nervous about wanting to impress you."

Val studied him closely. "Was it me you wanted to impress, Sam? Or my dad? You know it doesn't matter to me if he approves of you or not."

"But it *should*. I don't want to be a source of tension between you and your family. Especially when your father is Admiral Archer's right-hand man. Besides—" He hesitated.

"Besides, what?"

Grev stepped in. Despite his habitually kindly, soft-spoken delivery, he could be as blunt as any other Tellarite. "Sam thinks it's not just your father who wishes he were tougher and more assertive. He can tell you get impatient with him sometimes."

Williams stared at Kirk. "Sam, is this true?"

He gazed back. "You tell me."

She let go of his hand, but only so she could pace sickbay while she gathered her thoughts. "Okay, look," she finally said. "Yes, I admit, I'm used to a more . . .

intense lifestyle than you prefer. I'm used to dating people who like the same. So this—the quieter times we spend just talking, or walking on the beach, or playing chess, or going to museums—it's a new gear for me. But it's not that I don't enjoy it." She came closer and took his hand again. "It's actually pretty refreshing. To slow down with you, take the time to listen to myself think and get to know myself better. It's soothing, and reassuring, and safe, and that's important to me with the life we lead.

"If I occasionally show impatience, if my attention wanders . . . it's not a judgment of you. It's just that it's not easy for me to drop out of warp. You help me find the quiet within me, but it's . . . a finite supply.

"But that's okay. I don't feel we always have to stay moving at the same pace . . . as long as we keep heading in the same direction."

There was nothing Kirk needed to say in response. He simply held her gaze, and it was all they both needed. But Grev tilted his head and folded his hands before his chest. "Oh, well said, Val! I'm going to write that one down."

6

"SO MALTUVIS WASN'T EXAGGERATING about the size of his fleet after all," Bryce Shumar remarked as he examined the scans of Psi Serpentis IV's orbital space on the bridge situation table. The tactical display showed dozens of small but powerful ships in orbit of the watery planet, enough to cover every possible approach route. Telescopic scans showed them to be spindle-shaped craft with large airfoils, resembling something out of the twentieth-century space adventure fiction that Caroline Paris had enjoyed; yet they also bore more modern features, including multiple weapon emplacements and wing-mounted nacelles that looked like warp engines. And what they lacked in advancement, they made up for in sheer numbers. "Even if it's meant more for controlling his own conquests than defending against aliens, it's still a formidable blockade."

A whistle came from the science station on the port side of the bridge. The captain was still getting used to seeing Alvaro Coelho there instead of Steven Mullen. "I'd call it sheer overkill either way," the tan-skinned Brazilian lieutenant said. "How much did he have to impoverish his people to build so many ships in such short order?"

"That's one of the things Commander Mullen's team will determine," Shumar told him, "assuming we can get them past those ships." Coming around the table and moving forward into the main section of the bridge, he faced the tactical station on his right. "Their armaments, Ensign?"

"Consistent with the resistance footage, sir," Jamala Mahendra responded. She was another less familiar face, as the regular armory officer, Morgan Kelly, was standing by with Mullen's team down in the shuttlebay. "Primarily plasma cannons, supplemented by X-ray lasers. A number of ships are specialized as bombers—mostly ultritium signatures, but I detect plutonium fission bombs on some of them. No shields, but they have polarized hull plating."

"Hmm." Shumar turned to the black-haired young woman at the helm. "Ensign Moy, move us into their detection range. And remember to make it look like we're trying to avoid detection."

"I understand, Captain," Melissa Moy answered, but there was uncertainty in her Hong Kong–accented voice. "But it'll be hard to find a weak spot in their orbital coverage."

"That doesn't matter," Shumar said. "Our goal is to *create* a weak spot. If they think we've already found one, they'll redirect other ships to shore it up."

"I get it now, sir. I just need to make us look overconfident."

"Hmp. Yes, exactly."

Whatever Moy did to create that impression, it appeared to work, since it wasn't long before several of the Saurian craft accelerated outward onto intercept trajectories. "They're hailing," Miguel Avila advised from the communications station.

"On-screen, Lieutenant."

A bulbous-eyed, smooth-skinned reptilian face appeared on the viewer, its violet complexion marking it as a member of Maltuvis's ethnic group, the M'Tezir. *"Federation ship! Your kind is no longer wanted in our space. Turn back now or be driven back!"*

"This is Captain Bryce Shumar of the Federation vessel *Essex*. Perhaps you recall us from the first Federation diplomatic mission to your world. We are here seeking to renew a dialogue with Emperor Maltuvis." It took all his discipline to utter the title and name without disgust.

The Saurian commander smiled. *"Driven back, then. I hoped you would be stupid enough to choose that."* He cut the transmission with no further ceremony.

Moments later, Mahendra called, "Three ships closing to attack range. Their weapons are charged and free to fire."

"Polarize the hull plating, but hold off on shields. Ensign Moy, evasive course toward the planet. Get us as close as you can." Both officers acknowledged the orders in turn.

Of course, moving toward the armada ensured that the ship would come under attack. But getting close enough to send aid to the surface was necessary in both their feigned plan and their real one. Luckily, the salvos the ships unleashed against *Essex* were not particularly severe, causing only minor and localized damage to the hull plating.

"Bring us closer, Moy!" Shumar ordered. "Draw as many ships out of formation as you can."

Moy gritted her teeth and continued to spiral the ship in toward the planet, while dodging and weaving enough both to elude fire and to tempt more of the silver-hulled defense ships to break orbit and come after them. At tactical, Mahendra was clenching her fists, unhappy to be holding return fire while the hull plating continued its gradual erosion. "The aft plating is down to thirty-two percent," she announced after a while.

"That's where we want it weakest," Shumar reminded her.

"Nearing optimal range," Moy announced.

Shumar tapped his command-chair controls to open a channel to the main shuttlebay. "Bridge to Shuttlepod One. Stand by for launch."

"We're braced and ready, sir," Steven Mullen's voice replied.

Shumar leaned over Moy's seat. "Time to make your mistake, Ensign."

The young flight controller sighed, reluctant to show imperfection even under orders. Shumar admired her discipline and pride in her work, but he found himself thinking that Caroline Paris would have had a lot more fun with putting on this show. He felt a twinge of regret that she was no longer around to lighten the mood.

Still, Moy carried out her error with clock-work precision. *Essex* swerved right into the path of a plasma barrage that struck the very rear of its cylindrical secondary hull. "Now, Steven!" Shumar ordered.

As soon as the barrage ended, *Essex* rocked from an internal explosion. The viewscreen showed the feed from a rear sensor as the hangar doors blew open—or rather, as a thin dummy plate impersonating the hangar doors was detonated from the inside. Assorted chunks of metallic debris were blasted out into space by the explosive decompression of the atmosphere within. The Saurians' sensors were no doubt limited, so that the radiation, vapors, and shrapnel released by the explosion would interfere with their resolution, but they should be able to determine that the debris consisted of various refined metals and polymers of the type used in spaceship bulkheads, as well as gases and liquids that would be found in a life-support system. They would probably even be able to detect several human-sized objects registering as animal tissue, though hopefully their sensors would not be advanced enough to differentiate real human flesh from synthetic meat created by a protein resequencer. They would register that the debris was on a trajectory that would carry most of it into Sauria's atmosphere, but as it would no doubt burn up before reaching the ground, they would have no cause for concern.

Thus, with any luck, they would fail to notice that one of the largest chunks of debris was the size and shape of a Starfleet shuttlepod.

"I think that's enough of that," Shumar said. "Time to limp away with our tails between our legs."

"Aye, sir," Moy said, her expression grim as she put the ship onto a wobbly retreat trajectory.

Shumar patted her shoulder. "Buck up, Ensign. You performed superbly. It isn't easy for a skilled practitioner to fail so convincingly."

She looked up at him, offering a grateful but somewhat abashed smile. "Thank you, sir."

The captain turned to Mahendra. "Status of pursuers?"

"Following but falling behind, Captain," the armory officer replied.

"As we thought, they seem to be short-range ships only," Alvaro Coelho added. "Warp capable, but it's first generation, barely more than the *Phoenix* had. Based on their emission profiles and ion-trail composition, I'd say they aren't even using dilithium-regulated annihilation—more likely an antimatter-spiked microfusion drive, which makes sense given the Saurians' inability to manufacture antimatter in large quantities. No use for anything more than interplanetary hops within the system, a fraction above warp one for a matter of hours before they exhausted their antimatter reserves." He raised his eyebrows. "Ironic—they have all that dilithium in M'Tezir, and they don't even have the ability to use it yet."

"Why even bother with warp drives, then?" Shumar mused. "It seems unnecessary for planetary defense. Let alone for controlling a surface population."

"More power for his weapons?" Mahendra suggested.

"A dedicated reactor could achieve that more efficiently without the need to power warp coils," Coelho told her. "Then again, given the speed with which he developed these ships, his Orion backers probably just sold him some existing first-generation warp-drive plans, reactor and all. Something his people grafted onto an existing surface-to-orbit aircraft design, from the look of the things." The science officer tilted his head thoughtfully. "Not so different from the *Phoenix*, actually—Cochrane's team converted that from an old nuclear missile."

"There's also the propaganda benefit," Shumar said. "Maltuvis's rule is predicated on Saurian superiority. He has to persuade his people that his regime can achieve everything outsiders can. As long as he can broadcast imagery of Saurian ships with warp nacelles, their actual performance barely matters."

Mahendra checked her readouts. "The pursuit ships are breaking off. Decelerating onto orbital reinsertion trajectories—but slow ones, relying more on gravity than thrust. It'll take them a while to get back into position."

"Good," Shumar said. "Commander Mullen's team

will have the entry window they need. Ensign Moy, once they return to formation, circle back round to take up our monitor station."

"Aye, sir."

"Mister Coelho, make sure you provide her with an up-to-date plot of the fifth planet's ring system. We may be hiding there for quite a while, and I don't want any accidents."

"Understood, Captain."

Shumar looked around the bridge. With both Mullen and Kelly on the infiltration team, Miguel Avila was now the only other person here who'd been on the alpha-shift bridge crew for more than a few months. Mahendra had been the gamma-shift armory officer for the better part of a year, but she and Shumar had rarely been on the bridge at the same time. Moy had transferred aboard after the Klingons had killed her predecessor last October. Coelho had been the supervising officer of the science labs belowdecks until Mullen's promotion to first officer mere weeks ago. The captain hadn't experienced this much crew turnaround in such quick succession since the Romulan War. And the new faces seemed to keep getting younger and younger.

After a moment, he shook off the surge of nostalgic regret. The new personnel deserved the chance to prove themselves, and so far, they were performing as well as Shumar could have asked. Rather than regretting the changes in *Essex*'s crew, he decided, he should be grateful for the opportunities they provided for new officers to gain experience and make names of their own.

Captain Shumar had no reason to doubt that the men and women around him now would make quite a name for themselves in the years ahead.

Sauria

Getting past the orbital blockade was only the first of the challenges Steven Mullen's team faced in reaching Sauria. To avoid being tracked and shot down, they had to maintain the appearance of debris as they spiraled in through the gap in the blockade, their unpowered course carrying them a third of the way around the planet while the team sat tensely in their safety harnesses over several dozen minutes, hoping they had been correct about the range limitations on the Saurians' sensors.

Well, most of the team sat tensely. Across from Mullen, Lieutenant Morgan Kelly looked almost bored. "Don't drift off on us, Morgan," Mullen teased her, mainly to distract himself and the rest of the team. "This is your plan, after all." He tried to keep any accusation out of his voice.

From the look on the armory officer's dark brown, square-jawed face, he hadn't entirely succeeded. Though her tone was stoic as she said, "I went through drops like this a few times back in the war. Either we make it or we don't. Best to save our energy for when we need it."

He studied her. "So I guess it hasn't changed your perspective much," he ventured.

Her expression barely changed, but she knew what he meant. "Transitioning, you mean." He nodded. "Not about things outside myself, no."

"May I ask . . ." She waited patiently, so he continued. "If you weren't comfortable being anatomically male, why wait so long to change? Most people I know who've transitioned did it fairly young."

"You're from Earth," Kelly replied.

"Toronto born and bred."

"The Altair colonies have more traditional ideas about gender roles. That happens on a lot of frontier worlds—you need a high birth rate to build a stable population, so it's considered proper for women of childbearing age to focus on family. That's why my big sister Janelle left to enlist in Starfleet—so she could be an engineer instead." She shrugged. "But when I enlisted, it was to fight in the war, and I guess I brought that baggage with me. I thought I'd be a better soldier if I kept up the pretense of being cis-male. And the testosterone, the stronger body, didn't hurt."

"You still look plenty strong to me, Lieutenant." He tried to keep it from sounding flirtatious. The fact that Kelly had been essentially male in physiology until five years ago did nothing to detract from her striking attractiveness as a woman; if anything, it was part of what made her so distinctively compelling. When Mullen was with her, it was difficult to remember that his new status as first officer made it inappropriate to pursue a romance with anyone under his command. His girlfriend Melina, formerly the ship's chef, had been abruptly transferred to Starbase 12 as a consequence of his unexpected promotion, as Captain Shumar would not allow them to continue their relationship while serving on the same vessel. The resultant argument between Mullen and Melina had led to their breakup, rendering it a moot point anyway. The last thing he needed now was to let his rebound attraction to Kelly disrupt the mission.

Kelly's expression made it clear that he'd again failed to hide his subtext from her, but she chose to ignore it. "I have to work at it a bit more," she said. "But it's worth it. This is the body I always belonged in. I realized that when I was nearly killed at Tenebia. The physical therapy afterward, relearning how to use my body . . . I fought the therapists at every step. One of them finally smacked some sense into me and helped me see that I was fighting my own body—that it was the wrong body for me, and I'd always known it. It was making me weaker, not stronger. I didn't have time to get the surgeries until after the war, but just accepting that I was a woman, regardless of my anatomy, was what I needed to heal. In more ways than one."

Mullen stared at her admiringly. "Well . . . I'm glad you found the right path. I think it suits you. A-as an officer, I mean. You're . . . very good at your job."

Unexpectedly, Kelly softened and gave him a small, wry smile. "I know what you mean. And thanks."

Once the pod sank deep enough into Sauria's outer atmosphere for a plasma trail to begin forming around and behind it, the pilot was able to extend the wings and stabilize the small vessel's flight—yet he still had to maintain a steady course like an incoming bolide to avoid attracting attention. Only once they set off the charge to simulate the bolide exploding in the upper atmosphere, blinding any sensors, did Crewman Roget fire the engines in a quick burst to take the pod away from the explosion site and onto a stealthy low-altitude course for Lyaksti. Large meteoric explosions in the upper atmosphere were a daily event on most planets, statistically more likely to occur over ocean or empty land than a populated area. Roget had timed the blast to occur over one of Sauria's many wide stretches of open ocean, where it was unlikely to alarm anyone.

Lyaksti, the largest of Sauria's dozens of small land masses, was a rainforested continent, much like Brazil in size and ecology. That meant there was abundant cloud cover to shield the shuttlepod's final approach. With the capital city in ruins, the leaders of the resistance had retreated upriver to the ancient city of Akleyro in the inland rainforest, one of the few enclaves that had managed to retain some degree of autonomy due to its remoteness and harsh surroundings, as well as its historical and religious significance. Mullen looked forward to seeing it. Although he was no longer a science officer, he was still an explorer at heart.

The landing coordinates the resistance had provided

were for a small mesa on the edge of the canyon carved by the Vasakleyro River, under the near-perpetual shadow of the canyon's northern wall (for Lyaksti was in the planet's southern hemisphere). There, Mullen, Kelly, and the rest of their team were met by an armed squad consisting of two salmon-skinned Saurians, a massive Rigelian Chelon, and a stubbly-chinned young human with black hair and olive skin. After trading introductions, the human—Antonio Ruiz, evidently the man who'd documented the devastation of the capital city—looked over Mullen's party unhappily. "Is this all Starfleet has for us? A half-dozen people?"

"It's our first step," Kelly said. "It's not easy to get past Maltuvis's blockade."

"And we can't just send in an invasion force without making Maltuvis's propaganda about aliens seem justified," Mullen added. "We're going to help free Sauria, but it's going to take time and patience."

"Tell that to all the people who are going to die in the meantime," Ruiz said. "Luckily you aren't the only ones who've come to help."

Mullen furrowed his brow. "What do you mean?"

"Come with us," Ruiz said, "and you'll see."

The resistance members led the Starfleet team on a hike upriver, along the increasingly narrow shore between the Vasakleyro and the canyon wall. The walls' sheer faces on both sides of the river were notched with deep vertical fissures carved by the steady trickle of water from the rainforest above, giving them the aspect of enormous stone teeth. Atop the cliffs, the roots of the rainforest's massive trees curved over to hug the walls, while the tree canopies on both sides stretched far outward overhead, nearly meeting in the middle and providing the canyon with the kind of constant shade that the nocturnal Saurians relied on for their permanent habitations. It was no wonder Akleyro had been built here—and that the resistance was centered here, for the canopy and canyon walls also provided excellent cover from the sensors of orbiting battleships and spy satellites.

"Keep your night-vision scopes on and your phase pistols handy," Ruiz cautioned. "Sauria's a harsh planet, and we humans are a lot more fragile than the natives, or than Coraniach here," he said, slapping the Chelon on his dorsal shell. "There are serpents in the water that attack if you get too close. Oh, and keep your eyes on the rock fissures. There are giant crustaceans that hide in them, lying in wait for prey."

Kelly looked around warily. "So don't get too close to either the river *or* the walls. Exactly how narrow is the safe path between?"

"Depends on how hungry they are," Ruiz said.

"Right," the statuesque woman replied. "Single file, everybody."

Either Ruiz was bluffing or the local fauna had already dined, for the group made it to the city without incident. Akleyro did not disappoint. It was carved right into the vast stone teeth of the canyon walls. Within the twilight of the chasm, thousands of windows, archways, and galleries within the living stone gleamed with multicolored bioluminescence. The plazas carved from the more expansive fissures were crowned by large firewasp nests overhead, ensuring that many of the glowing, bioengineered insects congregated around them. Hundreds of rope bridges, made (according to Ruiz) of specially bred plant fibers nearly as strong as steel cable, formed precarious catenaries across the gorge, yet numerous Akleyro citizens traipsed across them as confidently as Mullen would stride down a starship corridor.

"That looks like fun," Kelly remarked, and Mullen couldn't tell from her dry tone whether she was kidding or not.

"In the dark?" he muttered back. "No, thanks."

"We've got night scopes," Kelly replied, tapping the glowing monocular lens that covered her right eye.

"Yeah, but it's all green on green." He fidgeted with his own scope briefly, then shrugged. "On second thought, I'd probably hate it even more if I could see clearly."

She moved in closer. "If we do have to cross one of those, just keep your fears to yourself," she murmured. "Remember, you're our leader now. Your doubts become your crew's."

Mullen nodded. "Right. Thanks." The reminder of his inexperience embarrassed him—but at the same time, he felt grateful for Kelly's support.

Fortunately, Ruiz's destination proved to be on the north side of the river, sparing the *Essex* team from the need to reconnect with their brachiating-primate roots. It felt more like reverting to the stage of burrowing rodents as the resistance members led them through the dark, twisting passages carved deep into the rock, finally emerging in a large, low-ceilinged chamber. The room was moderately well lit, no doubt to accommodate the offworlders of various species that Mullen noted among the group, so the *Essex* team members were able to deactivate their night scopes and fold their lenses back.

Ruiz and Coraniach led the team toward a large central desk where a wizened, green-bronze Saurian female sat surrounded by advisors. Mullen recognized her as Moxat, the deposed presider of the Saurian Global League and leader of the government in exile. She rose to greet them, the dignity in her bearing undiminished. "Lieutenant Commander Mullen. It is good to see you again."

He shook her hand. "It's commander now, Presider. I'm *Essex*'s first officer, and leader of this party." He proceeded to introduce Kelly and the rest of the team.

"I trust no harm has befallen Captain Shumar or Commander Paris," Moxat said.

"On the contrary, ma'am. Commander Paris was recently promoted to captain. I'm trying to fill her shoes as Captain Shumar's exec."

"Shoes?" Moxat asked, tilting her head quizzically. Even Saurian leaders rarely covered their webbed feet.

"Um, just an idiom, ma'am. What I mean to say is,

we're here to provide whatever assistance we can, and to lay the groundwork for future Starfleet aid toward the restoration of freedom to the Saurian people."

Moxat's wide-set, bulbous eyes caught him between them. "I note you take care to emphasize the positive goal, rather than the act that we both know will be necessary to achieve it: the death of Maltuvis."

Mullen fidgeted. "His removal from power, certainly. I'm sure you'd like to see him stand trial for his crimes, if possible."

"That is the ideal, according to my upbringing and the principles of the Global League. But in practice . . . I recognize that there is no way a tyrant like Maltuvis would let himself be taken alive, and I admit to being glad of it. I would not have admitted that a month ago, perhaps not even to myself. But after what his ships did to my home city, Commander, I admit it freely."

Kelly spoke up. "That's your right, Presider. We're not here to tell you what to do, but to help you do it yourselves."

"I know, Lieutenant Kelly. That is why my government chose to welcome the Federation in the first place. If you had come as conquerors . . ." She paused. "Well. Perhaps my people have proven more passive in the face of conquest than I would have believed before."

"When it's one of their own," Antonio Ruiz interposed. "And when he spins it as a common defense against aliens."

"Then we have to remind the people that the aliens aren't their real enemy," Mullen said. "That's why I want to focus on the positive, ma'am. On providing relief, medical aid, whatever we can do to repair the breaches of trust that Maltuvis engineered between your people and ours. A military victory over Maltuvis won't last unless it's legitimate in the eyes of the people."

Moxat looked pleased. "I think I underestimated you, Commander. That is an excellent point." She sobered. "Nonetheless, military victories will be essential. Most of all, we must direct our efforts toward destroying Maltuvis's orbital ships and the factories that create them. More of those factories are under construction even now, being built in conquered territories and using slave labor—forcing the oppressed peoples to participate in creating the engines of their own oppression."

"We'll do what we can to assist with that as well, Presider," Kelly said. "But for now, until we can devise a more reliable way past the blockade, there's not much we can offer militarily beyond advice and training."

"Luckily," Ruiz put in, "we already have some help on the guerrilla side of things."

After getting Moxat's leave to withdraw, Ruiz led the team toward a corner where a group of Saurians and a few offworlders were unloading a large crate of phase rifles under the supervision of another offworlder—a broad-faced, hairless humanoid male with gray reptilian scales. Several low, parallel ridges of raised scales adorned his scalp and cheeks, and two others shaded his eyes. The species looked familiar to Mullen, but he couldn't quite place it. "Ahh, at last our Starfleet benefactors have deigned to arrive," the humanoid boomed in a deep, resonant voice.

"This is Commander Steven Mullen of the *Essex*," Ruiz told him, going on to introduce the rest. "Commander, this is Dular Garos of Maluria. His organization, the Raldul alignment, has been providing arms to the resistance."

Kelly stepped forward to confront the Malurian. "Garos! You were the one who helped the Orion Syndicate stir up the Vertian crisis. You destroyed an Andorian battle cruiser. And you tried to sabotage Rigel's admission to the Federation!"

"I *did* have an alliance with the Three Sisters, I admit," Garos replied in a mollifying tone. "It was a partnership of convenience. My alignment works to promote Malurian expansion into space, in the name of the long-term future of our civilization. In the ideology of our rulers, that makes us criminals, so we have had no choice but to ally with criminals to survive." He tilted his head back. "But if you know my record so well, Lieutenant . . ."

"Kelly," she reminded him. "Morgan Kelly."

"Then you should recall that I turned against the Rigelian faction behind the sabotage and provided intelligence that helped Starfleet prevail in the crisis."

"Only because your partners betrayed you first."

"Precisely. They forced me to employ my defense mechanism—which foiled the Sisters' plans as well as my own. Yet the Sisters are not known for their forgiving nature. They blamed *me* for the failure of their Rigelian scheme. They classified me and my alignment as their enemies." He crossed his arms. "So we have chosen to live up to their expectations. If helping Maltuvis in his conquests helps the Sisters' plans, then Raldul will support Maltuvis's opponents."

"And just how much is this 'support' costing them?"

"We still have to make a profit. But Sauria is a wealthy world. Its people can afford to sign away a few mining rights and trade concessions." Garos shrugged. "More than they can afford to live under a brutal tyrant. So you see, we're all on the same side here."

"But not for the same reasons."

"It's not as if the Federation's motives are selfless. Maltuvis would still be the despot of a small, impoverished land if not for your insatiable appetite for dilithium." His scaled face twisted into a smile. "So can we accept that we both have a vested interest in making up for past mistakes?"

Kelly bristled, but Mullen touched her arm. "It's the Saurians' world, so it's their decision. If they trust you," he said to Garos, "then that means our interests align, at least here and now."

"I appreciate it, Commander Mullen. That's the Starfleet spirit I've seen before. Perhaps someday my people will have the luxury of your ideals."

Once they'd parted from Garos, Kelly remained tense. "I'll work with him for the Saurians' sake . . . but I still don't trust him."

Mullen held her gaze. "Good. Because somebody needs to keep an eye on him."

February 20, 2166
Stameris (Lambda Serpentis VII)

The rendezvous site that Charles Tucker had transmitted to Devna two weeks before was on Stameris, an unaligned planet ten light-years from Sauria. There were several reasons he had chosen to meet with her near their destination rather than arranging to travel together. For one thing, Stameris was an obscure planet, as yet unexplored by Starfleet. Though less than forty light-years from Earth, it was more or less in the opposite direction from the Federation's recent growth, and its system contained no naturally habitable worlds. Tucker had first heard of Stameris some fourteen years before, when *Enterprise* had been hijacked by pirates from an unidentified species of diminutive, large-eared humanoids who had intended to sell its female personnel at a slave market on the planet. That market, he had since learned, was held periodically at a trading outpost on the otherwise barren world, far from the reach of any interstellar authorities. Naturally, the Orion Syndicate was one of the criminal organizations that patronized the slave market, and that gave

Devna an excuse to travel here without arousing suspicion.

The other things Devna might arouse were yet another good reason Tucker had not wanted to be alone with her in a small ship for two weeks. His bond to T'Pol had made him immune to Orion pheromones in the past, but he was unsure if that was still the case. Last year, an ordeal T'Pol had suffered on Vulcan had shut down their ability to communicate telepathically over great distances, and since that ability had been anomalous even for bonded Vulcan couples, T'Pol was inclined to doubt that it would ever return. Tucker was not yet sure whether his resistance to Orion pheromones had gone with it. Even if his resistance remained, Devna was still an extremely beautiful woman whose entire life revolved around seduction. He had no wish to be unfaithful to T'Pol, but there was no point in testing his resolve more than he had to.

Tucker attended the slave market disguised as a member of the Eska species—a people who relished hunting and were not always concerned with ethics. Devna had somehow managed to arrange for her master, an Orion male named Parrec-Sut, to assign her a mission to infiltrate an Eska criminal operation engaged in smuggling the skins and organs of endangered or sapient animals from multiple worlds, in order to assess whether it was worth the Syndicate's while to muscle in on the operation. Tucker's years of espionage training let him mask his distaste as he attended the slave auction as an interested customer. It took rather less acting to appear intrigued by Devna when Parrec-Sut brought her out to dance for him in extremely skimpy attire. The Orion spy was certainly lovely, with a lissome, agile frame, lime-green skin, almond-shaped eyes with large, emerald irises, and void-black hair that tumbled to the small of her back. But it was the grace and beauty of her dancing, the sense of liberation and joy he felt from her as she performed, that he found truly compelling. He remembered how trapped Devna had seemed when they had first met. There was no trace of that burden upon her now—though it returned once she stopped dancing.

Tucker's plan was that, when his mission on Sauria was done, he would tip Starfleet off to the Eska smuggling operation, providing a pretense for Devna's "rescue" and return to Orion, and incidentally saving the creatures the Eska murdered for sport. But even as he haggled with Parrec-Sut for the purchase of Devna, he hoped that he could persuade her to take the opportunity to escape slavery once and for all.

Once the sale was made, Devna came aboard Tucker's scout ship with no possessions save a small bag of even smaller garments, makeup and grooming items, and sexual paraphernalia. He showed her to a private cabin and invited her to select an appropriate garment from its wardrobe fabricator while he removed his Eska makeup. It was rather a relief to confirm that he still could resist her allure enough to leave her alone in the room.

When he emerged barefaced once more, he found Devna far less bare-bodied than before, attired in a short-sleeved, functional catsuit in dark red. Tucker couldn't help staring. "This is the first time I've seen you actually wearing anything to speak of," he explained at her inquisitive look. "It, uh, it suits you."

She was unmoved by the compliment. "It suits the mission," she replied in the breathy soprano lilt he remembered so well. "Personally, I find it confining."

"Well, I-I appreciate it," he said. "After all, this is a working partnership. I'd prefer to avoid any distractions."

"You're clearly still immune to my influence."

"To your pheromones, yes." *Thank God.* "But those are far from your only charms."

She gave him a smile that seemed oddly pitying. "I promise not to take advantage of your vulnerability, Charles. It's all right for you to relax."

"Yeah, that's not likely. Best if we just get a move on. The sooner we can get to Sauria, the better."

Tucker moved to the cockpit, where Devna joined him in the copilot's seat. Once they were under way, he turned to her. "How much do you know about the Three Sisters' plan to cause a disaster on Sauria?"

"Thanks to my mistress Maras's indulgence, I was on hand to hear much of their planning. I have all the information we should need to expose and prevent the plot."

"And frame my employers for initiating it. Don't forget how important that part is."

Devna's emerald eyes pierced his. "I had thought the most important part to you was to save lives. That that was why you did this." In his abashed silence, she went on, lowering her gaze. "Among the Dhei'ten—the Deltans—I gained a greater appreciation for . . . the unity of life. The shared value of it."

"Of course. You're right, that is why I'm doing this. And the fact that I needed an Orion spy to remind me of that is why I so badly need to get out." He stopped himself. "I'm sorry, I shouldn't have put it that way. If there's one thing you aren't, Devna, it's a typical Orion spy."

After a hesitant moment, she faced him again. "In fact . . . you are not alone in having an ulterior purpose. You seek to tie your employers to the Syndicate. My condition for helping you, Charles, is that, in doing so, you tie them solely to D'Nesh, the middle Sister. I have the information you will require to plant evidence linking to her—but only to her. Do you accept this?"

He studied her for a moment. "As long as my employers are compromised, it doesn't matter which Sister we use." A pause. "Can I ask, why D'Nesh?"

She considered her response. "No one who has been her slave would need to ask why."

Tucker nodded. "Okay. I won't pry. One thing about bein' free—you're entitled to your privacy."

"I'm not free, Charles. Technically, I belong to you now."

"Then consider yourself manumitted, Devna. I need a partner, not a pet."

Devna was skeptical. "It can't be that easy."

"Freedom is your right by birth. It always has been. All I have to do is acknowledge it."

After a tense moment, Devna shot out of the chair and moved to the rear of the cockpit. It was the first movement he'd ever seen from her that wasn't composed and graceful. After a few moments, she spoke even more softly than usual. "I would make a request of you."

"Anything."

"We both have a mission to complete. That is where I need my focus to be. I need a clear sense of who I am and who is in charge. These . . . larger questions . . . they are too much for me now. So . . . please, Charles . . . let me have the comfort of considering you my master. It gives me structure."

Tucker wanted to protest that the request caused him considerable discomfort. He was unsure enough of his ethics as it was. And absolute power over another being was a difficult temptation to resist. But by that same token, it would be selfish to place his own discomfort over hers. "All right, Devna," he said, feeling compelled to use her name, to remind them both of her personhood. "You can define our relationship however you want. And as far as chain of command goes, sure—this is my operation, so I give the orders. But I don't want you to be passive and unquestioning. You're smart, you're experienced, you're a keen observer—I expect you to contribute. Assert yourself when you have an idea or a question. Argue with me if you think I'm about to make the wrong choice." After considering his words, he smirked. "Like . . . you've already been doing all along."

"As you wish."

He pointed at her. "And don't even *think* about calling me 'master.'"

"Of course not, Charles."

"Trip. My friends call me Trip."

"As you wish, Trip."

He sighed. This was going to take some work. "Okay . . . what say we get back to the mission planning? Tell me what you know about the Sisters' plan. How is Maltuvis supposed to maneuver Starfleet into causing a catastrophe?"

Devna returned to her seat. "It will not be Maltuvis—not directly. Starfleet is aiding the resistance—so it is in the resistance that we have placed our key agents."

Tucker leaned back in surprise. "How'd they arrange that?"

"The agents play the role of arms suppliers and military advisors—just as the Sisters' chief male Harrad-Sar does for Maltuvis. By arming and influencing both sides, the Sisters can engineer the conflict to suit their goals."

"I can't believe the resistance would accept help from the Orions. Surely they know you're backing Maltuvis."

"Our agents in the resistance are not Orion. They are an ally the Sisters have used before—in fact, you and I first met when you foiled one of their plans. They are Malurians . . . led by a man named Dular Garos."

7

"THE TREES . . . ARE ALIVE?"

Hoshi Sato winced at Takashi Kimura's question. "Well, of course they're alive—they're trees," the linguist in her answered before the fiancée in her could make allowances for Takashi's language difficulties. On her desk screen, he winced in embarrassment. "Sorry," she said. "I know what you meant."

"Mean . . . they move. Walk."

"The *Jules Verne* crew calls them dryads," she said. She saw him straining to recall the word. "Like *kodama*," she clarified. "But more Greek."

"Ah. So . . . have spirits? In-intelligent?"

"That's what Starfleet's sending us to Birnam to find out. Apparently it's a topic of controversy among the *Verne* crew. Their science team found that the dryads' internal tissues have chemical properties that could lead to some powerful new pharmaceuticals and medical treatments. They could be worth a fortune."

Takashi nodded, understanding that well enough. In many ways, it was lucky for starfarers that the same basic DNA code and biochemistry had been found on planets all over the known galaxy, for it meant that habitable environments and edible foods were easy to find. But the downside of being able to eat a planet's foods was that its disease organisms could eat you in return. Not to mention that the Earthly germs you brought with you were constantly evolving in new planetary conditions or mutating from space radiation, so that even a disease thought long conquered could cough up, so to speak, a new strain resistant to conventional medicines. Hence the ongoing search for useful new drugs and remedies, which drove the "Space Boomer" crews of the Earth Cargo Service as powerfully as their quest for alien technology, dilithium, rare earths, and exotic foods and artworks.

"Their captain wants to start harvesting the dryads to extract it right away," Sato went on. "Which would require killing them, but their science officer says he's found evidence of intelligent behavior and communication. But he doesn't have hard proof."

Takashi smiled. *"So they called you. Who better?"*

Hoshi smiled back. "They called *us*. Their own science team couldn't agree on it, so they asked for an outside opinion. I'll do my part to examine the evidence of communication, but Elizabeth will probably do the bulk of the work."

"Hm. How would trees talk?"

"On a trunk system, of course."

He groaned. *"For making . . . log entries?"*

"You *wood* say that." She was glad to hear him making puns—it was good exercise for his impaired language and problem-solving skills. But she was also intrigued by the point he'd raised. "Seriously, it's a good question. From the reports, it sounds like they've detected chemical signals passing among the dryads. Many known plants do communicate through scent and pheromonal exchanges, but the science officer claims these signals are unusually complex. But whether that complexity is the right kind to be a potential language . . . that I'll have to see when we get there."

"Sounds like a great challenge. New kind of life . . . tough problem to crack . . . nobody shooting."

While that last might have sounded like self-pity to some ears, she knew Takashi was thinking more of her safety than his own traumatic memories. "It does sound like a fascinating world. I'm not sure how peaceful it'll be, though. Boomers don't tend to be too happy with Starfleet butting into their affairs. Things must be pretty tense between them already if they'd call us in to mediate."

"Don't worry," he replied. *"Once you talk to the trees . . . sure you'll be very poplar."*

Hoshi dearly wished there were a way to throw something at him over subspace.

February 24, 2166
Palais de la Concorde, Paris

"I agree that there must be a noninterference directive," intoned Percival Kimbridge, the dignified, dark-complexioned Federation councillor from Earth. "We may debate the ambiguities of contacts with starfaring peoples like the Partnership," the middle-aged human went on, his booming voice echoing off the pristine new walls of the conference room, "but when it comes to younger civilizations, our responsibilities are clear. History is replete with examples of the destruction wrought on primitive societies exposed to ideas they are not yet ready to understand."

"That is pure arrogance!" objected Councillor Kishkik Sajithen of Rigel, pounding the conference table with a heavy manus. "Most of the problems my people faced in our contact with the other Rigelian species," continued the Chelon female, "were a direct result of their condescending belief that they were more qualified than we were to make decisions about our own lives, our own environment. Had they respected our better understanding of our world from the start, the damage would not have been done."

"I fear Councillor Kimbridge is . . . overzealous," Commissioner Soval interposed. "The intention of the proposed directive has never been to discredit the ability of other civilizations to make their own choices, but rather, to respect it. I'm sure Admiral Archer would be glad to clarify."

Next to Soval, Archer jerked back to full attention on hearing his name. Chastising himself for growing distracted during the Federation Council's panel review of his noninterference proposal, he strove to catch up with the conversation as best he could.

"That's right. What's at issue here isn't other civilizations' wisdom—it's our own. We can't assume that just having more advanced technology makes us wiser, or gives us a better understanding of a civilization's needs than its own people. That assumption that we know better is exactly what creates the danger to other societies if we allow ourselves to interfere. It's not about whether they can understand our ideas, it's about whether we can understand theirs. We didn't understand the Partnership's symbiosis with the Ware. We didn't understand how unstable the political situation was on Sauria. But we assumed we knew better, and that's why we messed up."

"But those are different situations," Kimbridge objected. "One was an interstellar civilization already, the other a pre-spaceflight world with whom we made first contact. Surely there is a fundamental difference in their readiness for such contact."

"The principle is the same either way, Councillor. No matter how advanced another society is, they know their needs and values better than we do. Therefore, we have an obligation to respect their independence. In the case of pre-contact worlds, it's best to leave them to discover space travel and aliens on their own, so that they can develop their own understanding of science and not become dependent on us. Also, it's to protect *us* from the temptation of using our greater power to boss them around.

"But when it comes to post-contact, starfaring worlds, we have just as great a responsibility to respect their autonomy and freedom of choice. For instance, by not trying to force another culture to change a practice we dislike. Or not taking sides in a civil war. History shows the dangers of that kind of intervention in other nations' politics—the ways that misconceptions of their cultural dynamics and needs can cause the intervening nation to do more harm than good. We can interact with worlds like that, trade with them, be good neighbors—but part of being a good neighbor, or a good friend, is not butting in where you aren't invited."

"But isn't that just what we're currently doing on Sauria?" asked Nasrin Sloane, the councillor from Alpha Centauri. "Favoring one side in an internal conflict?"

"I reluctantly accept that as a necessary measure to correct the mistake resulting from our initial intervention," Archer said. "But if the noninterference policy had been in place from the beginning, that mistake never would have been made. This directive is about preventing us from making such mistakes in the future."

Across the table, Admiral Shran leaned forward. "All this sounds very noble, Jon. But can you really expect people to understand all these moral complexities? People don't like to admit their own fallibility, even if you put a rule in place designed to remind them of it. Say this directive of yours becomes Federation law. You can explain it all you want in the press, teach the moral philosophy in detail at Starfleet Academy, and sure, maybe most officers will get it at first. But people are lazy. Give them long enough and they'll reduce any complex idea to its simplest level. How can you be sure that the next generation of officers, or the one after that, or the one after that, will still remember the humble principle behind the policy? What if they really do end up thinking it's about protecting 'primitives' from advanced knowledge? Just how far would they take that so-called protection? Would they refuse to give them medicine that would save millions of lives? Would they even allow a whole world to succumb to a natural disaster rather than reveal the existence of spaceflight and other worlds to them?"

Archer scoffed. "Come on, Shran, that's ridiculous. No one would ever be so twisted as to think it made sense to let a whole species die in order to avoid harming them!"

"They might—if they were more faithful to the letter of the law than its spirit. You know that's possible. Not everyone bothers to think about *why* the rules are what they are—they just do what they're told. That's why a rigid ban on all intervention is too dangerous. It gives people an excuse to follow the rules blindly and fail to apply their own judgment. If we want our captains to be responsible, we have to let them make these decisions for themselves, case by case. That way, they have to consider the reasons behind their choices."

Archer fell silent, unable to muster a good counterargument. Though he wouldn't admit it aloud in this context, he was starting to have doubts. The fact that both the Orion Syndicate and Section 31 wanted the noninterference directive to pass had kept him up nights wondering if he might be on the wrong side. Even if the principle were legitimate, the fact that others saw ways to corrupt the directive might mean that it was the wrong way of serving that principle. Maybe Shran was right that it might be misapplied by future generations, its original intentions forgotten. The directive was meant to minimize the harm that Starfleet crews could do to other societies, but what if it ended up causing equal or greater harm?

Soval did his best to continue making the case, falling back on the Vulcans' traditional arguments for their own longstanding policy of nonintervention. This only served to rile Shran, who pointed out the often self-serving and hypocritical ways the defunct Vulcan High Command had misapplied or disregarded that rule in their historical dealings with Andoria, Earth, and other cultures. The session only deteriorated from there, and Archer was no help in bringing it back on track.

Once the meeting adjourned, Soval led Archer into a vacant side office to speak to him privately. "Admiral, considering that this is your initiative, it does little to aid its chances if you are unable to muster an effective defense of it. Your attention barely seemed to be on the meeting."

"I'm sorry, Soval. I've just been . . . I've been distracted lately. It's a hard time for me."

Soval furrowed his brow. "Can you explain the nature of your distress?"

The human hesitated, but he couldn't dodge such a direct question. "It's Porthos."

The commissioner reacted with surprise. "Your canine companion?"

"My pet beagle, yes. He . . ." Archer sighed heavily. "The vet told me yesterday that he hasn't got long left to live. He's only eighteen, and with modern medicine, a lot of beagles make it to twenty or more . . . but Porthos is already living on borrowed time. He almost died back in '52, when a Kreetassan virus shut down his immune system. Phlox had to replace his pituitary gland with one from an alien lizard. The vet tells me it's actually pretty remarkable that Porthos has lived this long." He blinked rapidly. "But that doesn't make it easier to cope with the end coming."

Soval's gaze was stony. "Admiral—we are confronting an issue urgent to the entire future of the Federation and perhaps many other civilizations. You cannot afford to be distracted by your emotional attachment to a small animal."

"You don't understand. I've lived with dogs since I was a boy. Porthos has been with me through all the hardest and most important experiences of my adult life. The whole time I was aboard *Enterprise*, from Klaang all the way to the Battle of Cheron, Porthos was there."

"None of which is relevant to the role you must play now, Admiral. You may indulge your sentiment when you are not addressing far more important matters." Soval paused. "Do not forget all you have learned of Vulcan discipline. The needs of the many outweigh the needs of . . . a pet."

The admiral clenched his fists as Soval strode away. He should have known better than to expect the haughty commissioner to understand. But in his own condescending way, Soval had a point. With so much else to worry about right now, the need to face Porthos's mortality could not have come at a worse time. Or maybe it was the debate that had come at the worst time. He wanted nothing more right now than to be at home, keeping his dear old friend company in his last weeks (days?). But his duties kept getting in the way. And those duties were, indeed, too important to walk away from. It was an agonizing truth to face.

Archer strode from the room and headed for the orbital shuttle terminal. At least he could go home now and spend a little more time with Porthos. They could no longer play together as they once had; the little dog had even lost his appetite for cheese. But at least he could sit with his old friend in his lap, and keep him company while he could. The comfort that would bring Archer would be bittersweet at best . . . but giving comfort to the ailing Porthos was the thing that truly mattered. That was something Soval would never understand.

February 26, 2166
Akleyro, Sauria

The fact that the Malurians running guns to the Saurian resistance were double agents for the Orion

Syndicate made it relatively easy for Charles Tucker and Devna to get through the orbital blockade. Tucker presented himself as a Space Boomer arms dealer recruited by the Syndicate to supplement the Raldul alignment's supply effort, using Syndicate authorization protocols provided by Devna. In this way, they were able to hitch a ride with the Malurians on their next arms delivery to the surface, using Orion-provided clearance codes to gain safe passage through the blockade. Devna operated under the alias of Elevia, supposedly a slave provided to Tucker in payment for his services—and, implicitly, to monitor his activity on the Syndicate's behalf and assassinate him should he prove unreliable. Playing that role required Devna to adopt skimpier attire than she had worn aboard their scout ship, but she had gone with a compromise, an elaborately patterned red-orange halter top, abbreviated shorts, and calf-length boots. It was about as concealing as T'Pol's regulation underwear, but by Devna's standards, it was downright modest.

The trek from Raldul's secret landing site through the dense jungle surrounding Akleyro proved more hazardous than the passage through the blockade. The Malurians had been through the rainforest enough times to be alert to the local predators and quick on the trigger when they drew near, and Tucker's own intensive training served him in stead of such experience, enabling him to get off a phase pistol shot at a fierce-looking gliding lizard that swooped down on him from the lower limbs of the canopy overhead. But not all Saurian predators were as easy to spot. While the group rested against a tree bole as wide as *Enterprise*'s engine room, one of its supporting roots suddenly moved, revealing itself to be a huge serpent whose scales mimicked the bark of a root. The serpent wrapped its body around Devna, and Tucker was afraid to shoot for fear of hitting her. He tried aiming lower on its body, but the real roots surrounding it confused him.

Moments later, the serpent trembled and fell to the ground, its coils relaxing around Devna. Tucker rushed to her side and offered a hand to help her climb free—but she cautioned him to avoid the poisoned needle she held, then extricated herself lithely on her own. "I've been in more dangerous embraces," she said, seeming almost bored by the whole thing.

Tucker stared in amazement. "How can you be so calm about all this?"

She resumed the march, while the Malurians gathered up the arms crates behind them. "It's a survival trait for a sex slave," she explained. "I withdraw within myself. Detach from whatever is said to me or done to my body, from whatever motions I am trained to go through, so that it doesn't reach me." She gave a faint shrug. "As you see, it has other benefits."

The human shook his head. "I never know whether to be sad for you or impressed as hell."

"Whichever you choose, it matters little to me. Which is essentially the point."

Once they finally reached the resistance headquarters

and were introduced to Dular Garos, the Raldul operative was less than pleased to see them. "It was reckless of the Sisters to send a representative directly to me—especially with one of their agents at his side," the gray-scaled humanoid intoned. "If it were to be confirmed that Maltuvis has Orion backing, then your presence here could risk exposing the larger strategy."

Tucker spread his arms. "Plenty of Orion slave women out there. Not all of them are secret agents."

Garos's gangsterish features twisted skeptically. "Would you care to wager on the percentage?"

"Anyway, it's not something you have to worry about. You see, we're not actually here on the Sisters' behalf."

"Then what—"

The Malurian broke off at the sound of new arrivals at the entrance. Tucker turned to see a Chelon and a human entering—and his eyes widened in recognition at the latter. "Garos, good, I see the new shipment's finally here," Antonio Ruiz said. "Maybe if we get in some practice, it'll help distract from all the strategy arguments and—" He faltered, staring at the other human in the room. "Albert?" he asked. "Albert Sims?"

Tucker sighed. He didn't look quite the same as he had under that identity, but he and Ruiz had gotten to know each other pretty well during his previous visit to Sauria. "Hey, Tony. Been a while."

Ruiz rushed over to him. "Yeah, it has."

For the second time in two years, Tucker saw Ruiz's punch coming a mile away and let it hit home regardless. He deserved it no less now than he had then. "Good to see you too, buddy," he said as he rubbed his jaw afterward.

Devna swiftly interposed herself, stroking Ruiz's chest. "There's no need for that, is there? We're all friends here."

"It's all right," Tucker told her, regaining his feet. "Nothing I didn't have coming. Let him go."

After a probing glance at Tucker, the Orion spy shrugged and released Ruiz, who was visibly reeling from her pheromonal whammy. Meanwhile, Garos looked confused. "Sims? You told my men your name was Victor Lund."

"He's a Federation spy," Ruiz explained, his anger letting himself shake off Devna's influence. "At least, I figured he was. I guess I have my proof now. So why are you back, Al? Victor? Mal-toothless already cut off the Fed's dilithium gravy train, so you got nothing to gain by sabotaging the resistance. Or did your masters finally decide to close the barn door after the cows got slaughtered?"

"I have my own questions," Garos broke in, his commanding voice halting Ruiz's tirade. He crossed his arms and looked back and forth at his new visitors. "A Federation agent with an Orion agent? Which of you is the defector?"

Tucker gave a slight grin. "Would you believe both? Tony's right—my employers pulled me out two years ago because they didn't want me disrupting the mining deal with Maltuvis. They figured the Federation's material wealth was more important than the Saurians' freedom." He turned to Ruiz, not needing to feign his abashed tone. "You were right about me, Tony. I didn't have the courage to say no when I knew my orders were wrong, like you did. It took a few more wrong orders before I managed to find my spine. If I'd stood with you when you asked . . . well, the Saurians and a lot more people besides might be better off. I'm sorry."

The younger human looked wary—but Garos was even more so. "And you?" he challenged Devna. "What did he offer you to gain your defection?"

"The only thing I have ever truly desired," Devna replied. "Freedom. Which is why I join him in fighting for Sauria's freedom." She told the lie with a perfect facsimile of sincerity.

"Starfleet is here for the same reason," Garos said, turning back to Tucker. "How, then, are you in defiance of your Federation masters?"

"Not everyone shares Starfleet's goal," Tucker replied. "Some groups think they'd be better off if the intervention failed."

Garos studied him and Devna warily, afraid they intended to expose his true agenda. Instead, Tucker turned to Ruiz. "That's why Elevia and I came—to warn you about the risk of sabotage. We came to Garos first because his people had a way in . . . and because it might be tricky to explain my presence to the Starfleet team. I'm glad you found me first. It'll be easier to maintain my cover if I have your help."

"Why can't you just tell them who you are, if you're here to help?" Ruiz countered.

"Because I'm not 'Mister Bond,'" Tucker replied, invoking Ruiz's old nickname for him. "I can't be careless about revealing my identity, for a lot of reasons. In this case, it'd just make it harder to get them to trust me. And I need them—and you—to trust me if I'm going to help you."

"Why the hell should I trust you, after you let me down before? You talk a good game now, but you've changed your mind before when it suited you or the Federation. People like you—like me, before I spent the past two years in the thick of this—you don't know what oppression is. Your privilege keeps you safe, makes it something that happens to other people, something you can feel bad about but shrug off in the name of the bigger picture.

"Not like Garos. Not like his people. These guys, the Raldul alignment, they know oppression. They know what it's like to be branded as criminals, exiled from their homes and families, just for disagreeing with their leaders. They understand doing whatever it takes to survive and carry on the fight. Yeah, I know the things he's done in the past. I know what the Feds think of him. But I know he's fighting for survival, like the Saurians—not just for some abstract principle or a clear conscience. So I trust him." Tucker saw Garos's head tilt back and his shoulders straighten at Ruiz's praise. It was subtle, most likely involuntary, and Tucker filed that away for future consideration. "Give me a reason I should trust you."

Tucker held his gaze. "Because I'm trusting you. I could get in real trouble if you don't keep my secret from Starfleet. And as right as you are to be mad at me, I'm trusting in your sense of mercy and fair play. All I'm askin' for is a second chance. A chance to prove myself before you throw me to the wolves."

Ruiz brooded over the matter for a few moments before giving a heavy sigh. "All right. A chance. Because we need all the help we can get. But trust needs to be earned, 'Victor.'"

"I understand. For now, though, there are things Elevia and I need to discuss with Garos in private. If you don't mind."

"Okay," Ruiz replied slowly. "I just came to get some rifles for the exercises. I should get back to that anyway."

Garos instructed his underlings to assist Ruiz and the Chelon with the rifles while he led Tucker and Devna to his private office. Once they were alone, the Malurian crime boss spoke. "Well, you didn't expose my link to the Sisters. If that gesture was meant to earn my trust, it's succeeded to the extent that I won't just shoot you here and now. But what you've come to say to me had better be worth my while."

"You should think about being nicer to us, Mister Garos," Tucker replied. "Because we're here to prevent the sabotage the Sisters recruited you to perform. Now, we could do that just by telling the resistance what your real allegiances are. But I'd prefer to do it with your cooperation."

Garos studied their faces. "Because you aren't in it for simple altruism. You want to get something out of it for yourselves. Such as?"

"Like we established, the lady and I are both, shall we say, disillusioned with our respective employers. Hers are trying to engineer a catastrophe to make Starfleet intervention look bad, so the Federation will adopt a policy of noninterference—which they imagine to mean that Federation justice would leave their activities alone. My employers know all about it—and they want to let it happen. In their minds, an officially hands-off Federation will make fewer enemies, and they'll still be free to act secretly on its behalf when they need to. And neither organization much cares how many Saurians have to die for their convenience."

"So you want me to help you stop them. How? While I'm certainly open to negotiations, you'd need to pay me quite a bit to outbid the Sisters. And foiling the sabotage might embarrass the Sisters, but it would have no effect on your employers, Mister Lund."

Tucker went on to explain the rest of his plan—to fabricate evidence of collusion between Harris and D'Nesh in the planned sabotage, then publicize it before the disaster happened, thereby exposing Section 31 and discrediting D'Nesh within the Syndicate. "A bold plan," Garos said, taking in both Tucker and Devna with his smile. "You're not as soft as I suspected. Playing your respective superiors against each other, gambling with the lives of the Saurians to betray your own masters . . . it's brazen. Reckless. I like it.

"But how does it benefit me? What reason do I have to cooperate in this betrayal? My relationship with the Sisters is tenuous enough after Rigel. And I'm not in the mood to draw down the wrath of your employers either."

"I have a different question for you, Garos. What benefit is there in continuing to work with the Orions? What do you get from that relationship that's worth betraying what you believe in?"

Garos bristled. "I have *never* betrayed my beliefs! Everything I do is for the good of Maluria. *Everything!*"

"I know. You believe you're rebelling against an unjust regime. You think their policies are bad for your people."

"I don't just think, I know. They're trapped in an antiquated way of thinking that ends at the atmosphere. They can't recognize that a planetbound nation is doomed to be overrun in a galaxy of interstellar empires and syndicates and *federations*. Their laws and regulations are killing our people. Only the outlaws can save Maluria."

"These rebels are fighting for the same thing! They've been driven from their homes by an unjust leader clinging to antiquated ways and an insular view of the universe. They're willing to do anything it takes to save their people from that. I saw it in your eyes,

Garos—you're proud that people like Antonio approve of your efforts here."

Garos made a dismissive noise. "Your ability to read Malurian expressions is limited."

Devna stepped forward. "Mine is not," she said. "I may not be able to seduce your kind, but I and my sisters have had to tend to their other needs in the course of our alliance. I've had sufficient occasion to learn to read Malurian moods. My master is correct. You do recognize these rebels as kindred spirits." That silenced Garos.

Tucker took the opportunity to continue. "So how can you be okay with betraying them, discrediting them, probably getting thousands of them killed, just to help that tyrant secure his power?"

The Raldul boss glared. "It wouldn't be the first sacrifice I've made for Maluria. I've made deals with monsters. I've killed personal friends. I've done none of these things lightly."

"So it's all right to let others burn as long as you save your own people from the same fate?" Tucker shook his head. "I've tried that, Garos. I've been ordered to do that twice—once right here on Sauria. I was dense enough that it took me two tries to see the hypocrisy of it. What good is saving a society from its enemies if you become as bad as they are?" At the Malurian's sneer, the human went on. "I think you feel that too, deep down. You weren't comfortable helping the First Families tear down Rigel's civilization for their own profit. You helped Valeria Williams and Starfleet expose their plans."

"Only because the Families betrayed me first. Retaliation in kind was the only option left to me. And it brought no benefit to Maluria. Rigel's Federation membership has cost my alignment dearly in the Kandari sector. Our profits have taken a serious hit now that Starfleet law and order has engulfed the region. We need the remaining allies we have, and we need the profits from this arms deal—plus what the Sisters are paying for my assistance with their upcoming show."

"And what kind of an ally has the Syndicate been to you, really? Think back, Garos. Their plan to weaken the Federation by starting a war with the Vertians failed. Their attempt to sabotage the last Babel Conference was a fiasco. Their plans to undermine the Federation from within were exposed, and all the secessionist groups they supported are now either dissolved or discredited. They keep losing, Garos. Losing to the Federation, again and again. Can you really look at that win-loss record and still believe you've bet on the right team?"

Garos scoffed. "So you suggest that Raldul should realign with the Federation? The author of so many of our setbacks?"

"Setbacks to your plans to undermine us. Maybe if you tried working *with* us instead, it'd work out better."

"The Federation would never back a criminal organization."

"But it would use every legitimate means at its disposal to encourage reforms on Malur. Admiral Archer went there last year to try just that. Even though you tried to kill him once or twice, even though he hates your guts, he still tried to help your people."

"By *talking*. Then just walking away when, to no one's surprise, it achieved nothing. I prefer methods that actually get things done."

"Except we've established you haven't actually been doing that. Even before there was a Federation, you weren't able to make enough of a difference to change things on your world."

"And do you really believe," Devna put in, "that the Three Sisters have any true concern for the good of Maluria? They are simply using you for their convenience, just as they do with everyone else. They will betray you and your people as soon as it benefits them."

"Which is why I will betray them first—*when* the time is right."

"That time is now, Garos," Tucker said. "This is your opportunity. Stand with the Federation. Make the act a reality. We love a good redemption story. Show us you really want to help, and we'll do all we can to help you in turn."

Garos shifted his weight uneasily. "This is the second time one of you Federation do-gooders made me that offer. I have to admit, when Lieutenant Williams did it back at Rigel, I appreciated it in an odd way. To be offered aid by an enemy after my own allies failed me one by one . . . it did raise some questions." After an encouraging moment, though, he shook his head. "But the cost is too high. You're too obsessed with getting everyone to join your club—to put the good of the whole above their own needs. I would never subsume Maluria to your authority."

"You don't have to. The Federation has allies, not just members. Whether you join or not is up to you. Nobody's been forced in."

"And that's the other reason I wouldn't trust your help. You're too soft, too indecisive. You won't do whatever it takes to win." He smirked. "At least, not officially. Your employers seem like more pragmatic types. Maybe I should consider—"

Tucker preempted him, shaking his head. "Allying with them? Never work. They're just as gung-ho about protecting the Federation by any means necessary as you are about Maluria. If they wouldn't hesitate to let Sauria suffer a disaster for their own convenience, they certainly wouldn't hesitate to do the same to Malur or one of its colonies."

Devna moved in closer. "Neither would the Sisters. Navaar already considers your aid unreliable. D'Nesh resents you for humiliating her before Navaar after her Babel plan failed. And Maras? If your whole system burned, she would applaud the pretty fireworks. All they need is an excuse."

"And yet you ask me to give them one. If I fail them this time, do you imagine they won't retaliate?"

"I imagine that Victor's plan will weaken them badly. If the plot to implicate Starfleet in a staged disaster is exposed before it comes to fruition, and if both Victor's employers and D'Nesh are publicly revealed as conspirators in the plot, it will destroy D'Nesh. Navaar is like you—a pragmatist, willing to sacrifice those she loves for the sake of her goals." She gave a graceful shrug. "Those she loves, besides herself, number exactly two, but that will not stop her from halving that number."

Garos studied her. "Why D'Nesh? Why not all three?"

"As a united front, they could fight the charges. Even if they were brought down, one of their rivals would quickly enough seize control and take aggressive action to make a name for herself. But turn Navaar against D'Nesh, and the Sisters will be weakened, their image of an inseparable front broken. It will undermine them without breeding open chaos. Surely that could benefit Raldul as much as weakening the Federation would. A diminished, distracted Sisterhood might lose its grip on certain business opportunities. Raldul could move into the void."

Garos looked intrigued. "You should have let this one speak first, Lund. Her arguments are far more appealing. As, I admit, is the prospect of seeing D'Nesh brought down. I have some degree of respect for Navaar's raw cunning, but D'Nesh is crass, clumsy, and arrogant. She deserves to be humbled."

After a moment, Tucker dared to ask, "Does that mean you'll help us?"

"It means I'll give it serious thought. But in all honesty, I'm not certain how much help I can provide. The plan was made by Navaar and Maltuvis. They've only given me what information I need to play my part."

"Information such as . . . ?"

With a sigh, Garos went on. "Oh, very well. All I know is that I'm supposed to ensure that the rebels raid and sabotage one of Maltuvis's shipbuilding facilities, and that at least one of the more extremist factions of the resistance is included in the raid. Some sort of disaster will be triggered in the process, leading to Starfleet being blamed for recklessly putting dangerous technology in the hands of fanatics."

Tucker nodded. "And so that shifts Federation sentiment in favor of noninterference."

"In theory, yes. Navaar's plans do tend to be overcomplicated." Garos shook his head. "But I have not been provided with anything that could cause such a disaster. That must be something that Maltuvis's or Harrad-Sar's people are arranging. So if you hoped for my assistance in preventing the disaster, I must disappoint you."

Tucker exchanged a look with Devna. This was troubling news. "It makes things riskier," he said after a moment. "But maybe that doesn't matter. All we need to do is expose the plan in advance—and pin it on the right people. Once the public knows who's really behind it and what they were trying to do, there'd be no more point in actually going through with the disaster."

"You hope," Garos said. "Maltuvis seems the type who might go ahead with it out of sheer pique."

Tucker shook his head. "No. Maltuvis is a narcissist. He wants his people to love him, to admire him as the one who protects them from the evil aliens. If people know it was his idea, it would turn them against him."

"You assume his followers still know how to distinguish truth from propaganda. He has spent the past two years conditioning them to forget the difference."

"And I'm sure that in M'Tezir, whole generations have been raised not to know it. But it takes time to erode a people's ability to reason and recognize fact. It requires conditioning them to mistrust sources of information besides the state. Most Saurians grew up in countries that had good schools and a free and responsible press. Those habits of thought can't all have been eroded in two years, no matter how hard Maltuvis's propagandists have worked."

Garos considered his words, then nodded. "All of that is probably true, I grant." Then his gaze sharpened. "But does Maltuvis know that?"

8

"*THIS . . . STARSHIP . . . is a piece of . . . crap!*" Caroline Paris cried as she pounded futilely on the turbolift door.

Malcolm Reed clasped her shoulders from behind. "Calm down, Caroline. It's just a stuck lift. The repair team will get us out of here soon enough."

Paris struck her fist against the door one last time as punctuation before slumping back into Reed's comforting embrace. "I know, but it's not just that. It's everything. It's been a month since I got this ship, and it still isn't working well enough to leave this damn dry dock!"

"Well, at least it's the shortest month." His comment evoked a laugh from Paris despite herself. "Remember, we had comparable troubles getting *Pioneer* up to speed. *We* almost got crushed inside a Jovian atmosphere."

She turned to face him, leaning back against the gray-paneled lift wall. "Yeah, and discovered an amazing new life-form in the process. At least you got some excitement. I can't even get the car out of the garage." She sighed. "I should've known a ship named after the biggest silicate asteroid would get off to a rocky start."

Reed groaned. "How long have you been waiting to use that one?"

"A while. But I can't afford to vent like this in front of the crew."

Reed leaned against the wall alongside her. "Maybe I chose the wrong day to come for a tour. Things will probably be better tomorrow."

Paris quirked a brow at him. "Since when were you the optimist in this relationship?"

He stroked her shoulder. "Since you needed me to be."

It was a wonderful feeling to hear him say that, especially when their romance was the only thing that was going right in her life at the moment. So Paris made a decision. Taking a deep breath, she said, "The thing is . . . I asked you to visit now because I know you won't have the chance for much longer. The investigations are done, your refits are wrapping up. You'll be taking *Pioneer* out again soon, and whether this hunk of junk ever starts working or not, we won't be able to spend as much time together."

Reed fidgeted. "Well. That's the way it is with service romances, right? You make the most of the time you have, and you cherish the memories when it's time to move on."

She met his eyes intently. "Is that all this has been to you, Malcolm? Just a casual fling?"

"No, I . . . I didn't mean it like that. These past

weeks have been . . . extraordinary. You've given me more happiness than I've known in a very long time."

"But you've still kept your distance. At first I thought it was out of deference to me, to my hang-ups after Delta. But we're well past that now. You've certainly cured me of my lingering issues with inti-macy," she added with a bawdy grin. Then Paris grew serious again. "So when are you going to tell me about your damage? About why you pull away every time the conversation starts nudging toward commitment?"

Reed spoke hesitantly. "It's . . . not that I wouldn't welcome a . . . a lasting relationship with you, Caro-line. It's just that, before we move forward, you should be aware—not that it would necessarily become an issue, I wouldn't want to assume that—"

"Malcolm."

He gathered himself. "A few years ago, I was di-agnosed with transporter-inflicted genetic damage. In fact, it was my case, along with Admiral Archer's, that led Doctor Phlox to discover the flaw in our trans-porter technology. You see, he and I had been the heaviest early users, so—"

"What kind of genetic damage?" she asked, not letting him avoid the issue any further.

He sighed. "The kind that would prevent me from ever having children."

For a moment, she just blinked. "That's it? I mean . . . not to belittle your feelings about it, but it's not something that would have to be a deal-breaker for a relationship."

"No, of course not. But . . . well, I was something of a womanizer in my younger days, I admit. I had . . . rather a few casual dalliances. But they always meant something to me, and I was always looking for something more. Something deeper, something lasting. I kept hoping to find the person I'd be happy spending my life with—ideally, the woman who would be the mother of my children. You know how important the Reed legacy is to me." Paris nodded.

"So when I found I could never father a child," Malcolm went on, "it made me feel, well, as if there was no longer any point in looking for companionship. I haven't been with anyone since then. Maybe I haven't felt . . . entirely adequate as a man."

Caroline stared. "Are you listening to yourself? Oh, Malcolm, just because we like old movies doesn't mean we have to live in the damn twentieth century. You're not less of a man if you can't get a woman pregnant. The human population is large and stable enough that there's no absolute imperative to procreate; love and connection should be enough for their own sake. Besides, lots of wonderful men are married to other wonderful men. Or are single fathers who adopt. There are plenty of kids who need adoption, even today. That's as real as any other kind of parenting."

Reed nodded. "Yes, Phlox and others have made the same point to me. But it still feels different."

"You mean it's not what you were hoping for. Welcome to living in the universe."

"But doesn't it matter to you? You were raised in a family with just as strong a sense of lineage."

"My big brother had a son and two daughters before his ship was lost in the war. James Junior's already applied to Starfleet Academy, and Taylor intends to follow him when she's old enough. So the family tradition's taken care of, whether I contribute to it or not. And that frees me to pursue my own aspirations." She was compelled to pace within the lift, though its confines offered her little release for her need to move. "I've seen what happens when societies place too much value on procreation. I've been to Earth colonies like Vega and the Altair worlds, where the need to grow the population has caused a resurgence in traditional parenting roles—women of childbearing age expected to devote themselves to that function above all others, men coming to see them as a precious resource to be sheltered at all costs for the good of society. It's led to a resurgence of gender inequalities that I'd thought were long extinct, the kind of things we make fun of when we watch old movies.

"When I've seen those societies, I've had to wonder: What will happen to future generations, say, fifty or a hundred years from now, when people raised with those colonial attitudes become a larger percentage of the Federation's population—of its electoral base? How might their values come to feed back into the larger society, or influence politics?"

"That hardly seems like a plausible concern," Reed said.

"Well, you have the luxury to think that because you wouldn't be affected by that kind of a change. I would be. Malcolm, just because we've built a world where equality is prized and respected doesn't mean we can't backslide. And I, for one, am not going to be part of that. I'm not going to define my identity *or* my relationships based on childbearing potential."

She moved closer and held him again. "Malcolm, I decided a long time ago that the only expectations I needed to satisfy were my own. I just wish you were able to feel the same way about yourself. Because I think we could have a future together . . . if you believed in yourself enough to embrace it."

He blinked away tears. "Then maybe I need you to teach me how. I hadn't allowed myself to believe that was really possible . . . that you'd want a future with me. So I didn't allow myself to think about . . . how much I want that too."

When the turbolift repair crew found them, the two captains were locked in a passionate kiss, oblivious to the lift's restored movement. The repair crew stepped back, let the doors close, and waited a while before declaring the lift open for service.

Birnam (GJ 1045 I)

"Just so we're clear," Zang Liwei said as he led the *Endeavour* landing party out from the *Verne* crew's base camp, "it was Farid's idea to invite you here, not mine."

Captain T'Pol absorbed the information dispassionately. "I believe you made that adequately clear already, Captain Zang. Yet we would not be here had you not acceded to his suggestion."

The burly, middle-aged Boomer captain wrinkled his mustached lip in reluctant acknowledgment. "Just because he wouldn't let this go. The sooner we get this resolved, the better."

Hoshi Sato was just glad to be here. She hadn't expected a half-frozen world under a dim red star that never moved in the sky to be so beautiful. True, the light here was subdued, nothing like the warmth of Earth's sun shining through the treetops on a clear spring day. Not only was the star itself (which the Boomers were calling Dunsinane) dim and broad and low in the sky, but its light was diffused by a near-perpetual cloud cover that only got thicker the closer you got to the sunward pole. But Birnam's woods were substantially brighter than those of Dakala, the geothermally heated rogue planet she'd visited in her first year aboard *Enterprise*, and her eyes adjusted readily enough that the lighting seemed more gentle than gloomy. Perhaps it was the nature of the surrounding vegetation that helped create that impression. The plants came in many unusual shapes and colors, tending toward deep, rich purples and blues that gave the forest a regal air. The vegetation was spaced widely enough to keep the setting from feeling oppressively dark—probably because so much of it was mobile, able to crawl or slither or walk or even glide away from any obstruction that blocked the heat of Dunsinane too long (for it was the star's infrared heat, more than its feeble visible light, that was its main boon to the life of this planet). Indeed, maybe the very liveliness of the plants here was what made the environment feel so stimulating.

"It's the oxygen."

Startled, Sato turned to see the Boomer science officer, Farid Najafi, striding alongside her with his hands in his pockets, offering a boyish grin that sat well on his handsome, dark features. "What is?" she asked.

"Sorry, but that look on your face—we've all had it from time to time, especially on the first days before we adjusted. All these plants converting carbon dioxide to oxygen, no animals to respire it back the other way—the O-two levels are pretty high around here. Even with the frequent rainfall, fire's a big risk. And it has a way of making people giddy when they're not used to it."

Sato giggled, realizing that she was proving his point. "And when you do get used to it?"

Najafi tilted his head. "More a general sense of well-being. A lot of energy."

Zang stared back at him glumly. "Or heightened irritability—if someone gives you reason."

"Let's just say we haven't needed much coffee since we got here," Najafi finished, visibly resisting the urge to rise to the bait. Then he smiled at Sato, and she felt a thrill that she hoped was just the oxygen talking.

"But don't worry—what's over this rise will be plenty stimulating."

He raced ahead, and Hoshi barely remembered to glance at T'Pol for permission before jogging after him. Soon, she caught up at the top of the rise, and the dryads came into view below her. There were dozens of them, maybe a hundred or more, generating a deep, creaking rumble as they made their slow migration through the wide dale below, along the banks of a small brook.

The dryads were not standard-issue trees. They were certainly tall, averaging something like ten meters high, but about a third of the way up from a broad base of root-legs were several dozen thick, vine-like tentacles emerging from all around the trunk. Atop each dryad's trunk was a single, broad, roughly circular deep-blue canopy like the brim of an inverted sombrero, tilted at a rakish angle to face the never-moving sun. "Are those their . . . leaves?" Sato asked, for want of a better word.

"Essentially," Najafi answered. "Our scouts have found other dryad populations elsewhere on the planet—the angle of the 'leaf' varies depending on the angle of the light in various regions, naturally. A given population can't migrate too far north or south—well, unless they follow a ring-shaped path around the sub-stellar pole." He shrugged. "Or maybe we're wrong—maybe the supporting branches can grow over time and change the angle if they migrate slowly enough. We'd need a broader genetic comparison to find out—unless we just wanted to watch for a few decades."

Elizabeth Cutler had caught up with them as he

spoke. "I don't know," the slim, honey-haired science officer observed. "It hardly seems to have the surface area to collect enough sunlight."

Najafi pulled a compact magnifier scope from a pocket and handed it to her. "Take a closer look at the texture."

Cutler put the small binocular scanner to her eyes. "Kind of spongy and convoluted, it looks like."

Najafi grinned. "Increases its surface area, lets it gather more light. Besides, it's mostly absorbing infrared, and that can penetrate deeper."

"There's more," Cutler reported. "In the middle of the 'leaf' is sort of a funnel, filled with water." She handed the scope to Sato.

T'Pol and Zang soon caught up, and Sato passed the scope to her captain. On locating the funnels for herself, the elegant Vulcan officer said, "I see. I would hypothesize that the funnels collect rainwater, so that the dendriforms do not need to depend solely on moisture absorption through their roots."

"Exactly, Captain," Najafi said. "After all, those roots were made for walking. And that's not all they do. Come on."

He led them down to the trampled path where the massive creatures had previously trodden. "What do you see here?"

"A lot of mush, basically," said Sato.

"A lot?" Cutler added. "Maybe, but not as much as there should be."

Najafi just stood there grinning, letting them size

things up for themselves. Recognizing this, T'Pol looked at her science officer. "How would you account for the discrepancy, Lieutenant?"

Cutler cleared her throat. "As Hoshi said, Captain, this stuff is pretty mushy. The plant matter gets crushed, even liquefied by the creatures' sheer weight. And roots absorb liquid."

Sato stared at her. "They're grazing?"

"That's right," Najafi acknowledged, smiling at her. "They absorb the crushed plant matter and use its nutrients and sugars, instead of depending entirely on their own photosynthesis. Another reason the 'leaf' on top doesn't have to be so big. It seems that's the only way a plant that big and mobile could manage."

"So that is why they bypassed your campsite, as described in your initial report," T'Pol said. "The ground was bare thanks to your landing, so the site offered nothing for the dendriforms to consume."

"Exactly," said Zang. "As long as we keep the ground surrounding the camp clear of cover the dryads can feed on, we're safe from their herds."

"Copses," Najafi corrected. Zang just rolled his eyes, as if tired of an old argument.

At Najafi's urging, the group followed this cluster of dryads (whatever term one might use) along the course of the brook until they reached a wide pond. The humans and Vulcan watched patiently as the dendriforms began to sink into the mud under their own weight. "Watering hole," Cutler observed.

"In a weird sort of way," Najafi replied.

"Not all of them are settling in," T'Pol said. "Observe the ones on the outside."

The specified dryads had remained in motion, Sato realized—slowly but deliberately circling the perimeter of the herd. "I'd swear they're standing guard."

"Exactly," the Boomer scientist replied, his excitement growing. "The way the others sink in, it takes some time for them to get unstuck. The outside ones keep watch for predators, protecting their immobile fellows. They even do it in shifts—eventually, once the inside ones are sated, they'll relieve the sentries and let them sink their roots."

"Social behavior," T'Pol noted. "In vegetative organisms. Truly intriguing."

"As far as it goes, yes," Captain Zang acknowledged. "But hardly evidence of sentience. Many animal species, even insects, show behavior like this. There's nothing to it that can't be raw instinct."

Najafi glared at him. "You know there's more. Come on—what I want to show you is on the other side of the pond."

It took several minutes to circle the resting copse of dryads, but in this oxygen-rich air, Sato hardly felt winded when they reached the other side. It was due as much to her sense of wonder at this world as to the oxygen in the air.

Najafi gestured widely to encompass the area before them, including a wide pile of boulders that formed one edge of the pond. "What do you notice about the pond?"

Cutler narrowed her eyes. "Nothing special. Just a widening of the brook, created by that rock formation acting as a natural dam."

"Natural?" Najafi asked. "Look around, Lieutenant. Where did the rocks come from?"

The three women from *Endeavour* surveyed the area, but Sato could see no similar boulders. A moment later, Cutler confirmed, "There's nothing in the immediate vicinity that matches. Maybe they were deposited by glaciation—but no, wait, the climate would be constant, barring a major change in stellar activity. And this doesn't look like a glacially formed landscape."

"Have you looked closely at the dryads' tentacles?" Najafi said. "They're strong and thick—and they end in three digits apiece. The minimum number necessary for fine manipulation."

T'Pol's brows went up. "Do you propose that the dryads constructed this dam?"

"I'm certain of it."

Zang crossed his arms. "Even if that's true," he said, "beavers build dams. Birds build nests."

"And people build things too," Najafi countered with some heat. "You can't assume they aren't intelligent just because you don't *want* them to be."

T'Pol interposed. "With all due respect, Captain Zang, it does seem wise to err on the side of caution until we know more."

Her calm delivery served to damp the tension between the two Boomers. Visibly gathering himself,

Zang turned to her and asked, "Is it cautious, Captain T'Pol, to deprive the Federation of the medical benefits the dryads could provide us? And not just potential new pharmaceuticals. My people think that study of their neural tissues could lead to new nerve regeneration treatments. Imagine if we could regrow nerves from cuttings as easily as a, a tomato plant."

Sato looked up sharply at that, thinking of Kimura. *Could harvesting the dryads lead to a treatment for his impairment?*

But would he be willing to be healed if it came at the expense of a sentient being's life?

Even as Hoshi wrestled with her conflicting thoughts, T'Pol asked, "Can the beneficial compounds be synthesized without killing the dryads?"

"They're very complex. We haven't found a way to do it effectively. And it's far more efficient and economical to extract them from the dryads' own bodies." Zang sighed. "Look, I'm not proposing we slash and burn the whole species. Obviously I want to do this sustainably. These organisms could be a cash crop for a long time to come. If anything, cultivating them— herding them, whatever you call it—could increase their population. We'd take good care of them."

Najafi fumed. "Until the time came to murder them, suck out their innards, and dissect their brains."

"A few stacked rocks don't prove they can think."

Sato touched Najafi's arm calmingly. This atmosphere could indeed make sparks easier to set off, it seemed. "Look—the reason I'm here is because you reported there was evidence of communication. Why don't we go back to base so you can show me your data?" She gave a sheepish smile. "I wouldn't mind getting back into some more normal air. This is bracing, but the three of us aren't used to it yet, so . . ."

The suggestion allowed the Boomers to save face, so both Zang and Najafi agreed to it readily. As they strode back toward camp, T'Pol sidled over to whisper at Sato. "You may have a future in diplomacy," she said. "Still, I doubt it will be easy to convince either of these men they are wrong."

Sato was tempted to speak out in Najafi's defense; to her, the lanky young science officer seemed far more reasonable than the gruff captain. But she was learning to second-guess her impulses while under the influence of Birnam's atmosphere. Was there some other reason she wanted to leap to the defense of the Boomer scientist? Perhaps that he was funny and charming and had a gorgeous smile, not to mention being rather fun to watch from behind as he strode eagerly and athletically back toward camp?

It's the oxygen, Hoshi told herself, forcing her eyes down to her fingers as they stroked her engagement ring reassuringly. *It's just the oxygen.*

February 28, 2166
Akleyro, Sauria

Whatever his issues with Charles Tucker, Antonio Ruiz had chosen to cooperate with him for the good of the cause, at least to the extent of supporting his persona as the arms smuggler Victor Lund, with the modification of presenting Devna (or rather, Elevia) to them as his partner rather than his property. Commander Mullen, Lieutenant Kelly, and the rest of the *Essex* team had seemed to accept him on the recommendation of Ruiz and Garos, and none of them seemed to be enough of a *Casablanca* fan to notice anything familiar about his alias.

But Mullen and Kelly had little time for him, since wrangling the Saurian resistance factions was a full-time job. Saurians were a confident, self-reliant people on the whole, an understandable attribute given their great physical robustness. They had evolved in response to a harsh, dangerous environment, and that response had essentially amounted to "Oh, yeah? Take your best shot!" They had unusual strength, endurance, and robustness; heightened senses including infrared vision; and the ability to withstand extreme temperature shifts and toxic gases. They could even function underwater for extended periods. Their evolutionary ancestors had made one concession to the planet's fierce conditions, adopting a nocturnal lifestyle to avoid the searing heat and overpowering storms that often swept the planet in the light of day. Nonetheless, the Saurians had shown great ingenuity in overcoming the limitations of a nocturnal species in order to develop technology. After initially relying on the planet's abundant volcanic vents and hot springs as their main sources of heat, they had eventually realized that sheets of volcanic glass could shield their sensitive eyes enough to allow them to harness fire. Their civilization had literally begun with the invention of sunglasses, which was not a bad symbol for their attitude as a culture.

That attitude made it a challenge for offworlders like Mullen and Kelly to convince the Saurians to respect their ideas. Even those who nominally rejected Maltuvis's xenophobia often had an unconscious perception of offworlders as intrinsically weak—though the no-nonsense military manner and combat prowess that Morgan Kelly had demonstrated in her training drills had gone a long way to counter that perception. But it looked like the greater challenge might be getting the different Saurian factions to find common ground. While Maltuvis had many foes, they had been pursuing separate resistance campaigns in service to distinct priorities and ideologies, and on several occasions, they had gotten in each other's way or even come into conflict over their old grudges. It had taken until now for the Starfleet advisors to convince the heads of several resistance groups to meet and discuss coordinating their efforts toward a common goal—specifically, a joint operation to destroy one of Maltuvis's new shipbuilding factories before it went online. Such a blow against the emperor's ability to construct the ships that let him oppress and terrorize the entire planet would be a major military victory as well as a propaganda victory, proving to the Saurian people that Maltuvis's power was not absolute and that resistance could succeed. The hope was that the very public de-struction of one factory would inspire the slave labor-ers at the other factories to commit their own acts of sabotage, if not to destroy the other factories, then at least to slow them down or introduce exploitable flaws into the ships they built. Surely this was a plan that all the resistance groups could get behind—which was presumably why Garos and the Three Sisters consid-ered it the ideal bait for their trap.

The summit, however, was not going smoothly. When Moxat, the presider-in-exile of the Global League, spoke of following up the raid with an out-reach campaign to the oppressed masses within Maltuvis's home nation of M'Tezir, both to inspire the sabotage of military facilities therein and to pro-vide relief and rescue for those suffering worst under the dictator's heel, it provoked an angry response from K'vizhano, the head of the resistance faction from the conquered nation of Veranith. Tucker recalled from his previous visit that Veranith and M'Tezir had been traditional enemies for centuries. "You're fools to waste your sympathy on those people," K'vizhano insisted. "They've accepted dictatorship for genera-tions because it suits their character—rigid, intoler-ant, authoritarian, paranoid. They could have risen up against their monarchy long ago, but instead they wel-comed it. They're all part of M'Tezir's military ma-chine, indoctrinated from birth and fanatically loyal. They supported the previous Basileus, even gladly cooperated, when he expelled or executed all Veranith immigrants during the Third Oceanic War. Hostility and cruelty are the nature of all their kind."

"Your fire sprays too widely," objected Porsalis of the R'Ganik, a Global League nation belonging to the same lilac-skinned ethnic minority as the M'Tezir, yet with its own long history of enmity with that state. "It is not their 'kind' that is to blame—it is the antiquated culture that the Basilic line of rulers has kept alive long after the rest of us embraced modernity and democracy. If all you see when you look at them is the hue of their flesh, how does that make you any less intolerant?"

"How dare you accuse me of only seeing the surface?" K'vizhano shouted. "I am not some Clear Light cultist with my membranes cut out!"

Next to him, the representative of Clear Light made an outraged noise. "I am sitting right beside you! I should have known. Why did I think we would receive any respect here? Your nations have never welcomed us any more than Maltuvis did." Apparently Nekze's sect was a philosophical fringe group (few Saurians held religious beliefs per se, at least not of the theistic variety) that practiced a form of self-mutilation, severing the nictitating membranes that allowed them to block out visible light and see purely in infrared. Tucker wasn't entirely clear on why they did this, though he gathered it had something to do with finding it invasive to see inside others' bodies. But most Saurians saw the practice as an induced disability, finding it repellent—even abusive, since the procedure was performed on children in infancy. Lightists generally had to hide their nature from other Saurians, though Nekze's faction had been openly campaigning for acceptance in the Global League, arguing that its inclusiveness meant nothing if it didn't extend to every group.

"The M'Tezir are far worse," K'vizhano insisted. "They execute your kind for their disabilities."

"While you merely outlaw us and attempt to 'cure' us of our purity!"

"Purity?" The disbelieving cry came from Kobekla, the spokesperson for an even more extremist sect called the Untainted. "You corrupt the purity of the body, weaken yourselves as much as those who rely on cities and guns and spaceships. At least these others merely *use* such abominations—you turn yourselves into abominations!" Most Saurians tended to rely more on their own robust abilities and less on technology than humans typically did—which was why they were not a starfaring power despite having a much older civilization than Earth's—but the Untainted took it to an extreme, rejecting all advanced technology and relying on their own innate abilities or on tools they built from natural materials. Kobekla and her supporters didn't even wear clothing aside from a few handmade straps and carrying pouches. Nonetheless, they had managed to wage a long-running guerrilla campaign to prevent civilization from encroaching on their territories, using their own resourcefulness and strength to drive out or kill intruders and smash their technology—sometimes siccing predatory animals on them or redirecting herds of megafauna to smash their outposts. The Untainted could be formidable allies, but even getting them to the table had taken all of Mullen's diplomatic skills, with help from Garos—who had cooperated in recruiting the more extreme sects like the Untainted and Clear Light as potential scapegoats for the impending terroristic catastrophe.

K'vizhano simply ignored the Untainted leader's protest. "The point," he went on, "is that we must not hobble our ability to strike at Maltuvis's seat of power because we fear harming the civilians around him. Now, I wish no more loss of life than necessary, but all M'Tezir should be considered legitimate military targets."

"We can't define the enemy by ethnicity!" Porsalis objected. "Already some R'Ganik citizens have been subjected to violence by those who mistook them for M'Tezir. The resistance must take a stand against such profiling!"

"You're too preoccupied with your own sense of victimhood! This is about saving our world!"

"Saving it for whom?"

"*Hold it!*" The forceful shout from Morgan Kelly silenced all the Saurians. "Debating which of you is more oppressed won't get you anywhere. It's what Maltuvis wants! The only way this alliance can advance is if you recognize that your concerns are intersectional. The dynamics of one form of oppression or intolerance are the same as the dynamics of another, even if the specific excuses are different." A couple of the Saurians attempted to object, but Kelly continued to speak in loud, relentless tones. "And a key part of that dynamic is pitting different oppressed groups *against* each other so they won't recognize their common ground and *unite*. You need to stop dwelling on the ways you're unlike each other and recognize that you all share a common fear of being punished for your identity, marginalized for your way of life. Those ways are different, but the fear of losing them is the same. And the threat Maltuvis poses to all of your independence is the same."

"What do you know of it, outsider?" Kobekla demanded, her own stridency rivaling Kelly's intensity. "You, who are further removed from your nature than any of us. You, who are not a part of this world and can leave it as you choose."

"My nature *is* what I choose to make it. Who we are isn't some accident of birth, it's a creation of our will."

Now Antonio Ruiz stepped up. "She's right. I *am* part of this world. I may not have been born here, my people may not have evolved here, but I've made it my home. The gravity's too high for me, the climate's too hot, my eyes are weak in the dark, but Sauria is where I feel I belong, and its people are my family. And I'm not the only one. Many offworlders have chosen to live here, and Maltuvis is killing us just as he's killing you. Yes, I'm an alien, but I'm also a Saurian. We aren't all just one thing."

Kelly nodded. "Are there no Clear Lightists in Veranith? No Untainted in R'Ganik? There were even Veranith in M'Tezir once—and how can you protest their expulsion," the armory officer challenged K'vizhano, "if you don't believe that dual identity was the way it *should* have been? If those Veranith chose to live in M'Tezir, then they made that part of their identity as Veranith! Just as all your groups intersect with other identities, whether national, ethnic, or philosophical. If you look for the ways members of *your own* groups and causes are different from you, then you can see that those differences don't keep you from working together. And that helps you to recognize that your differences with *other* groups are not insurmountable."

Tucker sensed Devna moving alongside him as Kelly spoke. "A surprise," the Orion said, "to find that Lieutenant Kelly is as adept at discoursing on the politics of resistance as she is at drilling fighters and field-stripping plasma rifles."

"Yeah," Tucker replied with a chuckle, "especially since she talks more like a drill sergeant than a professor."

"I do wonder how you humans know so much about these matters, though. You pride yourself so much on your freedom and equality."

"Only because we had to fight so hard to achieve them. Or—well—some had to fight the rest of us." He grimaced. "The ugly truth is, not much more than three centuries ago, my ancestors might've owned her ancestors as slaves."

Devna stared at him. "You had slavery that recently?"

"Afraid so. And even after we outlawed it, the attitudes that had evolved to justify slavery—the beliefs that some humans were genetically inferior to others—those went on poisoning our society for almost another two centuries."

"How did you finally overcome them?"

"It took a lot of hard work. A lot of courage and resistance from people who refused to have their rights denied. A lot of sacrificed lives, too."

Devna absorbed that quietly. "And was it worth the suffering and dying . . . to win those rights?"

He held her emerald gaze. "They already *had* those rights. We're all born with them. They were fighting for the recognition of something that was always theirs." He looked back at Kelly, Mullen, and Ruiz. "And folks like them . . . like my brother Albert and his husband . . . they wouldn't be free to exercise their rights today if their forebears hadn't fought those battles."

"But the battles are won. You have the privilege of being your own masters. Why, then, do you not simply enjoy the fruits of your victory?"

"Because if we ever forget what we owe to our ancestors . . . if we take our freedoms for granted . . . then we can start to lose them." He turned to her. "And because there are always others who have their own freedoms to fight for. The Saurians, the Partnership, the Orions . . . if we don't stand up for all of their rights, then we're forfeiting what our ancestors fought so hard to win. Ultimately it's all the same fight—only the battlefield shifts."

Devna looked within herself. "On Delta . . . they taught me that all beings are part of one another. That we share a common spirit, a common dignity. That what hurts one hurts us all."

"And that's why you helped the Deltans escape your master, right?"

"Yes . . . though I still have my doubts about whether it applies to everyone. But what you say . . . it's surprisingly similar. Even though it's much more aggressive." She frowned. "I never thought of aggression and empathy as going together."

"I think maybe they *need* to go together. To balance each other out."

After pondering that for a moment, Devna returned her attention to the negotiating table. "Kelly's methods seem effective. None of the factions has stormed out yet."

"You sound impressed."

"I could've done the same more easily . . . if Saurians were receptive to my wiles. She has only the truth to work with. It is difficult to persuade people with the truth."

"Maybe," he conceded. "But it lasts longer."

"It only needs to last until the factory raid. Rather, until we create your frame and expose the planned sabotage of the raid." Devna turned her head to study him. "How long do you suppose that untruth will last?"

Tucker fidgeted, aware of his hypocrisy. "It's in service to a deeper truth. Harris *does* support the Sisters' plan—just not as directly as we're going to make it look."

"And that is truth enough for you?"

He looked away. "In this line of work, it's about as close as we can get."

9

San Francisco

"I STILL SAY we should put transporters back into regular personnel use," Kivei Tizahr said to the other *Pioneer* personnel seated with her at the restaurant table. "I mean, nobody's actually *died* from a few minor assembly errors, and most people aren't affected at all. Anyone who shows signs of damage could just be advised to reduce their transporter use from then on. And how can we redesign the system for greater accuracy if we can't gather enough data on the specific effects it has on the body?"

Travis Mayweather sighed. He'd managed to convince the intense young Rigelian to try taking a break from her work and getting better acquainted with some of her crewmates, and he'd managed to rope two other members of the command crew, Rey Sangupta and Regina Tallarico, into joining them at one of his favorite restaurant-bars in the Bay Area. But so far, Tizahr had only discussed engineering matters. And her views on those could be a bit callous, it seemed.

"I don't know about Rigelians," Sangupta said, "but humans get a bit touchy on the subject of experimenting on actual people."

"Nonsense. Just flying starships into unknown space is a dangerous experiment," she told the science officer. "And we face more risk of genetic damage from ordinary cosmic radiation than from transporter use. It's a manageable risk; the only thing making people unwilling to use it is irrational fear. Boldness is what gets things done, people."

"So how exactly would you get people to be so bold with risking their bodily integrity in transporters?" Tallarico asked.

"Easy," Tizahr said to the blond flight controller. "Just tell them the system's been fixed. Say it's safe now. It's not that far from the truth, and with the new data we gathered, we could make it true soon enough."

Tallarico shook her head, a shocked grin on her face. "You are unbelievable!"

"I'm just practical. And you'll be glad of it when the ship's under Orion or Nausicaan attack and you find out just how fast you can dodge and how well the shields will hold up, thanks to me."

Mayweather chuckled. The fact that her confident proclamations were made in such a matter-of-fact, casual tone, with no affectation or bombast, helped soften them. She wasn't boasting, just making an honest assessment of her ability, as unfiltered as anything else she said. "Okay, I think that's enough engineering talk for tonight. We hardly know anything else about you, Kivei. What do you like to do when you're not on duty?"

Her response was a bit less animated than usual.

"You mean social stuff? Personal life, that sort of thing? Never been too good at that, honestly. I was always years ahead of my classmates, my peers couldn't follow my interests, my family didn't know what to do with me besides shipping me off to trade school. At least when I'm working, I'm with people who love the same things I do. Who share my need for things to make sense." She shrugged. "And being the boss means I can yell at people without them taking it personally. Much cleaner."

"Well, I don't know about that," Mayweather ventured. "Sure, all your engineers understand you're just trying to improve efficiency, but they still have feelings. It doesn't hurt to take that into—"

"Hey, Boomer!"

The interruption came from the larger of a pair of drunks who'd wandered over from the bar. From the looks of their attire, and from the hint of the accent Travis caught, they were Space Boomers like himself—and given how much they were indulging themselves, they were probably Earth Cargo Service crewmen on furlough after a long tour. "Can I help you, friend?" he asked with a cautious smile.

"I know you, right?" said the large man, who had South Asian features and a close-shaved head. "Mayflower. Mayfellow."

"Mayweather. That's right." Well, not *quite* right, but he let it slide in the hope of keeping things amiable. "Have we met?"

"We recognize you. Know you by reputation. The Boomer who went Starfleet."

Wow, Mayweather thought. *That's an old tune.* As more and more Boomers adjusted to the new era of faster warp drives and more widespread interstellar contact, they were reassimilating into the larger human community—still existing as a distinct subculture, fortunately, but generally not as insular as they'd been back in the day, when Travis's craving for a less-constrained existence had led him to leave the *Horizon* for Starfleet.

The smaller, olive-skinned man grinned, brushing back his long bangs. "Oh, my friend doesn't mean anything by it, man. Hey, you made it big. Increased our vibiz . . . vizziblillity. You're, like, our mascot, man!"

"That's right," said the bigger man. "You're an important guy now. That's why we wanted to know what you think about this interference thing. This new rule your boss Archer wants to pass. You're against it, right?"

Mayweather took a moment. "What makes you think that?"

"Because you're one of us! You know we depend on first contacts, trade with new aliens. We have to stop at ports . . . at any ports we can reach, 'cause we can't all go fast and far enough to get to a fancy Federation starbase." His tone grew more intense and self-righteous as he went on. "Only way to fix the warp drive is to convince some stone-age tribe to let us mine their sacred mountain? Then that's what we gotta do."

"Sure!" the smaller man said, rather more facetiously. "And, hey, if we happ'nta find a planet of prehic—prehysterical wild women ready to worship us as gods an' obey our ev'ry command, well, where's the harm in that?"

Travis controlled himself tightly. He'd seen how the Ware infection had brought destruction to the Kyraw, a raven-like people whose readiness to wage holy wars over it had led to their virtual annihilation. He'd seen how even the early stages of infection had disrupted the Vanotli, allowing one corporation to dominate the society and exploit and endanger its people—including a woman he'd come to care for a great deal. So the Boomer's casual joke offended him deeply. It was just the sort of exploitative attitude that the noninterference directive was meant to constrain.

Still, arguing with these drunks would just provoke a fight, and the other patrons of the restaurant didn't deserve that. "I don't think this is the right place for this discussion, fellas," Mayweather said. "I'm sure the admiralty is considering all sides of the issue."

"Yeah, but you should be up there, making our case," the big man said, poking his shoulder. "Why aren't you up there? You haven't forgotten where you're from, have you? You don't actually agree with Archer, do you?"

Travis let a bit of steel into his voice. "Sir, I'm going to have to ask you to lower your voice and step back."

"You do! You've turned on your own kind! Sell-out!" He pulled his arm back, and Mayweather tried to size up whether he had room to dodge the coming swing or would be forced to block it and escalate.

To his surprise, Kivei Tizahr shot out of her seat, caught the man's arm, and twisted it a certain way.

The Boomer was half again her size, but he yelled out in pain and fell to his knees, ending up with Tizahr's slim left hand pushing his face into the tabletop while her right kept his arm wrenched back. The smaller drunk stumbled back in panic, fell on his rear, and scrambled away.

"That's enough, Kivei," Mayweather advised as the big drunk continued to moan.

"Oh, he's just being a crybaby. Don't worry, sir, I'm an engineer. I know how to apply just the right amount of force to get the job done." She let the drunk go, then leaned closer to speak loudly into his ear. "Wouldn't you agree?" Nodding meekly, he shuffled away on his knees, then rose to his feet and ran after his friend.

"There," Tizahr said, brushing her hands as she resumed her seat. "Problem solved."

Sangupta was grinning at her with something strongly resembling lust. "Commander," he said to Mayweather, "would I be out of line to say I think that was awesome?"

After giving the Rigelian engineer a pointed stare for a moment, Travis relaxed. "I guess it could've gone worse. Thanks, Kivei."

"Just the most efficient way to resolve the situation, sir." She shook her head. "Really, I don't get politics at all. All this moral and ideological bickering over intervention. As if it were a binary choice between free intervention and complete prohibition. How is that useful?"

"So you don't support the directive?" Tallarico

asked. "Just so you know, that won't be a popular view on *Pioneer*, not after what we all saw in Ware space."

"Regina, I think we all know I'm not looking to be popular," Tizahr said. "I'd rather find solutions. You don't solve problems by avoiding them, you do it by engineering them." She leaned forward. "Look. Starfarers have been making first contacts for millennia. Not to mention all the historical first contacts between cultures of the same species. That gives us precedents to work with. Let's compile a database of contacts—their successes, their failures, the methods that proved most successful or most harmful in a given set of conditions—and construct some optimization algorithms. When a new contact situation comes along, the algorithm compares its parameters against the database and models the best approach. Takes sentient error and bias out of the equation."

"But it's the same problem as with the transporter," Sangupta replied, cheerfully getting drawn into the argument. "People aren't that meekly rational. They care about what feels right, what the moral thing to do is."

"Fine—then we just include probable moral reactions in the algorithm and model those as well. Find solutions that are nondisruptive to the contacted culture *and* that feel ethical to the contacting one."

"And what if there isn't one that satisfies both parameters?"

"Then obviously you weight actual impact over perceived morality. What should matter is what actually works."

"What about the new culture's *own* perception of morality? That's one of the biggest pitfalls of first contact, the risk of tripping over indigenous taboos or misunderstanding their values. How can you reliably model the ethical parameters of a society you've only started observing?"

"Like I said, you compare it against known cultures already in the database. There are only so many possible configurations a culture can take and still be viable. Okay, the assessments might be inaccurate to start with, but further interaction will quickly allow improvement and suggest ways to correct any earlier missteps. And as we accumulate more contacts, observe more cultures, the database will become fuller and more reliably predictive."

Mayweather listened to the developing conversation with interest. It was a much more agreeable non-interference debate than he'd expected to have in a setting like this, thanks entirely to Tizahr's rather unusual view of the world. He doubted her ideas would spread very far beyond this table, or that they would be effective in real first-contact situations. But they were certainly interesting. And for the first time, Mayweather was confident that Kivei Tizahr would mesh well with *Pioneer*'s crew.

Birnam

On *Endeavour*'s second day at Birnam (shipboard time), Captain Zang invited T'Pol, Sato, and Cutler to dine with his team on the planet surface. T'Pol stiffened when it became evident that the meal being served was made from the local flora. "Don't worry," said Maya Castellano, the resident biologist who doubled as the *Verne* crew's chef. "I'm not serving you anything taken from a dryad. Anyway, there's nothing on this entire planet that a vegetarian couldn't eat."

"The nature of the organisms on this planet renders that distinction ambiguous," T'Pol replied. "Vulcans are vegetarians because we reject the infliction of violence upon any organism capable of perceiving painful qualia or emotional distress."

"Just because the plants here can move around and prey on each other doesn't mean they have sentience," Zang countered. "I'll grant that the dryads have fairly complex instinctive behavior, but nothing else we've observed—or used for food—shows any similar complexity."

Elizabeth Cutler spoke up. "Humans observed chimpanzees for centuries before discovering their capacity for language and culture. Sometimes it's hard to know what to look for, especially when your preconceptions get in the way." Nonetheless, she had already begun eating the contents of her plate. "Still—this is really good," she admitted with a mild blush.

Sato nodded, chewing on her own portion. "Like a vegetarian curry, but with a meaty overtone. It's a fascinating blend."

"Glad you like it," said Castellano. "Birnam's potential as a food source could be as lucrative as its medical possibilities. I know Vulcans have to manage their diets carefully to ensure they get enough protein without eating meat. These myophytic organisms—plants with muscle-like tissues—could solve that problem." She glanced at *Endeavour*'s captain as she finished speaking.

T'Pol sighed and decided she might as well sample the fare. Logically, her refusal to eat it would not bring the constituent organisms back to life; it would only render their demise pointless and wasteful. It was much the same logic that had enabled her to tolerate humans' consumption of meat sourced from live animals—a custom many humans persisted in to some extent even though they relied primarily on more humane and efficient methods such as tissue cloning and protein resequencing. Life was life, and all animals (and some plants) must consume life to continue living. Even the life that was consumed could be said to continue in an altered form. And the flavor was, in fact, quite agreeable.

"Elizabeth does raise a valid point," T'Pol said after washing down a portion of her meal with fresh local water. "Numerous species have been hunted or herded for food before it was discovered that they were sapient entities—from the *moantar* of Lorillia to the whales of Earth to the Wraiths of Dakala. As the Federation expands into space, there will unquestionably be others. So we must ask ourselves: In cases where the sentience or intelligence of a new species is ambiguous, is it ethical to presume its absence, engaging in the hunting or harvesting of a new species and risking the slaughter of self-aware beings?"

"So you'd rather risk depriving those beings that we *know* are sentient of medicines that could save their lives," Zang countered, "just because there's a chance that something's intelligent?" The burly Boomer shook his head. "That's not just caution, that's paralysis."

"The question is one of our own entitlement versus the rights of other beings. What justifies us in assuming the former has priority?" T'Pol paused. "This strikes me as a similar matter to the noninterference debate currently ongoing in Starfleet Command. Do we presume we have the right—and the wisdom—to intervene in the lives of other beings we may not fully understand? Or do we default to granting them the same primacy over their lives that we insist upon for our own?"

Her question reminded her of Trip's current efforts on Sauria. Knowing that he was facing a potentially dangerous situation with virtually no backup was a distracting source of concern for her. In the past, she would likely have been able to connect with him telepathically in her meditative state and assure herself of his safety—even offer him advice and guidance should he need it. He, in turn, would often provide her with thoughts and suggestions that proved beneficial to her decision-making, however rustic and emotional they might initially sound. His perspective on the dryad situation would have been beneficial to her—if only to see the look of wonder in his eyes on hearing of their existence. But as more months passed with no trace of their long-distance psionic connection returning, T'Pol found it increasingly doubtful that the link would ever be restored. She would simply have to trust that he would survive Sauria on his own and eventually return to her. The fact that this was normal for most separated couples did not make it any more agreeable.

"It's easy for Starfleeters to dwell on abstractions," Maya Castellano was saying, "with your cushy government paychecks giving you the luxury. We Boomers actually have to *earn* a living. Yes, I'm a scientist, I'm interested in what we can learn, but it's a means to an end. For me, it's about making sure my boy Alec has a future. And that means making sure the Boomer way of life continues to prove it has value."

"And we aren't reckless like the Eska hunters or the old whalers of Earth," Zang added. "We have advanced science now. Scanners that can detect complex brain activity, translators that can flag alien language." He gestured at Sato. "You helped create those translators, as I recall."

"Yes," Hoshi acknowledged, "but they can only recognize patterns they're programmed to find. They can crack most humanoid languages quickly because most humanoids have similar brain structures that lead to certain common syntactical schemas . . ." She caught herself. "The point is, just because a language isn't something we recognize yet, that doesn't mean it doesn't exist."

Farid Najafi touched Sato's arm. "You told Captain T'Pol about the chemical signals we detected, right?"

Sato moved that arm to take a sip of water. "I did, but I think it's inconclusive. With fewer than two dozen distinct pheromones, I'm not sure there's enough complexity for language. And computer analysis of their subsonics shows there's no way they could carry enough information to qualify as language."

"The Roman alphabet has only twenty-six letters, but it can make plenty of words. The dryads' chemical signals have the potential for even more complexity, since they can combine simultaneously as well as sequentially. We've already found hundreds of repeating patterns."

"Come on, Farid," Castellano objected. "You can't even be sure which pheromones come from which individual. You're making a rookie mistake, inventing spurious patterns out of randomness because it's what you hope to see."

"You just admitted you have a personal stake in getting the result *you* want to see!"

"No," the biologist countered. "I don't. I have a stake in profiting from the medicines and materials we can harvest from the dryads. I consider the question of their intelligence independent and irrelevant to that."

"You're saying you don't care if we're killing intelligent life?"

"I'm saying it's not a likely enough possibility to worry about. The dryads are just too big. Too much of their brain mass must be devoted to sensation and motor control—there can't be enough left over for reasoning."

"Their size is deceptive," Najafi replied. "Only the tentacles and leg-roots can move. And the trunk's mostly hollow, due to the resonating cavity and the water reservoir."

"They have dozens of tentacles and roots. The computations to maintain their balance alone would take up a lot of brain space."

"But we've seen social behavior. Their cooperation at the river, some of them guarding the others from predators." He turned to Sato again. T'Pol raised an eyebrow, noting that he seemed to pay far more attention to Hoshi than to the other *Endeavour* officers. "We saw one of the guards attacked by a carnivorous— sorry, predatory plant. It was a kind of large mat that folded upward when stepped on and wrapped itself around the dryad. Several others came to its rescue and pulled the mat off, and not a moment too soon, because there seemed to be acid burns on the dryad. And it seemed like they'd done it before, because they did it very methodically and smoothly."

"Which could be an evolved instinct," Castellano said, "not learned behavior. Red dwarfs are very long-lived. If this planet's been here long enough for evolution to produce mobile plants, it's long enough to produce complicated instincts as well."

"Or to produce intelligence?"

"That, you have to prove."

Zang turned to T'Pol. "Captain, you can philosophize all you want about respecting other beings' primacy and erring on the side of caution, but as I see it, we're weighing the very real medical benefits that dryad products could provide for millions of people who are *certainly* sentient against the remote and highly improbable suspicion that a species of mobile plant *might* be sentient. Is there a remote chance that the dryads have minds? Maybe. Sure. But whenever I take my ship to warp, there's a remote chance my crew could be struck by an asteroid or sucked into a wormhole. There's always a risk my decisions could kill someone—but if it's a remote enough risk, nobody would call it unreasonable for me to take it. I have a responsibility to my crew to take action rather than living in fear of the improbable.

"Every day you and Farid delay our harvesting of the dryads because of your ethical concerns, Captain T'Pol, you prevent me from taking action for the good of my crew, and for the good of many others besides. My people are eager to get to work, and so am I. I've been patient with Farid so far. I've let him call you in to speed up the process. But if you and he don't find some kind of result soon, I'm within my rights to ask you to leave and proceed with my harvest. Given your fondness for noninterference, I trust," Zang finished with a pointed look, "that you will respect that."

"That is your right," she conceded. She then rose from the table. "I trust you will excuse me, Captain

Zang." T'Pol left without looking back at the unfinished meal on her plate.

March 1, 2166
Akleyro, Sauria

"Nearly all the pieces are in place," Charles Tucker said. "I've provided the Malurians with Harris's physical specs and a recording of his voice. They've already fabricated the mask, and their man Tanag is working on his impersonation. It won't be perfect on short notice, but since Harris has been so careful to stay out of any public record for years, it should be close enough. That's also why we don't have to worry about him having an alibi. The only people who could corroborate his whereabouts for the past few weeks are also part of the organization, and they can't defend him without exposing themselves, which is just what we want.

"So what we'll do is to stage a scene of Harris and D'Nesh discussing their plan over subspace. Garos has recordings of his own prior conversations with D'Nesh, and his people are altering them to create the simulation. It'll look like subspace interference is lowering the image clarity and causing the occasional glitch, to hide any imperfections. Elevia will be part of that little confab in disguise, after which she and the fake Harris will meet with the Untainted, to make it look like they're conspiring to arrange the catastrophe during the factory attack. They're the ones Garos plans to pin it on, since they're the most extreme sect. Now, to really sell it, Elevia will be wearing a bracelet she managed to swipe from D'Nesh. The plan is that Navaar will recognize that bracelet, and it'll help convince her that Elevia is D'Nesh's operative. And that's where you come in."

Antonio Ruiz studied Tucker skeptically, crossing his arms. "Because you need me to catch it on my imager and beam it out to the galaxy."

"That's right."

"Why can't you do it yourself?"

"Because it'll be more convincing if it comes from a known advocate of the resistance. And I need to keep myself out of it. I explained why." That was an incomplete truth, just as the explanation itself had been. There was much that Trip wanted to tell his friend but still could not—and much more that he would be ashamed to admit even if he could. But it was a relief even to come clean to Antonio as far as he had.

Ruiz shook his head. "Don't you get it, man? All these lies and tricks—how are they supposed to make anything better? Why not just come out and tell the truth about who you are, what you know?"

"I would have, years ago, if I could. But I . . . I have too many bad decisions on my hands. Decisions that Harris and his people could easily pin on me so they could avoid exposure."

"You mean they're blackmailing you into silence."

Tucker winced inwardly, ashamed at how close that was to the mark. "Call it what you like. But it's effective. It's how they keep their own hands clean—by maneuvering their operatives into doing the dirty work for them. And Harris is too careful to ever let himself be implicated. That's why we have to *create* the smoking gun."

"And you really think you can lie better than the master liars? That they won't be ready for this?"

"I'm not in this alone, Tony. My allies and I have come as close as we can to building a case against Section Thirty-one, but we have to tie Harris to it somehow. And this is the best plan we've managed to come up with."

"And that alone should tell you how screwed you are."

"You think I don't know that? This is a Hail Mary. But it's a gamble I'm willing to take. I can't stand idly by any longer." He clasped his old friend's shoulder. "You helped show me that. And that's why I need your help now."

"It's too risky," Ruiz protested, shrugging off the gesture. "If you know there's a major disaster being planned, you can't hide that. You can't gamble all those lives for the sake of your spy games. We should take this to Mullen and Kelly right now."

"And convince them how? You think they'd believe this story coming from me, a man who's faked being dead for eleven years? I've got no way to prove it. They sure wouldn't believe an Orion spy. And Garos wouldn't confess his involvement, not unless it's after he's had a chance to get away. Besides, if we scuttle their plan here, the Sisters might just try again later. The only way to stop it is to expose their goals publicly so they no longer have a reason to try it."

Ruiz began to pace. "If these Section *hombres* are responsible for half the things you said, then yeah, I want to see them get what's coming to them. And I'm up for anything I can do to save Saurian lives. But this plan—it's so crazy. How's it gonna hurt this D'Nesh lady if her sister catches her conspiring to do the same thing they were *already* conspiring to do?"

"Because it'll look like she's conspiring with someone in the Federation, behind Navaar's back. Maybe Navaar will think she was making a side deal, like she did before with the Babel Conference. More importantly, if the footage of their collusion gets exposed and the sabotage is foiled, then it'll look like D'Nesh's incompetence bungled the operation. Even if Navaar believes her denials, she may still have to write D'Nesh off as a liability."

Tucker's rationales sounded feeble even to his own ears. Bringing Devna and Garos in had been necessary, and he still felt the former could be a real asset; but balancing all the conflicting agendas was making this plan much more convoluted than he would have liked.

He sighed. "Look, honestly, that's the least important part to me. That was just the condition for getting Elevia's help. It's more important for the Federation to see Harris conspiring with the Syndicate. He's the one who needs to be discredited."

Ruiz looked him over. "You really hate this guy, don't you?"

Tucker held his friend's gaze. "Honestly? No, I don't. I hate what he's done, and I really hate what he's made *me* do. But in his own way, he's trying to do good. He really believes he's helping the Federation in a way nobody else can. He's just too willing to rationalize letting other people get hurt in the process."

The resistance fighter scoffed. "That's pretty much the definition of privilege. That bad things are only unthinkable if they happen to your own kind." Ruiz thought it over. "I like the idea of bringing this guy down. But my broadcasts are about getting out the truth. Against Maltuvis's propaganda, the truth is the most important weapon we have. You're asking me to taint that. Maybe lying's gotten so easy for you that you can't appreciate how hard that is to agree to."

Tucker lowered his head. "I deserve that. And I hate asking you for it. But it's the only way I know to bring out a deeper truth—that Section Thirty-one exists and is doing more harm than good. They need to be brought into the light, and they need to be stopped."

The younger man stepped closer. "And what will you do if you manage to get that truth out?"

"I'll get out of this life. Most likely, I'll disappear again—fake my death so even they can't find me. One more lie, but after that, I won't have to hurt anyone ever again. If I have to, I'll even come forward, tell the whole truth . . . and face the music for it."

It was some moments before Ruiz spoke again.

"Okay," he conceded. "If this is your only way out . . . then I'll do it. Because I believe we should help out our friends when they need us."

Tucker blinked rapidly, suffused with gratitude. "You don't owe me anything, Tony. I haven't been that good a friend."

"It's about how good I want to be to *my* friends. You made mistakes. I'm still pissed at you. But that doesn't mean you aren't still my friend, Al. And that means I'll be there for you."

Tucker grinned and clasped his friend's hands warmly. "Trip," he said. "My friends call me Trip."

Ruiz laughed. "Trip. You certainly are that, man."

When Devna signaled Tucker to let him know that she and Garos were done with their preparations, he brought Ruiz to the chamber the Malurians had rigged for their dramatization. To his surprise, Devna wore no disguise beyond a hooded cloak. "I expected you'd be in a mask of your own," he said.

"It will suffice," Devna said, her voice an even quieter whisper than usual. "Owners rarely look that closely at their slaves' faces."

Garos turned to the younger human. "You, Mister Ruiz, will be stationed behind this vent," he said, leading him over to a large grille at the rear of the chamber. "A city carved into a cliff needs plenty of air shafts, which are more than roomy enough to let an intrepid journalist eavesdrop on a secret conversation. The viewscreen that will display the D'Nesh simulation is positioned to give you an ideal vantage point." The Raldul leader studied Ruiz. "I trust you aren't claustrophobic."

That brought a laugh. "I was a mining engineer in my old life," Ruiz said. "I've crawled through tighter spaces plenty of times."

"Excellent. My men will help you inside." As he spoke, one of his Malurian subordinates removed the grille while another moved in to give Ruiz a leg up.

"What about the fake Harris?" Tucker asked.

"A good mask is an intricate creation," Garos said, moving back toward him. "Our masksmiths prefer to keep touching them up until the last possible moment. But I guarantee you will be amazed at the result."

Grinning, Garos moved to the side door and opened it. "Tanag! Time to take the stage."

In the corner of his eye, Tucker saw Devna look away and lower her head. He wasn't sure if it was that or Garos's increasingly smug grin that first made him feel that something was wrong.

When the Malurian impersonator Tanag entered the doorway, Tucker could see that he was suitably attired in the spare black uniform of Section 31. As he moved into the light, it became clear that the mask he wore was a perfect facsimile of the face of a Caucasian human male.

But the face he wore was that of Charles Tucker III.

"What the hell is going on here?" Tucker cried.

"Calm down, Agent Tucker," Garos intoned as more Raldul operatives moved into the room, covering him with Malurian phase pistols. "My revision to your plan will work best if you're alive, but I have contingencies for the alternative."

"Hey, what's going on?" Ruiz cried from the air shaft, but the operatives closed the grille and held it there to trap him.

Tucker almost asked how Garos had learned his real name, but years of intelligence training stopped him. Besides, he got his answer when Devna turned to him. "I'm sorry," she said.

He stared at her. "You betrayed me!"

"Oh, please don't hold it against her, Charles," Garos said. "I'm afraid I found it necessary to blackmail the young lady into cooperation, lest I reveal her treason to Navaar. I regret that I couldn't follow through with her plan to destroy D'Nesh . . . but stability within the Syndicate is better for Raldul's goals."

Tucker's angry gaze fell back upon Garos. "So you didn't have the guts to break free of the Sisters' control after all."

"Please, don't be crass. You'd understand if you were Malurian. If your females were largely sessile, unable to move far from the places of their birth. It makes my mate a sitting target for the Sisters' retaliation—and my mating bond makes it a biological imperative to protect and serve her. I never had the option of betraying Navaar. You were a fool to think I could."

"You always have such a righteous-sounding excuse for your crimes."

"Think what you will, but I cannot afford to let my own usefulness to Navaar be undermined any further. I have to help her ensure the success of *her* plan—a disaster large enough to shock the Federation into embracing noninterference, if not complete isolationism. Even better if the mishap can be blamed on the reckless, heavy-handed meddling of the same secretive Starfleet cabal that engineered the Partnership's destruction and chose not to stop Maltuvis's rise to power in the first place."

"And if the agent whose bungling led to the catastrophe is a Starfleet legend who falsified his own death at the start of the Earth-Romulan War," added Tanag in a flawless imitation of Tucker's voice, "it makes Starfleet's humiliation even greater."

"That's why you need me alive. As a scapegoat."

"Exactly," said Garos. "I've spoken to Maltuvis—he's very eager to get his hands on you for a show trial to prove the evils of the Federation. Kind of you to let yourself be seen among the rebels, and to leave your genetic material behind. It's convenient the way you mammals shed your hair and skin flakes everywhere you go, if somewhat disgusting."

"So why do you need to impersonate me at all?" Even as Tucker asked, the answer occurred to him. "No, wait—you need to take me out of the way before I can expose your plan, but you also need to make sure I'm still seen working with the resistance up until the factory raid."

"More than that," Tanag said. "I—or rather,

you—will be quite helpful in convincing the resistance to walk into our trap."

Tucker shook his head. "How can you live with yourself, Garos? I know you're a killer, but you like to insist it bothers you. Now you're talking about killing maybe millions of innocent civilians. *Children.* If you can go through with this, it renders all your claims of conscience meaningless."

"Even conscience has priorities, Agent Tucker," the Malurian leader replied. "I'm not happy about the fate of all those Saurians—especially since they're fellow reptilians. But I have to give more weight to the survival of Malurians. In a choice between the two, my first loyalty must be to my own kind."

Tucker shook his head. "That is exactly the excuse my employers always use."

"And I respect them for it," Garos said. "Just as I respect you for your own loyalty to your people. This is nothing personal." He shrugged. "But someone must win the game."

10

WHEN DAYLIGHT CAME and Akleyro slept, Garos's operatives smuggled their human prisoners out of the city and into the rainforest above. Tucker and Ruiz were marched forward at gunpoint, forced to keep up a pace that was difficult for the humans to bear in the sweltering heat and humidity, especially shackled to each other wrist to wrist by a half-meter chain. The Malurians, by contrast, seemed energized by the heat.

Nonetheless, Tucker felt obligated to consider options for escape. "We have to get back to the Starfleet team," he whispered to Ruiz. "My plan's blown—warning them about the attack is our only chance to stop it."

"You're thinking of making a break?" the Cuban whispered back.

"This jungle provides plenty of cover."

"Yeah, for a bunch of hungry serpents and pterosaurs that would have us for lunch."

"You've been here for years. You know the terrain."

"Not *this* terrain. I only know enough to know

I don't want to be here without a lot of reinforce-ments."

Tucker considered. "Okay, then," he breathed. "They're probably taking us to a ship—maybe we can make our move then, try to take it over."

Indeed, it wasn't much longer before a heavy shuttle of Malurian design came into view, parked in a clear-ing barely large enough for it. "Get ready," Tucker whispered.

A phase pistol burst came from behind them and felled Ruiz. Tucker stumbled as the other man's weight pulled him down. Coming to his knees, he checked to verify that his friend was merely stunned. The leader of their escorts arrived above them, smirking. "It might interest you to know that Malurian hearing is quite sensitive at high frequencies. Now, pick him up and get him into the shuttle."

Tucker had no choice but to comply. Still, he cursed to himself as he dragged his friend into the landing craft. This might have been their best chance to escape. Once they were in the hands of Maltuvis's soldiers—facing guards considerably stronger and more robust than themselves, confined by restraints and cells de-signed for equally strong and robust prisoners—escape might be next to impossible.

But Tucker refused to accept that. He'd escaped near-certain death repeatedly during the Romulan War, while serving Section 31 for the greater good. Now that he was *fighting* Section 31 for the greater good, surely he could find a way to do it again.

He tried not to think about how many of those escapes had been due to dumb luck.

Birnam

Hoshi Sato had resisted the urge to ask Cutler or one of the Boomers to come along as a chaperone when Farid Najafi had invited her out to gather more data on dryad pheromonal communication. Yes, he was a very attractive man whom she would be alone with in an almost Edenic landscape . . . but she was a grown woman, she loved her fiancé, and she had the discipline of a Starfleet officer. As long as she recognized her excited state as an artifact of the high oxygen content of the atmosphere, she should have no trouble containing herself. As for Farid—well, he was a Boomer, not a barbarian. The era when a human woman had to be concerned for her safety when alone with a man was generations in the past.

Indeed, Najafi seemed to be reserving his excitement for the dryads as he escorted Sato through the perpetually daylit, if usually overcast, woods. "Our projections show that the dryads keep growing throughout their lives, like normal trees. About four to five centimeters per standard year."

Sato's eyes widened. "I'd think they'd eventually get too big to move!"

"You're not wrong. Here, it's just ahead." He took her hand and pulled her into a run toward the top of the low ridge they were climbing. She let him.

Once they reached the crest, Sato saw that beyond the sunward side of the ridge, between it and the local river, was a grove of the largest dryads she had yet seen. They stood in an orderly array, spaced widely enough to ensure that none was in the shadow of another. Hoshi realized that this was not a watering stop like the one she had witnessed before. There were no mobile dryads patrolling the outer perimeter; they were hardly needed, because these dryads were too huge to be preyed upon. As Najafi led her down the slope to get a closer look, she realized that the ground around the giants' roots was smooth, as if it had not been disturbed for quite some time. Indeed, many of their tentacles had grown long enough to extend into the ground, becoming roots themselves—though a few remained free and mobile. Sato saw one dryad languidly batting at a small flying plant creature seeking to land on its trunk.

"I call it an elders' grove," Najafi said. "Once they reach twenty to twenty-four meters, they travel to a site like this, where they stop moving, grow out their root systems, and live out the rest of their lives like normal trees." He grinned. "There's a kind of symmetry to it, since it seems they also begin their lives in a sedentary phase. Apparently they reproduce with seedlike spores that grow in the ground for, oh, probably ten to twenty years before they fully develop their nerve and muscle analogs and become mobile."

"Do they just drop their spores anywhere?" Sato asked.

"No, we've found the seedlings planted in dedicated sites—I guess you'd call them nurseries in both senses of the word." They both laughed. "The grown dryads of their copse watch over them until they become mobile."

"Do the mobile dryads tend the old ones too?"

"They seem to let nature take its course with the elders, even when the elders are attacked by predatory plants. But they often communicate with them. I get the sense the mobile dryads are, you know, seeking the wisdom of their elders. Listening to their stories while they're still around."

She studied Najafi. "Are you seeking something, Farid? Is that why this is so important to you?"

His ready smile was abashed this time. "Nothing so profound. It's just . . . Well, you know what Boomer life was like. Growing up on starships, crawling at low warp from planet to planet." She nodded. "I was born on the *Verne*, near the start of a two-year voyage to a system that was nothing but asteroids and a few tight-orbiting superterrestrial planets too hot or too high-gravity to set foot on. Then a year setting up a mining colony, and sixteen-month round trips to a Draylaxian trade outpost on a frozen-over rogue planet. I was eight before I finally got to set foot on a planet with its own life. My mom took me down to this vast, endless forest . . . I'd seen pictures for years, but I'd never believed they were actually real. It was like finding out Santa's workshop really existed."

Hoshi widened her eyes in jest. "You mean it doesn't?"

Najafi laughed. "For me it did, at that moment. I fell in love with nature, with trees. To be in a place where everything was alive. . . . Before, the living things around me had been mostly people, thinking beings that could talk to me. That's what living things meant to me, and it took a while to realize that trees weren't people too. I tried talking to the trees, but they never talked back." He gazed in awe at the sessile dryads looming above them. "These trees might have something to say."

"We're a long way from proving that."

"That's why we're here." He frowned. "Sensors say there should be a small copse headed this way—I wanted us to take scans of their pheromone exchanges with the elders. I guess they got delayed."

Sato chuckled. "Or we ran too fast. All this oxygen does throw people into high gear, doesn't it?"

"That it does. Though I would've been just as excited without it."

She blushed, noticing that his eyes were on her rather than the dryads. She turned toward the dendriforms, hoping the ruddy light had masked her response. "I was the opposite," she said. "I grew up on Earth, surrounded by nature, and didn't set foot on a spaceship until my Starfleet training. I mean, it's not like I lived in the woods—Kyoto's a major city. But it's surrounded on three sides by mountains covered in green, and there are plenty of parks. Nature was never very far away. I guess I took it for granted. Always had my nose in a book or a computer, studying one language after another. I often neglected to look up at the world and appreciate what was around me—and who was around me. It wasn't until those first training flights in space that I realized how *rare* it was in the universe to be surrounded by living things."

The Boomer watched her expectantly. "And it gave you a new appreciation of nature?"

She laughed. "I thought it did. After I decided Starfleet wasn't for me—before Jonathan Archer talked me into coming back to serve on *Enterprise*—I went to teach in Brazil, partly because the Amazon rainforest was there. But when I went on a river cruise to see the wildlife . . ." She shuddered. "Let's just say I'm glad there are no anacondas on this planet."

"Wait. You're Hoshi Sato. You've faced down Xindi-Reptilians without blinking."

She tensed, lowering her head. "Oh, I blinked. And a lot worse."

He stroked her arm lightly. "But you still triumphed. I can't even imagine. And after that, you're still afraid of snakes?"

"Not just snakes! *Really big* snakes!"

They laughed together, somewhat longer and more hysterically than was called for. Finally, Najafi cleared his throat and gathered himself. "Uh, look, I'm just gonna go see what's keeping that copse of dryads." He frowned. "We need a better word. Like 'copse,' but more mobile."

Hoshi pondered for a moment. "Traffic copse?"

They both broke down giggling again. "Perfect!" Farid managed to get out before he retreated upstream.

Once he was out of sight—and she'd gotten her giggling under control—Hoshi turned slowly to take in her idyllic surroundings. It was rather extraordinary for a native of modern-day Earth to be surrounded by untouched wilds and know that virtually the entire planet around her was free of any trace of civilization. She had experienced such planets many times before, but usually in the company of *Enterprise* or *Endeavour* landing parties. Out here, kilometers from the base camp, she could imagine there was nothing human on Birnam besides herself. There was a comfort in that solitude, reminding her of the quiet isolation in which she had spent much of her childhood. She had been lonely at times, but she had valued the freedom from distractions, the space in which to contemplate her beloved languages.

To enhance the illusion, Hoshi unfastened her science-blue uniform tunic and stripped down to her tank top, then removed her boots so she could walk barefoot. It was a relief in this hot, humid climate. She wandered through the glade, delighting in the warm breeze against her skin and the soft, dewy ground cover beneath her feet as she contemplated the question of how a pheromonal language might be organized. She tried to look at Birnam as Najafi did, as a mythic place imbued with living spirits—like the *kodama* she had mentioned to Takashi, or the other animistic forest denizens from the stories her grandfather had shared with her in her youth. Maybe some adorable little cartoon sprite would amble out of the woods and lead her to a spirit realm where she could speak to the dryads directly. She laughed, feeling giddy from all the oxygen, and imagined she was walking on air.

Then she realized she was, in fact, falling through the air. Her burgeoning shriek was cut off by her impact with a damp, squishy surface. Looking up, she saw an opening three meters overhead, flanked by four organic-looking flaps carpeted with the local ground cover. Hoshi realized some sort of trapdoor plant buried in the ground had captured her for dinner.

She struggled to her feet, stumbling as the slippery surface moved beneath her, and tried to grab one of the slowly closing flaps, to no avail. Reflexively, she reached for the sleeve pocket that held her communicator . . . but she touched only bare skin. She'd left her tunic on the ground above. *Stupid!*

Hoshi screamed for help at the top of her lungs, but soon the flaps shut completely, leaving her in blackness. She screamed louder, praying her cries could penetrate the flaps, for the pit was already beginning to fill with what had to be digestive acid.

After a panicked minute, she heard a muffled voice calling her name, followed by the whine of a phase pistol. The creature convulsed, knocking her over, and the flaps fell limp. *Thank God,* Hoshi thought as she saw a vine being lowered. She scrambled up its length, gladly grasped the hand extended to her. Moments later, Najafi pulled her up and out, toppling backward as he did so. She fell atop him, panting hard along with him. "Thank you. Thank you so much."

She couldn't stop herself from kissing him. She didn't want to. And once she started, she didn't want to stop—and clearly, neither did he. Somewhere along the way, he managed to mention between kisses that her uniform trousers were covered in pitcher-plant acid, so she might want to remove them, whereupon she invited him to help her do so, then started to remove his clothes just in case any acid had splashed on him . . .

"What am I doing?" She pulled away, finally, just before matters reached the point of no return. "No. This is wrong. I'm—I'm engaged. I have a fiancé. I have a ring, see?" She held up her ring. "I have a ring."

Najafi nodded understandingly, looking away, handing her back what he'd removed. "I'm sorry. I didn't . . . I never would've . . ."

"It's the oxygen," she gasped as she began to dress again.

"Of course. Just the oxygen."

"And the intensity of the moment . . . I was grateful . . ."

"I understand. Only natural. Don't worry about it."

"No. No! Why should I? I wasn't myself."

"Me neither. It's the oxygen."

"Just the oxygen. Sure."

U.S.S. Endeavour

"It wasn't just the oxygen," Hoshi moaned as Doctor Phlox examined her for injury or harmful aftereffects of her close call with the pitcher plant. "Or the danger. I've been attracted to Farid from the start."

"I can't blame you," Phlox said cheerily. "He's an extremely attractive and charming young man."

"I *have* an attractive and charming man in my life. A man I'm going to marry. A man I *want* to marry. This isn't supposed to happen." She sighed. "I guess I shouldn't expect you to understand."

Phlox patted her shoulder. "It's true that your cultural preference for monogamy is somewhat odd from a Denobulan point of view. To us, romantic love is not a finite resource that must be—heh—husbanded, but something that you have more to give the more people you share it with. Even in humans, some degree of promiscuity is more the norm than the exception, judging from actual statistics and behavioral observation as opposed to cultural ideals."

"You must think I'm being silly, then. To feel guilty over just *wanting* to be with someone else."

"Not at all, Hoshi. Just because I don't share this particular ideal, that doesn't mean I can't respect what it means to you. It's not unlike Vulcan logic, in a way. It's hardly the default behavior of the species, and that makes it difficult to achieve in practice—yet that very difficulty is why it is considered worth striving for. It's seen as an attempt to rise above instinctual appetites and behave in a manner one has earned through dedication and commitment." He met her eyes. "And that means you're entitled to regret falling short of that ideal—but it also means that such shortfalls are a normal experience for human beings. What matters is not that you have these urges, but what you choose to do about them."

Sato thought it over, then nodded. "Right. You're right. I just have to avoid being alone with Farid again. Especially out in that atmosphere."

Phlox gave her a stern look. "You already know it wasn't about the atmosphere. It wasn't even about Mister Najafi. Part of making the right choice is understanding the real source of the problem."

She winced, closing her eyes. "I love Takashi. What happened to him hasn't changed that."

"Of course it's changed that." She stared at Phlox in shock, and the doctor clarified his words. "It hasn't ended your love for him, but your love has changed, because he has changed. The nature of the future you would have together as wife and husband has changed. Our recent return to Earth gave you a taste of what married life with Takashi would entail. It was abstract for you before, but now you've experienced it more directly." He checked the readouts on his scanner. "Ah. You'll be pleased to know there are no harmful aftereffects from the pitcher plant's digestive juices—just a slight dermal irritation to your feet, but I have a salve that will clear that up in no time. You may get dressed now."

Sato leaped off the exam table and began to pace. "Oh-h, Phlox, you're right. I hate to admit it, but you're right. Having to help him with his limitations . . . to be patient with his struggles . . . to have to be strong for him all the time, when I was so used to knowing I could rely on *his* strength. Phlox, I don't know if I have what it takes to handle that. It scares me."

"Hoshi, when we first met, you were afraid that you would fail as a Starfleet officer. You very nearly gave up and returned home after your first crisis on *Enterprise*. You've always doubted your ability to handle new challenges. But those doubts have always proven to be unfounded."

"But what if I'm the wrong person to take up *this* challenge?" she asked as she pulled her tunic back on. "Takashi needs someone who can be strong for him. Someone who'll love him unconditionally. I don't know if I'm that person. I loved him so much for his quick wit, his thoughtfulness, his gift with words, his grace and prowess . . . his fantastic body . . . and now all of that is tainted. And I'm ashamed to admit it, but I think it's made me love him less. I play the good, supportive fiancée, I try to be selfless because it's the right thing to do . . . but deep down, I'm having second thoughts. Maybe my love was too superficial to be what he needs. Look how easily I get tempted by another great body and easy smile."

"Hoshi . . ."

She finished pulling on her boots. "Maybe you Denobulans have the right idea. Maybe it's better to have three spouses, because it's so hard to find any one person you can truly rely on." She strode out of sickbay before Phlox could answer.

March 3, 2166
M'Tezir, Sauria

Maltuvis's prison turned out to be as great a challenge as Tucker had feared. The doors were heavy and the locks were strong, and since the Saurians had always tended to rely more on their own inherent gifts than on technology, the locks were strictly mechanical, with no electronics for a former starship engineer to hack or hot-wire. By the same token, the prison's security system consisted of live Saurian guards with superior strength and keen senses. Escaping would take considerable ingenuity—and that was the optimistic assessment.

For his part, Ruiz tried to appeal to the guards on a personal level, arguing that his cause would benefit their own freedom and that of their families. But either his grasp of the M'Tezir language was inadequate to convey subtle ideas, or Maltuvis selected his prison guards for their simplemindedness and lack of empathy. Ruiz's exhortations fell on deaf earholes, earning nothing but threats and silencing blows from their captors. It was only when they started hitting Tucker in response to Ruiz's urgings that he stopped trying.

After they had been left alone for a day with no provisions for their physical needs, Maltuvis himself finally arrived to gloat over them. "Please," Tucker urged, "we need food. Water."

The dictator scoffed. "You mammals. So fragile

and needy. How unjust, that such an inferior breed should master the stars. One day, you will surely succumb to your betters."

"It's our cooperation that makes us strong," Ruiz told him. "Our respect for each other. You'll never understand that, Malvolio."

"Cooperation. Is that what you call it?" His bulbous eyes darted to take in the two humans. "Your friend's organization endorses the Orions' efforts to sabotage Starfleet. He works against his organization to stop them. Even within your own race, you are fragmented by differing agendas. This is what happens when there is no singular will to guide all—when the masses are allowed to dissent and question. It is that same lack of unity that made it so easy for me to undermine the so-called Global League and bend its subjects to my will. That same tolerance of abnormal beliefs that permits the existence of groups such as the Untainted, who will make such convincing scapegoats for the impending disaster. Along with Starfleet, of course," he concluded with a humorless smirk.

"How can you do it?" Ruiz demanded. "How can you be so willing to let millions of your own people suffer and die just so you can get ahead?"

"My people?" Maltuvis looked disgusted. "The Lyaksti, the Veranith, the Narprans? They are not *my* people. They are inferior breeds that, like yours, have managed through a fluke of history to gain an advantage over their betters and who imagine that this is their destiny for all time. You have seen how easily they were mastered as soon as fortune shifted back toward those with the strength to take advantage of it. For centuries, they undermined the greatness of M'Tezir—infecting us with their weakness, draining us through economic trickery, using the crutches of technology and industry to gain power that the truly strong would have taken by conquest. Now they are finally getting the punishment they deserve. In one stroke, I will break the resistance, discredit and humiliate your precious Federation, and prove the superiority of the Maltuvian Empire for all to see."

"Yeah," Tucker said, "thanks to all the help you've gotten from the Orions and Malurians. Make sure you don't forget to give them credit in your victory speech."

Maltuvis gestured to a burly guard who stepped forward and began to beat Tucker. An uncertain time later, the agent became aware of Ruiz shouting at the Saurian to stop. Tucker was filled with relief when the pain stopped—so much so that he hesitated to cry out in protest when Maltuvis gestured to the guard to begin beating Ruiz instead. Ashamed of his weakness, he tried to summon his voice, but he could barely catch his breath.

Then he realized that the fear of weakness was what drove Maltuvis to these atrocities, all out of the pathetic need to compensate for that fear. He realized that he needed to forgive himself for his vulnerability, that it was only human. It was his ability to face his own vulnerability that enabled him to empathize with others' pain and dedicate himself to alleviating it. Ruiz was right—true strength came from cooperation, from recognizing one's own limitations and the need to join with others whose strengths could balance them. If T'Pol's voice were still in his mind, she might remind him of the Vulcan IDIC symbol representing diversity in combination. For all that Vulcans disdained the expression of emotion, there was a surprising depth of empathy underlying their core teachings. The love she shared with Tucker—the love that let him endure moments like this and keep on going—was part and parcel of her Vulcan nature, not a violation of it. That was what made it so extraordinary a thing for a human to be allowed to share.

Tucker might not be able to spare Ruiz from pain now. But by holding on to his empathy, he could still be there for his friend in whatever way he could.

For his own part, Ruiz remained defiant. "Torture me all you like, Malt Liquor," he panted after a time. "I won't tell you anything."

Maltuvis looked confused. "Tell me? What does torture have to do with interrogation?" He pondered it for a moment, as if the idea had genuinely never occurred to him. "No, really, the two would only get in each other's way. You couldn't get reliable information from someone whose mind was addled with pain and fear, and you couldn't get the most satisfaction out of inflicting pain if you had to keep the victim coherent enough to answer questions. Really, the ideas you aliens come up with.

"No, I have all the information I need about your pathetic resistance thanks to the Malurian toady in their ranks. Your torture, Mister Ruiz, is merely what you deserve for being such a nuisance—exposing my disease gambit, stealing the cure, fomenting resistance with your propaganda campaign, and just generally being a piece of alien filth that keeps evading my efforts to cleanse you from my world. Your companion here shall be punished as well for his involvement in your troublemaking, once he has played his role in his upcoming trial. But you have been an irritant to me for far longer, so the—irritation—I cause you in turn shall be commensurately greater. Nothing you might tell me would alter that in any way.

"The only thing I hope to learn from your torture is just how much punishment humans can take before they die. I don't expect it will be very much, but it's important to know these things for the future."

"Why?" Tucker asked. "What do you have planned for the future?"

"Isn't it obvious, you stupid creature?" Maltuvis replied. "I already said your kind would inevitably succumb to your betters." He gestured to himself. "Who else did you imagine I was talking about?"

11

March 4, 2166
Oakland, California

EVEN THOUGH MARCUS WILLIAMS had made it clear that he found Sam Kirk unworthy of her, Valeria Williams had continued to bring the historian with her when she visited the captain's home. After all, her father had not raised her to retreat from a challenge. Both of the men made an effort to be civil when they were together, out of regard for Val's wish to have them both included in her life, but there remained a distance between them that Val feared she might never find a way to bridge.

Still, she tried her best. "You should come with us to Sam's lecture at the university next week," she suggested to her father at dinner one evening.

Captain Williams looked skeptical. "This is that presentation you said he's been working on?" he asked. "About the Partnership of Civilizations?"

"That's right, sir," Sam replied. "An overview of their history and culture, based on the accounts we managed to gather during the mission, plus a discussion of the questions that . . . well, that we may never be able to answer now."

"Hm," the captain said. "Accounts. Based on their Ware databases? How trustworthy do you think those were?"

"Based on that, on written histories we managed to document, and on oral interviews with Partners of several different species. Naturally no source is ever presumed to be absolutely trustworthy by itself, sir, but it's still important to preserve every account we can for posterity."

"It's actually a pretty interesting process when you get to know it, Dad," Val said. "It's like detective work, gathering evidence and witness statements and building a theory of the case."

"It's more than that," Sam added. "A whole civilization has died. Partly due to our mistakes. We have an obligation to do whatever we can to preserve their voices—to make sure they aren't forgotten."

Val clasped his hand across the table. "It's been pretty rough going for Sam, facing that loss every day. I think it's very brave of him to stick with it and make sure the stories get told." Kirk smiled at her and squeezed her hand back.

"Well, sure, no question it was a tragedy," her father said. "But it's not like some good hasn't come of it. If it leads to Starfleet adopting a noninterference policy, so nothing like it ever happens again, then it's better in the long run for the Federation and a lot of others."

Val felt the sudden tension in Sam's hand. "Better, sir?" he asked. "How can you say that? Millions of people died. Billions more have been stripped of their whole way of life, their ability to create a culture and travel the stars and communicate with one another."

"I'm not denying that. But it's like I've said before— sometimes sacrifices are necessary for the greater good."

"That's easy to say when you're not the one who has to make the sacrifice," the historian went on with rising heat. "Especially when you're the one who benefits from it. But the Partners weren't allowed to make that choice for themselves. Try to see it from their perspective, sir. Imagine your entire civilization was stripped away overnight, and you had no way to rebuild it or even preserve the knowledge of it. Imagine you no longer had a way to give your children an education or protect them from predators and disease. Would you see a 'greater good' in that, sir? Would you call that sacrifice justified, just because someone else you'd never know, someone who'd lost nothing in the process, got to learn a moral lesson from it? Would you take any comfort in their conviction that the sacrifice of your children's future was worth it?"

"But how much did they really lose, Sam? Their culture wasn't their own, it was sold to them by the Ware in exchange for their bodies and brains."

"Their mechanisms for creating culture came from the Ware. What they created came from them. From their history, their beliefs, their own unique ways of thinking and relating to the universe."

Kirk went on to tell Williams about the amazing cities and communities he and Val had walked among during their time in the Partnership, and about the diverse and fascinating individuals they'd conversed with in their investigations and striven alongside during the Klingon invasion. The Monsof, humanoids of limited manual and verbal dexterity who had lost their homeworld to the enemies of the Ware, but who had been taken in by the avian Hurrait, repaying their kindness by providing them with the hands they lacked and forming a symbiotic relationship that let them both achieve more than either could alone. The Sris'si, a sightless aquatic species of solitary predators, appearing at first to be lacking in social instincts, but capable of surprisingly selfless effort on behalf of those with whom they shared common goals. The Krutuvub, tree-grazing herbivores who saw all members of a herd as fragments of a single soul, and who had instinctively extended their definition of their herd to include the other Partnership species.

These were the same experiences on which he would base his upcoming lecture, but right here and now, he did not have to keep a scholarly distance. So he was able to imbue it with all the emotion he had felt at the time—the wonder at the extraordinarily different civilizations and the ways they had devised to live together, and the pain he felt as the individuals he had spoken with, dined with, and traveled with over his months in the Partnership had been stripped of their homes, their cities, their ability to communicate with one another, and even their lives.

Val joined in once he spoke of the destruction of

Oceantop City, an ordeal the two of them had endured together. Before, she had spoken of it to her father only to refer to Sam Kirk's heroism in the evacuation and the courage he had shown in their joint rescue efforts, leading to their first kiss and the onset of their love affair. Neither she nor Sam had wanted to dwell on the lives they'd failed to rescue, the thousands of Partners they'd seen drowned or crushed by debris or vaporized by Klingon disruptor fire. Now, though, Sam refused to shy away from those memories any longer. And that gave Val the courage to speak of them as well. She hardly remembered the words she used. All she remembered was the catharsis of pain and anger, her fury at the injustice of a galaxy that had allowed these things to happen. And she remembered ending up on the couch, crying onto her father's big, strong shoulder while Sam held her from behind, crying with her.

"Philip Collier may have thought he was helping the Federation when he gave the Klingons the means to destroy the Ware," Val said at length, "but in the end, he only hurt it. We saved our civilization by becoming accomplices in the murder of another, and that original sin will be with us from now on.

"Should we learn from that? Should we dedicate ourselves to never doing it again? Absolutely. But we can't do that if we just wash our hands of what we did and chalk it up to a learning experience. We need to do something to atone." Breathing raggedly, she shook her head. "But for the life of me, I don't know what we can do."

March 5, 2166
M'Tezir, Sauria

Maltuvis had apparently not been lying about using
the torture of Tucker and Ruiz to assess humans'
physical vulnerabilities. The two men were stripped
naked and hooked up to various sensor leads as they
were subjected to excessive heat, freezing cold, drown-
ing, electrocution, and other torments over what felt
to Tucker like days or weeks, though he had no confidence in his sense of time under these conditions.
Section 31 training had conditioned him to resist
breaking under torture, but it was based on the assumption that the goal of the torture would be to extract information, not simply to be an end in itself
(even though torture was always ultimately an end
in itself, whatever the excuses offered to justify it).
Tucker's nominal ability to withstand the ordeal was
moot when he had no specific goal for which to withstand it—beyond simply being there for Ruiz, helping him through it as best he could, and watching for
some chance to help the younger man escape, whether
or not Tucker managed to get away with him.

At times, Tucker found his thoughts turning to
Devna, in whom he had invested such high hopes, but
who had ultimately failed both him and herself. He
had thought she really understood the ideas he'd tried
to share with her, but in the end, she'd fallen back on
the habits she'd been programmed with, obediently

serving her masters in spite of everything. He'd tried to forgive her, to tell himself that Garos had black-mailed her, but it didn't erase the fact of her betrayal. He'd been betrayed by allies before—it was part and parcel of the espionage game—but he had let himself believe that Devna was different, that there was a bond of understanding between them. In the end, he'd been as gullible a mark as any of the numerous men and women she'd seduced.

He had to admit, though, that Devna's conditioning to find physical pain pleasurable was something to envy in his current situation. Perhaps that, more than resentment, was the reason his thoughts kept turning to her.

So when he saw Devna's lovely green face floating before him as he lay naked on the cold stone floor of the cell after a torture session, when he heard her soft, whispering voice calling his name, it seemed like just one more hallucination. As he felt small but strong hands shaking him to consciousness, as the impression of her presence strengthened rather than faded as he recovered his reason, he gradually realized that Devna was actually with him in the cell. "Here . . . to see your handiwork?" he managed to get out.

"I deserve that," she said, "but this is not the time, Charles. We have a limited window to escape."

He blinked as she moved over to assist Ruiz. She lifted his head and held a small flask of water to his lips; Tucker realized his own throat was less parched than before, suggesting he'd been conscious enough to drink already but had forgotten it. "Escape?" he managed.

"Yes. I would have come sooner, but I needed to arrange this in a way that won't expose my betrayal to Navaar. Helping Garos betray you was the only way to preserve my cover."

He was recovered enough to muster annoyance as he said, "Well, thanks ever so much for your loyalty."

"My first loyalty is to my mistress Maras. That is why I help you now—we still need to carry out your plan."

Once she got the two men on their feet, she handed them a pair of guard uniforms and helmets meant for Saurian proportions. The black garments fit poorly but were better than nothing, aside from the lack of shoes. "Where did you get these?" Ruiz asked.

"From the guards I killed outside. We must leave before they are found."

Ruiz winced. "Did you have to kill them?"

"Maltuvis would torture them to death for their failure anyway. I at least spared them pain."

"That doesn't make it right," Ruiz said, and Tucker admired him for his reflexive compassion for those he had every reason to hate.

"It was necessary," Devna said. "Now we must go, or it will have been for nothing!"

The Orion spy led the humans swiftly through the prison corridors, seeming to know the route by heart. "How did you get in here?" Tucker asked.

"I presented myself as an operative of Harrad-Sar.

He is the Sisters' chief slave, the one who handles Maltuvis."

"I remember him," Tucker said. "All friendly and reasonable on the surface, even as he slips in the knife."

"Yes. His name gave me some access, though not the authority to walk you out of here openly. This way."

She led them to the prison laundry, and Tucker was almost touched to see that the old Earth prison-break clichés were alive and well on an alien world. Luckily, the lack of electronic security meant they could sneak out in the back of a laundry truck without their bio-signs being detected. But Devna stayed behind as she helped the two men into the laundry bin. "Aren't you coming?" Tucker asked.

Devna shook her head. "I must be observed leaving the prison and returning to Harrad-Sar's harem before you are missed. Once you are clear, you must find a way to return to Akleyro on your own. Your Malurian impersonators have done their parts; the resistance has no idea you have been taken, and their planned strike is only days away. The new factory in Veranith is their target, and they intend to attack before it goes online. You must hurry if you hope to stop them. With luck, I will meet you there in a few days."

Tucker was hesitant to trust her. Could this be some sort of trap? Was Maltuvis's approach to torture more elaborate than he let on? But under the circumstances, he had no choice. He gave her a cautious nod. "We'll see how things turn out."

Devna nodded back and hurried from the laundry

room. Tucker and Ruiz lowered themselves into the bin and shut the lid. After a few moments, Ruiz whispered, "*Amigo* . . . is it weird that I'm excited she saw me naked? I mean, under the circumstances?"

Tucker laughed weakly, welcoming the release of tension. "My friend, let me explain a few things about Orion women . . ."

March 6, 2166

Devna had placed a great deal of faith in Tucker and Ruiz's resourcefulness. Even with their guard uniforms and helmets, Tucker knew, it would be next to impossible for two humans to blend in with a population of Saurians in the heart of the planet's most xenophobic nation. Once they slipped out of the back of the prison laundry truck while it was stopped at a railway crossing in a largely empty, run-down neighborhood, the two men made for an abandoned building and forced their way inside. "We'll wait here until sometime after daybreak," Tucker said. "Most of the Saurians should be asleep by then. After that, we'll try to find a sewer entrance."

"Okay," Ruiz said, unfazed; no doubt his mining career had inured him to tight, smelly places. "But where do we want to go?"

Tucker led him over to a half-barred window, inviting him to look through the gap. "There."

Through the grungy glass, they could both see the tall, delta-winged spindle shapes of several of

Maltuvis's orbital ships in the distance, accompanied by several cylindrical gantry towers and dozens of broad chimneys spewing thick clouds of smoke lit from below by the orange glow of factory forges. "One of *Malparido*'s spaceship plants," Ruiz said, using one of his favorite Maltuvian malapropisms, the Spanish equivalent of "bastard." "Are you *loco*, Trip? Why not just march into the Basilic Palace while we're at it?"

"Well, where else are we gonna find a ship that can get us halfway around the planet in time to stop the raid? Besides, we might learn something there. Garos didn't know just how the disaster was supposed to be triggered; maybe seeing the inside of one of those factories will give us a clue."

Ruiz considered. "Maybe we can even find a way to sabotage this one ourselves. If the resistance hears about it, they may postpone their raid."

"Or they may decide to go sooner, before Maltuvis heightens security. Too risky, even if we could pull it off."

Ruiz nodded. "Come to think of it, the way Malpractice controls the flow of information, news of sabotage in M'Tezir might not even reach the rest of the planet."

"Heh. 'Malpractice.' I like that one."

"I've got a million of 'em."

Basilic Palace, M'Tezir

Maltuvis sat hunched over the ornate desk in his lushly appointed private office, adding new revisions to the official state history text. After learning of the frustrating fact of the human spies' escape from his prison, he took comfort in the exercise of rewriting the facts to suit his desires.

The M'Tezir state's histories had been written to favor the Basilic line and suitably denigrate its rival nations for generations. But now that Maltuvis ruled the world, he felt it only right to apply a more personal touch to the readjustment of history. His predecessors had been too delicate in their amendments to reality, attempting to limit them to assertions that could not be disproven by self-evident facts. But they had missed the point of the exercise. The true mark of power was to compel agreement with whatever statements you made, regardless of the listener's knowledge of the facts. As Maltuvis's word was now unchallenged, he could assert whatever he wanted. He could claim that the sun was in the sky at night, and any who pointed out otherwise would be arrested for speaking sedition. Only those who bowed to his reality would remain entitled to live in it.

Not that he felt the need to go quite that far, at least for now. He could content himself with subtler redefinitions. The schools would still be compelled to teach them as the inviolable truth, after all—at least until he decided to change them again. But what new truths did he feel like inventing tonight? That all Lyaksti leaders had secretly been Clear Light cultists? That Veranith ritually sacrificed and devoured their young in public ceremonies? That humans had been genetically engineered as a slave race by ancient M'Tezir starfarers during their first conquest of the galaxy millennia ago? Now, that one had possibilities.

Maltuvis was annoyed when he heard a familiar sound—the opening of the secret passageway that connected to Harrad-Sar's hidden chamber within the palace. He turned to harangue the burly Orion for intruding on his entertainment, but was brought up short to see that his visitor was one of the females from Harrad-Sar's personal harem. "What do you want?" he barked.

The pale-skinned, black-haired female bowed and spoke in a breathy voice. "My lord Maltuvis. My name is Elevia."

"Yes, yes." He had no interest in her identity. He could not remember having seen this one before, but he could barely tell them apart anyway.

"I bear a message from Harrad-Sar. He apologizes for being unable to come himself, but he has urgent matters to attend to."

"As do I. Make it quick."

"My lord, it pertains to the spacecraft factory in Veranith, and the planned attack by the resistance. My master has approved an amendment to the plan. . . ."

12

COME MORNING, Tucker and Ruiz made their way to the ship factory via the sewer system and entered the complex through a drainage channel. The air grew increasingly foul as they moved deeper into the plant, and Tucker realized there was a flaw in his plan. "The Saurians can breathe this kind of stuff with no problem. They've got built-in filters, so they don't need any kind of masks or pollution controls."

Ruiz coughed. "So how are we gonna survive in there?"

"If they're mostly shut down for the day, the worst of it should've cleared out by now. We can probably manage for a little while."

"But what then?"

They soon emerged within the fabrication section of the complex, which was still running at reduced capacity for the day shift. Stifling heat and vapor rose from a row of foundry vats containing molten steel and aluminum to be poured into molds for casting the ships' superstructure members. Opposite them, long strands of carbon fiber were being drawn through an elaborate series of heated rollers, high-pressure furnaces, oxidation ovens, and electrolytic baths, the chemical fumes further fouling the air. Beyond were large, intricate looms for weaving the carbon fibers into mats that were then coated in resin and molded into strong, lightweight fuselage components. Even in low-power mode, the heat and fumes from the fabrication units were nearly unbearable. Tucker and Ruiz tried to breathe through the fabric of their uniform collars while Tucker searched for a plan of the complex.

Finally, he found what he was looking for and led Ruiz there. The plant was empty enough that they were able to keep their distance from the Saurians they saw, who seemed unsurprised by the presence of people in security uniforms—and who stayed far enough away not to hear their coughing over the noise of the plant.

Tucker's destination was the cleanroom facility where the ships' fine electronics were made. Saurians might not need their air filtered, but the ships' computers and advanced circuitry certainly did. The pair of cleanroom suits that Tucker and Ruiz appropriated were designed to filter the air they exhaled rather than the air they took in, but they worked well enough, and they had the additional benefit of concealing the men's faces as they moved deeper into the plant.

They soon made their way out of the fabrication center into the assembly plant proper, and both men had to halt and stare in astonishment. The assembly area was a vast hangar that towered hundreds of meters overhead and stretched dozens of meters down below the balcony where they stood, one of fifteen stories' worth of balconies surrounding the assembly floor on three sides. Eight orbital ships in various stages of assembly, positioned vertically with their nose cones pointing to the arched roof, were evenly spaced across the immense floor in two rows of four. The pair nearest Tucker and Ruiz were bare frameworks, with each successive pair being closer to completion. Vast cranes slid on overhead tracks, several of them carrying nose cones, weapon emplacements, or nacelles awaiting attachment to the ship frames, while flatbeds on tracks in the factory floor carried the bulky reactors and exhaust nozzles to be attached from below. At the far end, the rails continued along a shallow ramp that rose toward a huge sliding wall whose base was at ground level. No doubt the completed ships would be rolled up the ramp to the launch gantries outside.

Fortunately, there was also a series of enormous ventilation fans mounted in the walls just below the vaulted roof. Tucker and Ruiz were able to take off their cleanroom masks and breathe relatively freely. "I thought the Saurians didn't need the ventilation," Ruiz said between pants.

Tucker laughed. "It's to vent water vapor, keep the humidity down. A space this big can develop indoor weather if you aren't careful."

"I'd be really impressed," Ruiz said, "if this all wasn't being done to murder and oppress people."

"Yeah, the Nazis were pretty great engineers too. It's not the technology's fault, it's the fault of the people who decide how to use it." He leaned forward over the rail to get a better look at the engine components below. "So go ahead, be as impressed as you want with the technology."

"I'm more interested in finding a *working* ship we can steal. And just how did you plan to get away with that, anyway?"

"Hold on," Tucker said. "Something's not right."

"They're primitive warp drives that barely even work. I bet there's a ton that isn't right."

"That's just it. They're *too* right."

Ruiz stared. "You having a delayed reaction from the torture?"

"Come on, we need to get a closer look."

It took several minutes to descend the stairs to the factory floor; Saurians generally didn't need elevators. They had to wait until a guard patrol went by, but they were finally able to make their way over to one of the half-assembled engines. "No, this isn't right," Tucker said as he inspected the unit. "There. The antimatter bottles are far too big." He climbed up the catwalk, Ruiz following close behind, until he found a gap in the unfinished casing that let him examine the interior structure. "And that's a dilithium articulation frame," he added, his heart sinking. "Tony, these are second-generation warp drives."

"What? You mean these things are gonna have interstellar capability?"

"Yeah. Nothing fast, no better than the early Boomer ships, but enough to reach other stars in a matter of months."

"My God. Maltuvis isn't content with conquering Sauria. That's why he's making so many ships. He wants to build an interstellar empire."

"Tony . . . that's not what worries me. I mean, yeah, it's bad, long-term. But there's a more immediate thing to worry about."

"Which is?"

"Where's he getting the antimatter? This many warp engines needing this much antideuterium . . ."

Ruiz furrowed his brow. "The Orions must be shipping it in."

"That'd be pretty hard to hide. It's easy enough to smuggle in a few agents, transmit the plans and engineering tutorials for this stuff. But bulk antimatter shipments would've been spotted, and would've given away that Maltuvis is getting offworld help."

"Which means . . ."

"Yeah. We need to hold off on finding that ship, Tony. There's something else we need to find first."

The layout of the plant was efficient, with direct physical paths from one stage of fabrication and construction to the next. That made it easy to backtrack to the source of the antimatter. The path led them through an annex with a long central passage bracketed by cylindrical assembly chambers for warp nacelles and antimatter bottles. Once they moved past those components, they discovered additional, smaller assembly chambers dedicated to the construction of something yet more alarming. "Torpedoes?" Ruiz asked in dismay.

"Yeah. And from the design of those casings, I'd say they're photonic. Antimatter-based."

"More antimatter. Where's he getting it?"

It wasn't long before they found out. At the end of the annex was a balcony overlooking a massive toroidal structure surrounded by multiple large, spherical fusion reactors configured to feed it power. Tucker shook his head grimly. "A quantum charge reversal system," he said, having to speak loudly over the echoing roar of the mechanism. "An antimatter generator."

"It's huge!" Ruiz shouted back.

"It has to be. Even our best QCRS generators have an efficiency of only a few percent—you need to put in thirty, forty times as much deuterium in as you get antideuterium out. That's why we build them on places like the surface of Mercury—plenty of raw solar power to make up for the inefficiency. This rig, I doubt it's as much as half a percent. It must be putting an incredible drain on the country's power grid. No wonder we saw so few signs of life out in the city."

He led Ruiz back out into the annex so they could hear each other better. "So that's good, right?" the mining engineer asked. "It means it can't be making very much antimatter."

"That's the thing about antimatter—you don't need much. That's the other reason we build them on Mercury—because if one of those things goes up, you don't want anyone living nearby."

Ruiz's eyes widened as the true horrific implications began to sink in. "Trip, this thing is right in the middle of a city! How stable is it? How safe?"

"Given how hard they have to be running it to power all these warp drives and torpedoes? Not very. It wouldn't take much to overload its containment fields."

The younger man crossed himself. "*Dios*. If the other ship factories have this kind of generator . . ."

Tucker nodded. The possibility had occurred to him as soon as he'd laid eyes on the QCRS, but his intelligence training had hardened him. Now that he saw the horror in Ruiz's eyes, he began to feel it too. "This is why the Sisters didn't give Garos anything that would trigger the disaster. It's already in the factory. The resistance will go in there to blow it up, not knowing the antimatter generator is there. They blow the plant, set off the generator . . ." His throat tightened. It was hard to say it. "It could blow up an entire city. The ecological disaster could ravage a whole country."

"And since these ships aren't supposed to have more than trace quantities of antimatter . . ."

"Maltuvis could claim that Starfleet provided it. That they recklessly gave it to an extremist group that wasn't afraid to use it. The Federation would get blamed for the cataclysm."

Ruiz clenched his fists. "And wouldn't that just give the tin-pot fascist the perfect excuse to start an interstellar war . . . and make the Saurians want it."

The possibilities were becoming clear in Tucker's mind. "He's still a long way from having the resources to attack the Federation directly. These ships would take years to reach Federation space. But with the Orions' help, he could begin to conquer nearer worlds. Use their resources and populations to add to his military strength, broaden his influence. Given time . . . it's possible he could build a big enough empire out here to pose a threat to the Federation in years to come."

"And even before then," Ruiz said, "the Federation would be blamed for letting it happen. Every conquest Maltuvis achieved would be one more stain on humanity's reputation. Could the Federation even survive that?"

Tucker didn't want to try answering that question. Either way, this had now become about something much bigger than Section 31.

Birnam

The *Endeavour* crew's study of the dryads had proceeded slowly, for the dryads lived slowly. Even mobile trees still went through life at a stately pace. But it was difficult for Hoshi Sato to continue working in such proximity to Farid Najafi. She had no choice in the matter; those were her orders, and attempting to get out of them for personal reasons would be dereliction of duty. And to his credit, Najafi had not attempted any advances over the past few days. "I'm a Boomer," he'd explained the first time they'd been alone together since the incident. "We live with the same people for years on end, even lifetimes. We understand how bad it is to disrupt a committed relationship. It can make things pretty toxic.

"But we also understand," he'd gone on, "that running away isn't an option. If you have an issue with a shipmate, you work through it or you get over it. You forget the past and focus on the next thing you have to do. So can we just do that? Focus on the dryads from here on?"

Hoshi was grateful to Farid for making it so easy for her. The problem was that the source of her emotional distress came from herself, not from him. She still couldn't help being attracted to him—and she couldn't help wondering if that meant she was looking for a way out of her commitment to Takashi. If she couldn't give him the selfless companionship he needed, maybe it would be kinder in the long run just to break it off.

She tried to distract herself from such thoughts by focusing on the dryad research. Yesterday, Captain T'Pol and Lieutenant Cutler had come up with a clever way to evaluate dryad brain activity. Cutler and Najafi had spiked the soil by the dryad watering hole with a low-level radioisotope. Once it was absorbed by the dryads' roots, it would be drawn up into their circulatory systems, where it could be used as a tracer for mapping their brain activity. A copse of dryads had reached the watering hole a few hours later, and now the team—with T'Pol observing—was patiently letting the vast creatures' slow circulation do its work. The amount of tracer already absorbed by several of the dryads had given some promising results as the dendriforms exchanged pheromonal signals to coordinate their watering and patrol shifts. But it would take days of observation of their brain activity in varied circumstances to gain a good understanding of their cognitive structure—and, if possible, to lay the foundations of a translation matrix for their chemical communication.

That linguistic challenge was just the problem Sato needed as a distraction from her personal issues, so she immersed herself gladly in the analysis of the scans. So she was not pleased when a ground skimmer approached from the direction of the Boomers' camp, creating a competing distraction.

The skimmer came to a halt and disgorged Captain Zang, Maya and Alec Castellano, and a pair of *Verne* security people. Sato noted with concern that most of them were armed.

"Captain T'Pol!" Zang intoned, marching toward her.

The captain stood her ground, her serenity unruffled by his belligerent approach. "What is the purpose of this show of force, Captain?"

"Merely a reminder that you are here only at our invitation. We have a rightful claim to this planet and its resources, and you are welcome here only as long as we see fit to allow it. And I'm afraid I have to revoke that welcome and ask you to leave."

"What?" Najafi cried, stalking over to them with Cutler close behind. "What's all this about, Captain?"

"What it's about," the elder Castellano interposed, "is that you and your Starfleet buddies are stalling. They've been here a week and you've found nothing to support your claims."

"Science takes time, Maya. I don't have to tell you that."

Zang turned to him. "And we shouldn't have to tell you, Farid, that we already have several buyers lined up for dryad pharmaceuticals. They won't wait indefinitely. I was willing to allow your experiments as due diligence, but my responsibility is to the good of the entire crew, and I can't afford to cheat them out of the profits they're entitled to for the sake of your hypotheticals."

Najafi turned to T'Pol. "Captain, you can't let him do this!"

"He does have the legal right to ask us to leave," T'Pol told him.

"In the middle of the experiment?" Cutler protested.

"The lieutenant makes a good point, Captain Zang. The procedure that we are now conducting may be most useful in resolving the question of dryad sentience, but it will require several more days to run, due to the slow passage of the radioisotope through these dryads' circulatory systems. If you will be patient for just that long before making your decision—"

"You're just making excuses," Maya said. "You can't

stand that Boomers made a discovery Starfleet didn't, so you're trying to ruin it for us by 'discovering' something bigger!"

Cutler's gentle face took on an unwontedly angry mien. "I'm discovering a big *something* right now, but I don't want to say what in front of the kid!"

"Please, calm yourselves," T'Pol advised. "Keep in mind the effect of Birnam's atmosphere on human emotional states."

"I am sick of your Starfleet condescension." Castellano stepped toward the dryad that Sato and Najafi had just been scanning. "So this is one of the dryads you're in the middle of studying? Fine." She brandished her plasma rifle. "Let's just cancel that experiment."

Maya fired before anyone could stop her. Eyes widening, Farid cried, "The water reservoir—everyone, get down!" He grabbed Sato's hand and pulled her into a run; trusting him, she followed, then let him push her to the ground and shelter her body with his.

That trust may have saved her life. A moment later, the dryad literally exploded. Dazed by the deafening sound, Sato turned over to see chunks of wood and softer tissues falling to the ground about its charred and shattered stump. She belatedly realized that the plasma beam must have pierced the dryad's trunk and flash-boiled the water in its internal reservoir, causing a steam explosion. The creature's toroidal brain had surrounded the reservoir; what was left of it would never move again.

T'Pol and Cutler had retreated quickly after Farid's warning, but the concussion had knocked Maya down, and she screamed as her skin was scalded by the burst of steam. Alec cried out to his mother, but he was on the ground in the sheltering embrace of one of Zang's guards, the other having pulled Zang himself back from the blast radius. With no one to help her or stop her, Maya's hand convulsed on the trigger in her agony, and the rifle fired wildly, starting several small fires.

"No! The dryads!" Najafi leaped off of Sato's back, recklessly running toward the endangered copse, though there was little he could feasibly do to assist them. Sato chose instead to go after the source of the danger, rising into a crouch and running toward Maya.

T'Pol beat her to it, reaching Castellano first and kicking the weapon from her twitching hand. Zang and Alec arrived right behind her and helped the biologist to her feet, with Sato arriving last. The middle-aged Boomer was dazed and moaning in pain, bleeding from several shrapnel wounds, including some with heavy splinters still embedded. "All right, Maya," the *Verne* captain said. "You've done enough damage."

"You could have stopped her before she fired," T'Pol told him coldly.

"It seemed like a good idea at the time!" Zang snapped. "I hadn't expected such an explosive reaction. I though the reservoirs were open at the top."

"There is a porous filtration layer between the

funnel and the inner reservoir—an inadequate outlet for the sudden increase of pressure."

"Look, who cares about the damn trees?" Alec cried. "We need to get Mom back to camp and treat her wounds."

"Um, that could be a problem," Cutler interposed. Looking around, Sato realized that the fires had already spread quickly in the highly oxygenated atmosphere, surrounding the cleared area occupied by the crews and the skimmer. Not only were several of the dryads on fire, but so were many of the other plant creatures in the area. Some were trying to make their way for the pond at greater or lesser speeds, but in some cases their panicked flight just accelerated the spread of the blaze. There was no safe path for the skimmer.

Zang strode over to the ground-effect vehicle. "Extinguishers, now! We'll clear a path." Sato realized it made sense that the *Verne* crew would always have firefighting gear on hand, an important precaution in this environment. "Alec, get your mother into the skimmer. The first-aid kit is under—"

"I know, sir." The youth gently guided Maya toward the vehicle. Cutler helped them, looking abashed by her earlier outburst.

"Hey!" came Najafi's voice. "I could use some help here!"

Sato looked about her, realizing she'd lost track of Farid in the confusion. She spotted him behind a second burning dryad, his path blocked by large, flaming chunks of the exploded dryad's leaf structure and upper branches. "There! He's trapped!"

"We must get to him quickly," T'Pol advised Zang. "Another explosive rupture seems unlikely, but we cannot rule it out." Nodding, Zang handed her an extinguisher. Together, they and the two guards advanced on the flaming debris, spraying firefighting foam to clear a path. The burning dryad posed an obstacle as it heaved itself out of the soil and attempted to move toward the pond. T'Pol pulled Sato out of the path of a flailing, fiery tentacle; then *Endeavour*'s captain held her ground before the dryad, dodging those same tentacles to spray foam on the vast creature, both to save it and to calm its struggles while the others circled around to reach Najafi and lead him to safety.

Soon, the others were back at the skimmer, save for T'Pol, who was finishing up with the dryad. "You okay?" Sato said to Najafi.

"I'm fine," he said, coughing. "At least for now."

Hoshi realized what he meant. In the time the group had spent saving him, the opportunity to clear a path for the skimmer had diminished. The fire surrounding them had spread further, and they had a smaller supply of foam left to fight it with.

"We must still do what we can," T'Pol said.

"Agreed," Zang replied, gathering the guards to him. "We'll advance against the fire. The rest of you, into the skimmer. Follow behind us."

The two captains moved forward side by side, dousing the flames with their extinguisher spray. Once

T'Pol's sprayer ran out, she resorted to removing her uniform tunic and using it to beat out burning brush and mobile plants and clear away their remains. Zang followed suit when his sprayer ran dry. Sato clutched the rim of the speeder's windshield, afraid that they would run out of the means to fight the fire before they managed to clear a path.

But soon, Najafi clutched her shoulder, calling, "Look! The dryads! They're fighting the fire!"

Lifting her gaze to the burning forest beyond, Sato saw that he was right. Dryads from all around were shuffling at top speed toward the fire line. Many, especially the larger ones, were tipping themselves over as far as they could and emptying their rain funnels onto the burning foliage—as well as the intact foliage in the fire's path. "They're trying to keep it from burning," Cutler said. "They're anticipating!"

Soon, the dryads' actions had quelled enough of the fire to let the humanoids finish clearing a path and get the skimmer out of harm's way—though it was unclear whether that had been by accident or design. As the four firefighters returned to the skimmer and the group retreated to higher ground, Sato turned to take stock of the dryads' activity.

Once the massive dendriforms had emptied their funnels, they rushed to join what had to be a bucket brigade—a line of dryads stretching to the nearby river, using their tentacles to fill some sort of large plant shells with water and pass them down the line. Meanwhile, others were stamping down and tearing out the undergrowth ahead of the fire—undoubtedly creating a firebreak to keep it from spreading further.

"I don't understand," Zang said. "We've monitored several forest fires from orbit since we arrived here. The dryads have always let them burn."

"Fire's part of the cycle of the forest," Najafi said. "But maybe they know this fire is unnatural."

"Or maybe there is something special they wish to protect," T'Pol added.

Cutler nodded, realizing what she meant. "The elders' grove is nearby."

"But we've observed their behavior around groves. Farid, your own report said they let their elders die without interference," Zang countered.

"When they die of disease, or when they're struck by lightning or drought," Najafi replied. "But we've never seen the whole grove threatened."

Sato looked at him in realization. "Sacred ground?"

"Who knows? It's possible."

"Whatever their reasons," T'Pol noted, "they are showing cooperation at a high level of complexity."

Zang pondered for a long moment. "Yes," he finally said. "That they are."

Soon, with a little more help from the Boomer camp, the forest fire had burned itself out. But the blaze had taken its toll. Three dryads would never move again. The others of their kind moved toward the smoldering corpses—followed by observers from *Endeavour* and *Verne*. Both Castellanos had returned to camp in the skimmer with one of the guards, but the other scientists and the captains remained to follow the dendriforms.

Several large dryads gathered around the splintered stumps of their late grovemates and carefully lifted them from the ground. Slowly, they began carrying them away. "I'm reading tons of pheromones being released," Cutler reported, studying her scanner. "If that's how they talk . . . they're talking up a storm."

"Or maybe chanting?" Sato suggested.

T'Pol turned to Najafi. "Have you observed behavior like this before?"

He shrugged. "We haven't been here long enough. They'd normally die as sessile elders in the grove."

They followed to see where the corpses would be taken. Intriguingly, the procession ended up in the elders' grove. "More pheromones," said Cutler. She and the others watched the readouts and the dryads for a long time.

"I'm not sure," Sato eventually reported, "but I think the elders are responding to the mobile ones."

"Why haven't they put the bodies down yet?" Zang asked.

"Maybe they're asking permission," Najafi ventured.

"I think you're right," said Sato. "The communication has stopped—and look." Indeed, the dryads were gently laying the corpses down amidst the elders. The dryads stood for a time, giving off more pheromones, and then slowly withdrew to get on with their lives.

The watchers stood in silence for a time. "What did we just see?" Cutler finally asked.

"A funeral," Sato speculated.

"But they just left them lying there, out in the open."

"Maybe where they're lying is what's important," Najafi said. "This is the elders' grove, where old dryads go to die. This is where they're *supposed* to die—which is why the others don't interfere. But these dryads died elsewhere, by violence . . . so they brought them here."

"And asked the elders to accept them in spite of the circumstances," Sato said. "Maybe the pheromone exchange was some sort of cleansing ritual—accept these dryads' spirits even though they didn't die on holy ground. And the elders agreed."

"And now that they lie on holy ground," Zang said in wonderment, "their spirits can rest in peace."

The others stared at the Boomer captain. "It sounds," T'Pol said, "as though you are reassessing the question of their sentience."

"After what I've seen today, Captain . . . I'm rethinking many things."

13

"WE HAVE TO FIND A WAY to contact the Starfleet team," Ruiz said as he and Tucker crept through the factory's underground maintenance ducts toward the launch area. Tucker's check of the factory manifest had shown that one spaceship had completed repairs and was scheduled to join the orbital patrol the following evening. The two men had agreed that stowing away on a ship already scheduled for launch would be less insane than trying to steal a whole warp-powered rocket plane and hope nobody noticed.

"Maybe we should track down a subspace radio, contact *Essex*," Ruiz went on, staying close to Tucker and speaking softly so his voice would not echo through the dark, cylindrical shaft. "Mullen said it's out in space, monitoring in case of emergency."

Tucker considered the suggestion warily. "I'm not sure that's a good idea," he said. "If it were *Endeavour* or *Pioneer*, I'd know who to trust. But I don't know anyone on *Essex*."

"What, you think your Section Whatever has a spy on board? Isn't that a little paranoid, man? I thought they were satisfied to let the Orions do their dirty work."

"That's what Harris *said*, but he always has plans within plans. If it's that important to him, he'd have an asset on hand, to observe if nothing else. And the Section has informants everywhere. People who agree with their goals, people they've pressured or tricked into helping . . . there's just no way to be sure." If anything, Tucker thought, Captain Shumar seemed like a prime recruit—the kind of captain who believed in the Federation's righteousness with almost religious fervor and whose wartime background made him willing to employ harsh or forceful measures. Granted, he was famously on the opposite side of the noninterference debate, but that would make him an ideal Trojan horse—and the Section had ways of compelling the cooperation of the reluctant. "If we tipped the wrong people off to the antimatter," Tucker went on, "they'd make sure nobody else got the message."

"Then we have to contact the resistance. Let them know without letting Starfleet know."

Tucker shook his head. "We couldn't prove it. They don't have the means to detect the gamma-ray signature of the antimatter, not with the limited resources they've scrounged and salvaged. Hell, we might not even be able to prove our own identities, with those Malurian impostors still there. And they'd probably just end up arguing over it until it was too late. I mean, just having these antimatter generators in populated areas is insanely dangerous. Wait too long and there could be a disaster with or without the resistance triggering it."

Ruiz stared. "How big a risk is that?"

"In the short term, not huge," Tucker admitted. "In the long term, closer to huge. It's still best if we act fast, though. If the resistance started debating it, then both Garos and any Section assets in the *Essex* crew would hear about it, and that could just provoke them to trigger the disaster sooner."

"Okay, Mister Bond, so what's your master plan? What the hell do we do?"

Tucker considered the question in grim silence for a few moments. "There's only one option. We have to get to Garos . . . and neutralize him before he can spring the trap."

Ruiz grabbed his arm, halting him. "'Neutralize'? Come on, man, have the spine to say what you mean."

The agent sighed. "Kill him. I mean kill him. Okay?"

"Oh, man. Are you sure? I mean, you were saying he wasn't such a bad guy, that you understood his reasons for doing what he does."

"It's not a punishment, Tony. It's a tactical necessity. Like it or not, it's the only sure way to neut— to prevent him from launching the attack. There are tens of thousands of other lives at stake, millions in the long term. Like the Vulcans say, the needs of the many outweigh the needs of the few."

Ruiz shook his head. "Never thought I'd hear Vulcan philosophy used to justify an assassination."

"You'd be surprised." Tucker looked him over. "So are you with me or not?"

The younger man took a deep breath and released it slowly. "We still need to get out of here and back to where we can do something. I'm with you on that. And if neither of us can think of a better way by then . . . well, I knew this was a war. I knew some people would have to die for the greater good. I just didn't think it'd be so calculated."

"I don't like it either, Tony. This is the sort of thing I was hoping this mission would let me walk away from." He lowered his eyes, absorbing that thought. "But at least this time I know it's for the right reasons. It's the only way to save all those lives."

Starfleet Headquarters

As more days passed without word from Tucker, Jonathan Archer grew increasingly concerned. The deliberations over the noninterference policy had been advancing slowly, but they were finally nearing a critical stage—and *Essex*'s reports from Sauria indicated that the resistance there was days away from a major strike against Maltuvis's facilities. If the Orions planned to sabotage the latter in order to influence the former, they would have to do so very soon. If Tucker failed to expose their scheme, then not only would something disastrous happen on Sauria, but Section 31 would still be in play, unhindered if its leaders wished to arrange even more mass deaths on other worlds in the name of Federation security.

Archer had only been able to discuss the matter with Captain Reed in vague and elliptical terms in the midst of conversations on other topics, out of what may or may not have been an excess of caution. But it had been clear enough that Malcolm was as deeply concerned as the admiral. Reed's very helplessness had made it clear that he had been unable to dig up any additional data on Harris and his associates, any smoking gun that could do the job of exposing their cabal if Tucker's fabricated evidence failed to materialize.

The admiral was thus on the verge of a fateful decision. If nothing broke soon, he would have no choice but to go public with what he knew about the Orions' plan. Doing so would surely mean exposing Tucker's betrayal to Harris, for he was the only one who could have revealed the specifics to Archer. And the admiral doubted very much that Harris would deal gently with a traitor. In order to save the Saurians, Archer might have to condemn one of his dearest friends to death.

He knew that was a sacrifice Charles Tucker would readily make. But that didn't make the decision any easier. If he could so easily throw one life away to save others, he would be no better than Harris and his cronies. But by the same token, he couldn't just stand by and let countless Saurians die when he had the power to deliver a warning.

What made his inner struggle even harder was that he had no one to share it with. Reed was too busy finishing *Pioneer*'s refit, and it was difficult for the two men to arrange opportunities to converse securely. T'Pol was dozens of light-years away, trying to establish a dialogue with a forest. Dani Erickson was safely out of the loop about Section 31, and he had no intention of endangering her by changing that. He couldn't even bring himself to discuss it with Porthos. The aging beagle might not follow the details of Archer's account all that well, but he would surely sense his master's distress, and that was the last thing he needed in his waning days. When he had time to spend with Porthos, Archer strove to make it as pleasant and soothing as he could for his old companion.

So preoccupied was Archer as he sat behind his office desk, struggling to reach a decision, that he took a moment to notice his aide striding toward him. "Admiral, could I speak with you?" Captain Williams asked him.

The big man looked unusually nervous and tentative. Archer realized that, in his concern for secrecy, he'd been keeping his aide at more of a distance than usual. Hoping to remedy that, he smiled at the captain. "Of course, Marcus. Anytime. Won't you have a seat?"

Williams lowered his muscular frame into the chair before the desk and fidgeted like a schoolboy before the principal. "Admiral . . . sir . . . I've been wrestling with this for the past couple of days, but . . ."

"Whatever it is, you can tell me, Marcus."

Williams folded his hands before him and cleared his throat. "Sir . . . there's something I need to tell you about . . . the fall of the Partnership. About how the Ware destruct protocol *really* fell into the Klingons' hands."

Archer stared at him, stunned. Not knowing what to think, he numbly said, "Go on."

"Admiral . . . years ago, around the start of the Romulan War, I was contacted by a man called Harris. A man I know you've had some contact with."

Williams went on to unfold a familiar story of being recruited as an asset, called on to provide certain information and assistance in service to what appeared to be the greater good of the Federation. "I was never actually a member of his organization, sir. More just a, a source that they drew on occasionally. I kept them aware of what went on in Admiral Gardner's office . . . and later on, sir, sometimes in yours." He lowered his head. "I always justified it to myself by accepting what Harris told me—that it was necessary for the sake of Earth and the Federation, that I was helping things get better in the long run.

"But what happened to the Partnership . . . I tried to rationalize it, sir. I figured, if it was the catalyst for your new directive, then some good had come of it, so ultimately Harris's people had done the right thing. But my Val . . . she was there. She saw it happen. And so did her boyfriend, Mister Kirk—a man I had sorely underestimated and who schooled me in no uncertain terms about what a selfish damn fool I'd been. With my daughter backing him up, and let me tell you, Admiral, that's a sobering experience."

Williams took a shuddering breath. Looking into his eyes, listening to the quaver in his voice, Archer doubted that his aide was a good enough actor for this to be some kind of trap by Harris to draw him out. "Marcus . . . I'm very disappointed to learn that you've been spying on me, even just 'sometimes.' Disappointed and angry. However—this isn't the first time I've had this experience. And I know how much courage it must have taken to decide to confess your involvement with Harris. You're taking a big risk by talking to me."

"Yes, sir. But I've had it knocked into my head that I don't have any business expecting others to make all the sacrifices for the Federation's well-being. Sometimes you have to take a hit for your team, sir."

Archer leaned forward. "What did you have in mind?"

March 7, 2166
Lower atmosphere of Sauria

Tucker and Ruiz had managed to reach the launch gantry undetected and stow away in the engine control bay of the ship scheduled for launch—fortunately one with a first-generation drive, so there was no risk of a significant antimatter explosion in the event of a crash. Which was good, since a crash was what they hoped to bring about . . . more or less.

Like the antique pulp-magazine space planes it resembled, the ship launched vertically using rocket propulsion, although the primitive warp drive was able to generate enough of an inertial reduction field to diminish the amount of thrust required to reach orbit. Still, the presence of two unauthorized human males on board meant that the ship was approximately 150 kilograms more massive than it was supposed to be, which meant that the launch was fractionally more sluggish than it was supposed to be—not enough to disrupt the ship's trajectory, but enough to register as an anomaly, which might tip off the M'Tezir military pilots and crew to the presence of stowaways. Thus, once the ship was in the air, Tucker acted fast, sabotaging the engine bay circuits to create a power drop-off in the engines that would look like a worsening of the initial problem. This would make it impossible for the ship to reach orbit, requiring it to abort and land at the first available site. Since they had already risen to a significant altitude and left the narrow land mass of M'Tezir hundreds of kilometers behind, that descent path would have to take them somewhere else. "So far, so good," Tucker said to Ruiz, whom he'd briefed on the plan during their wait. "I'm trying to time it so the optimal descent arc will bring the ship down in the vicinity of Lyaksti." He spoke softly, for they were in a small power systems access bay off of the main engine compartment, which was crewed by two M'Tezir military engineers. He was reasonably sure the crew would be unable to trace the engine fault to the circuits he was manipulating, but there was no point gambling on the acuteness of their hearing. He and Ruiz had made that mistake with the Malurians.

"How big a vicinity are we talking?" Ruiz asked just as softly, keeping his lips close to Tucker's ear.

Tucker met his skeptical gaze and fidgeted. "Significantly less than a hemisphere," he admitted.

"And what are the odds we'll even end up on land?"

"That's up to the pilots."

"Is real spy work always this improvisational?"

"Real spy work is mostly gathering information. Talking to people, reading, listening, cultivating contacts and assets. This kind of stuff is what happens when the plan goes very wrong."

"Is that what I am? A cultivated asset?"

"Started that way." Tucker grinned at him. "But you made yourself a lot more . . . Mister Leiter."

Ruiz looked touched for a moment, but he masked it. "Aww, I wanted to be Q."

"I'm an engineer. I'm my own—"

Perhaps they hadn't spoken softly enough after all, for the hatch swung open. A burly, purple-skinned Saurian shouted out, grabbed Ruiz's arm, and dragged him out of the access bay. Tucker rose from his crouch and drew his (or rather, his departed prison guard's) sidearm, but as he reached the hatch, the second engineer arrived to block it. Tucker had forgotten how swiftly Saurians could move.

And with that thought came the recognition that he would have no chance in hand-to-hand combat if the engineer managed to get a grip on him. The only choice he had was the one he took now—firing the weapon right at the Saurian's chest. The projectiles from its double barrel tore into her body, making her convulse and fall. Saurians were not easy to kill, but that meant their lethal weapons were designed to be especially potent. Even now, some life remained in the engineer; maybe she could be saved with immediate treatment. But that was not a prospect here. Tucker climbed over her and out into the engine compartment, where the other engineer was pummeling Ruiz. He fired again, this time at the Saurian's head.

Trying not to look at the results of that act, Tucker knelt by his friend and checked him over. "You okay?"

Ruiz groaned. "That . . . is the stupidest question . . . I've ever heard!"

"You're okay."

"Not . . . entirely."

Further examination showed that Ruiz had several broken ribs from the beating and a fractured ankle sustained when the engineer had tossed him to the deck. "No time to fix you up now," Tucker said, moving to seal the entry hatch. "I'm gonna have to speed up our crash timetable, keep the rest of the crew too busy to come back here."

While he saw to that, Ruiz tried to avoid looking at the engineers' bodies and failed. "Had to be done," Tucker told him.

"I know. Needs of the many." He grimaced, but not in pain. "I just . . . We're trying to save lives. It seems like a failure to have to take other lives to do it."

"For all you know, these guys helped bomb Lyaksti's capital. They might've killed thousands."

"Maybe. But they probably have people who love them. I can't help but wonder if we've just made someone feel like I felt when my girlfriend died in the Xindi attack."

Tucker remembered his sister Lizzie, vaporized in that same attack. He shook it off. "Better not to think about it."

"*Easier* not to think about it," Ruiz said. "Doesn't make it better."

The success of Tucker's sabotage was heralded by a strained whine and a bang from somewhere within the engine, followed by a sudden sinking sensation. "Was that a bad bang?" Ruiz asked. "I mean, worse than we want?"

"Just bad enough. The really bad bang, we'd never hear."

Luckily, this crude ship had crash harnesses built into the walls in case of emergency. He secured Ruiz and himself as best he could and waited. Tucker didn't have to wait long for the crash, although the noise and jostling were disorienting enough that he had little memory of it afterward.

The various sounds and smells of a crippled fusion reactor jogged him into action, though, and he hastily unstrapped himself and moved to extricate Ruiz. "We need to get out of here."

"Could the reactor blow?" Ruiz asked, alarmed.

"If you mean a fusion explosion, no—only way to make a fusion reactor blow up is to drop at least a fission bomb on it. But from the chill in the air, I'd say the liquid hydrogen is leaking—"

"And hydrogen's very flammable. Got it. *Vamonos.*" He put his arm around Tucker's shoulders and hobbled forward with Tucker supporting his weight.

Once they exited through the emergency hatch, they found that the space plane had come down in an arroyo in mountainous territory. The nose of the craft was uncomfortably near a sharp drop-off that might be a waterfall during the rainy season. In the other direction, the smoking hot, torn-up ground and debris from the crash blocked their path. Steep slopes covered by scree and brush bracketed the valley, with only one clear pass visible between them.

"This way," Tucker said. But it was slow going with Ruiz's injuries. Just before they reached the pass, shots began ringing out. Glancing back, Tucker saw that the remaining four crew members had survived and exited the ship by the cockpit's escape ladder. Two were already on the ground and running toward the humans, taking potshots. "Come on, faster, Tony!"

They got to the edge of a hill and ducked behind it, but the Saurians were still coming. That was lucky for the Saurians, since a massive clap rang out moments later; the hydrogen had finally ignited. Tucker peered over the crest of the hill to see that the ship's hull had been cracked open by the explosion, and now it burned from within, a funeral pyre for the engineers Tucker had killed. The other M'Tezir had been knocked to the ground, one bleeding from a shrapnel hit, but all four were merely dazed and starting to climb to their feet—a testament to Saurian robustness, but a bad sign for the humans' survival.

Tucker pulled Ruiz up from his crouch. "We have to move." Bits of debris from the blast were starting to rain down with some force.

"No use." Slumping back to his knees, Ruiz gasped for breath. "I'm only slowing you down, buddy."

"No, don't talk that way."

"Needs of the many, Trip! You said it yourself. Leave me the gun. I'll hold them off while you get away."

"Tony . . ."

Ruiz held his gaze. "I've known since the day I decided to stay and fight that I'd probably die here. I'm okay with that . . . as long as it makes a difference. Make sure it does, Trip."

Tucker quashed his emotions. The mission had to come first. All this was for a purpose.

He handed the gun to his friend, then clasped his wrist. Tony clasped his in return. "*Para Sauria. Para la libertad.*"

Tucker nodded. "*Vaya con Dios, amigo.*"

He ran, not looking back. Moments later, cracks

of gunfire began echoing through the pass. Soon it became a ledge running along the steep hillside. The cliff below was negotiable for a human, less so for a web-footed Saurian. And the sun was coming up in this part of the planet, illuminating the cliff face brightly. For once, his anatomy gave him an advantage over the locals. He lowered himself over the edge and began to climb down. Shots continued to ring out behind him.

There was an anguished, very human scream. It cut off abruptly, and the shots ended.

Tucker closed his eyes for a moment. Then he resumed his descent with grim efficiency. He still had a mission to complete—and he could afford no distractions if he wished to make it in time. He focused relentlessly on that purpose, reminding himself that all this death, all this sacrifice, was the only way to stop a catastrophe.

Starfleet Headquarters

"This could be it, sir," Malcolm Reed said as he and Archer reviewed the information Marcus Williams had shared with the latter the night before. That had included all the means by which Section 31 had surveilled Archer's office, so they were now able to be confident that all countermeasures had been taken and they could speak freely here. "The information Marcus had about Harris is sparse, but put together with my dossier and Trip's, I believe it's enough. It's the last piece of the puzzle we needed to tie Harris to the leak of the Ware destruct code and to at least a couple of other blatantly criminal acts. With this, we can go to the judge advocate general and get arrest warrants for Harris and most of his people. We can finally bring his cabal into the light of day!"

"And we can do all this without Trip's frame? We can do it the *right* way, with the truth?"

"With Marcus's testimony, and mine, yes, I'm confident we can. And I have no doubt there are others like us, officers who've aided Harris reluctantly and would be willing to come forward."

"Good," Archer said. "This needs to happen out in the open. Groups like this . . . the reason they insist on secrecy is because it's the only thing that lets them get away with their tricks, their crimes. They convince people it's for the greater good, but it's really just a license to get away with murder. If we don't play their games, if we refuse to hide the truth, then we can win."

Reed studied him. "There was a time when I wouldn't have believed that, sir. Now . . . well, the Partnership needs justice. The Federation needs to know its true role in this before we can atone."

"More importantly, we need to get the whole story out quickly, including the Orion plot on Sauria." He shook his head. "We took a huge gamble with their safety, Malcolm. Risked letting a catastrophe happen so we could play our own spy games. We should've revealed what we knew right away. The Sisters' plan depends on secrecy too."

"Well, now we can, sir. As soon as we have our warrants for Harris and his people, we can reveal everything."

Archer turned to gaze out the window at the predawn stars above. "I only pray we can do it in time."

14

March 8, 2166
Veranith, Sauria

AT LAST, THE RESISTANCE was ready to strike. Mullen and Kelly had managed to wrangle the various Saurian factions into cooperating in the raid on the newly completed spacecraft factory in Veranith—and just in time, for it was days away from starting production on a new wave of ships and weapons. Mullen had been impressed with how helpful Dular Garos had been in reining in the extremism of the Untainted. He wasn't entirely sure what the Malurian had said to their leaders to win their cooperation, but he was grateful for it. This would be the first major resistance strike against Maltuvis's machinery of terror, and it was essential that the opposition show a united front.

It had also been necessary to win the Untainted's support for assistance in smuggling the strike team into Veranith using the back-to-nature sect's wilderness travel routes, many of which had been kept deliberately hidden from civilized communities and were thus unknown to Maltuvis's forces. It had been a strenuous journey for the humans, with even Morgan Kelly looking exhausted by the time they reached the city on whose outskirts the factory had been built. But there was little time to rest and regroup. Presider Moxat was determined to destroy the plant before it went online and began churning out more death—and ideally before it was fully occupied by workers, so that casualties would be minimal. After all, most of the labor force would consist of enslaved Veranith.

Thus it was that Mullen and Kelly were crouched behind a boulder on a large hill near the factory, using their handheld scanners to gather intelligence on the plant's layout, guard postings and movements, and so forth. They also used the magnification settings on their night-vision scopes to supplement the sensor scans. But Mullen couldn't resist turning his gaze to the dark, quiet city beyond the plant. "Look at it," he muttered, shaking his head. "When I was here three years ago, this city was vibrant, bright, beautiful. There were firewasps and colored lanterns everywhere, music in the streets, farmer's markets . . . so full of life and confidence. Now they're huddled in their homes, keeping their heads down, afraid of what happens next.

"I just don't understand how people like Maltuvis can be okay with doing this to other people. Making so many millions suffer or die just so he, just one person, can get richer or more powerful. I can't imagine being that selfish, that greedy. That . . . *unfair*."

"He's a narcissist," Kelly replied. "Like most dictators. For a narcissist, nobody else really exists as a person. It's like . . . like being the only player in an

immersive simulation game. Everyone you interact with is just a character, so you don't have to care
about them or respect them. They're just obstacles to
overcome or resources to be used to get ahead in the
game."

Mullen pondered that. "Sounds pretty lonely when
you put it that way."

"Don't waste your sympathy. It's much worse for
the people around them." She went quiet, but Mullen
held his tongue, sensing that the armory officer had
more to say. "I had a childhood friend," she eventually went on, "who was always quiet, nervous, easily
spooked. She turned out to have an abusive father." At
Mullen's startled stare, she shrugged. "Colony world.
More stress than you get on Earth, less of a medical
or mental-health infrastructure to catch these things.
Sometimes it slips through the cracks.

"Anyway, when she finally got help, when she was
free of it and able to open up, she talked about what
it was like to live every day with an abusive parent—
someone who could lash out at any moment, triggered
by some random thing. Driven by his own demons,
but blaming you for every hurt he inflicted on you.
You never knew what he'd do or what would set it
off. You didn't even have a consistent sense of reality, because he'd make up lies and force you to agree
with them just as a power game. There was never a
moment's sense of safety or stability, anything to rely
on. I finally understood that when I went to war, felt
it for myself."

She paused in thought. "Life for people living under dictators is a lot like that. Like being abused by someone who should be taking care of you. Just imagine—whole nations, whole planets growing up abused. Traumatized. Just because one sick person thinks he's the only real thing in the universe." She shook it off. "We have to stop that bastard Maltuvis fast, or a whole generation of Saurian kids will grow up that way."

"No argument from me," Mullen said, turning his scope-enhanced gaze back toward the factory. "We have to show him that the Saurian people aren't his—" He broke off, noticing movement on the edge of the plant. "Trucks."

Kelly stared. "The people aren't his trucks?"

"No, look, there are trucks leaving the factory. Big ones."

The armory officer focused her scope where he pointed. "Got them. Looks like they're shipping something out of that heavily shielded annex off the main construction hangar."

"What would they be shipping out?" Mullen wondered. "They're gearing up to start manufacturing. They should be shipping things in."

"Whatever it is," Kelly answered, "it needs some kind of heavy-duty containment, judging from the way those trucks are built. So it's probably something dangerous."

Mullen raised his scanner and worked its controls to focus on the trucks, running a full spectroanalysis. "I'm picking up a faint radiation signature . . ."

"Faint is good."

His blood ran cold when he examined the readings. "Oh, my god."

"Commander?"

"The type of radiation . . . gamma rays and muons with these energy levels and distribution . . . Morgan, this is an antimatter signature."

Kelly's eyes widened. "The total amount of antimatter they should be able to produce on this whole planet in a year would fit into a single one of those trucks. I count five. From just one factory."

"They've got a starship-grade antimatter generator in there. They have to."

The lieutenant grabbed his arm. "Even if they got the specs from the Orions, there's no telling how unstable it could be. If we go in there tonight and try to blow things up . . ."

Mullen cursed. "We have to get back to the team *now*."

U.S.S. Essex

"It's good to hear your voice at last, Commander," said Bryce Shumar, who had been quietly going stir-crazy along with the rest of his crew over these past three weeks—though strictly on the inside in his case. The tradition of the stiff upper lip still served him well. "But isn't it risky to use the power to contact us at this range?"

"*It's a risk we need to take, Captain,*" Mullen said,

proceeding to fill Shumar in on the discovery of the antimatter generator at the factory. *"Naturally we've aborted the raid."*

"Of course. One containment breach and the whole city would be lost."

"Sir, that's likely to happen sooner or later even if we don't intervene. That's why it's necessary to break our silence. Presider Moxat has recorded an announcement to the Saurian people—we need Essex to transmit it planetwide. We have protocols that will get it past the automatic content blockers on the global information network, but we also need to beam it to every open receiver, make sure the word gets out. We need you to cover one hemisphere while we cover the other from the shuttlepod on an orbit antipodal to yours."

"You'll have to be in low orbit for that," Shumar said. "You'll be very exposed."

"It's a risk, sir, but the word has to get out. Hopefully the announcement itself will change things pretty quickly."

Shumar only needed a moment to decide. "Very well. Transmit the presider's speech to Mister Avila. Ensign Moy, break orbit, take us into optimum electromagnetic broadcast range of Sauria. Mahendra, ready shields and hull plating and charge weapons—those blockade ships will be going after both us and the shuttle."

The bridge crew gave their assents one by one, save Miguel Avila, who was already receiving the upload from the shuttlepod. Shumar stepped back to the situation table. "Relay the message here, Miguel. Let's hear it."

Presider Moxat's wizened face appeared on the tabletop screen. *"People of Sauria—Lyaksti'kton, N'Ragolar, whatever name you give our home. I am Moxat, Presider-in-exile of the Global League, and currently head of the resistance to the tyranny of Basileus Maltuvis of M'Tezir."* Shumar noted that she refused to acknowledge his self-proclaimed status as monarch of the Maltuvian Empire. *"I speak to you now because our movement has discovered something horrifying about the Basileus's actions and plans, pertaining to the shipbuilding plants he has had constructed with slave labor in several occupied countries. This discovery was made with the assistance of the United Federation of Planets' Starfleet, and I am transmitting their data to you now as proof of these revelations."*

Moxat went on to lay out the evidence for the antimatter generators, then continued: *"As many of you know, our people have made only the most limited progress in manufacturing antimatter. Most of the antimatter that Maltuvis uses to spark the fusion reaction in his warships is harvested from the sparse natural supply of antiparticles captured by our planet's magnetic field in its radiation belts. To go from those bare beginnings to the industrial-level antideuterium production now revealed to be occurring in the Veranith plant, and possibly in others, would be impossible in the short amount of time since Federation contact. Therefore, the only possible conclusion is that Maltuvis—he who has based his rise to power on the claim that he is the protector of our world from alien domination—must himself be in collusion with alien allies. Only they could have provided him with the technology to manufacture antimatter—indeed, as we now must recognize, the technology to produce such a large fleet of warships so swiftly. Far from protecting us from alien conquest, Maltuvis has had alien help in his own conquest.*

"And far from keeping the people safe, Maltuvis in his greed for power has directly endangered us by the hundreds of millions. These antimatter generators create a profound risk. Should one of them sustain a malfunction or a breach, the explosion could destroy the entire adjacent city and devastate the ecology of much of a country. Our resistance had intended to sabotage the Veranith plant in order to slow Maltuvis's conquest . . . but we cancelled our attack when we learned of the profound danger. We are grateful to our Federation advisors for saving us from a terrible mistake. And now we pay their kindness forward by warning you, the people of this beautiful world, of the depraved indifference that Basileus Maltuvis has shown for your safety, and the profound hypocrisy that underlies his self-created image as the defender of our people."

Strong words, thought Shumar. But they were words the people of Sauria needed to hear. It would be his privilege to ensure that they were heard.

March 9, 2166
Akleyro, Sauria

In the two days it had taken Charles Tucker to track down some of Antonio Ruiz's resistance contacts and recruit their aid in returning him to Akleyro, he had struggled with his decision to assassinate Garos. In his years with Section 31, and even before then in Starfleet, he had occasionally been ordered to take actions that would bring about the death of others. But it had usually been in the heat of battle, as it had been with the engineers aboard the Saurian ship, or in indirect ways that kept Tucker a step or two away from the actual killers, as it had been when Devna had killed the guards to free him and Ruiz. And it had almost always been under someone else's orders. Deciding on his own to commit a premeditated murder was a much heavier cross to bear. The bitter irony was that it was his desire to escape the immorality of the spy game that had led him to this point.

Yet he could see no alternative. Garos's plan to blow up the Veranith plant's antimatter generator would kill millions. Ruiz had understood that, and had given his life so that Tucker could survive and prevent it. If a life as noble as Ruiz's was an acceptable sacrifice to save those millions, then Tucker had no business feeling qualms about ending the life of Garos, a crime lord with the blood of thousands on his hands already. He had to terminate Garos with extreme prejudice, or Tony's sacrifice would have meant nothing.

And if he never got a good night's sleep again, it was still a price worth paying.

So it was that Charles Tucker returned to Akleyro, his mind focused, his emotions dammed in, his will directed by the overriding goal to prevent the disastrous raid on Veranith by any means necessary.

He was therefore completely staggered to discover that the raid had been called off while he had been crammed inside a shipping crate on a riverboat.

It was surreal. Through no action of his own,

apparently through sheer luck, the *Essex* team had stumbled upon the same intelligence he and Ruiz had found, because Maltuvis's forces had unwisely shipped out some of their antideuterium while the recon team had been on hand. The starship had helped beam the message all over Sauria, exposing Maltuvis's lies and hypocrisy. Naturally the dictator was denying the accusations of alien collusion, insisting that it was M'Tezir brilliance alone that had achieved the antimatter breakthrough, but there was nothing he could do to explain away his sheer recklessness in manufacturing and stockpiling antimatter adjacent to populated cities. His credibility had taken a massive hit, and the resistance had scored a major victory without firing a shot. More significantly for Tucker's mission, the abandonment of the raid, and Presider Moxat's pointed praise of Starfleet's aid in preventing a catastrophe, meant that the Sisters' plan to discredit Starfleet had failed without Tucker needing to lift a finger. All the killing, all the sacrifice, had been for nothing.

Tony Ruiz had not needed to die.

Tucker was still in shock when Devna, who had clearly had an easier time returning to Akleyro, found him and led him to Garos. "Ah, Mister Tucker," the Malurian greeted him cheerfully. "I'm impressed that you managed to survive in spite of everything. Well played, sir."

This was the man who had betrayed him and Ruiz and turned them over to Maltuvis for torture and execution. It was partly his fault that Ruiz was dead. But any rage Tucker felt was swamped by his confusion. "Why didn't you stop this?" he asked the Malurian. "You were working for the Sisters. You wanted the raid to happen. Why didn't you keep Starfleet from finding out about the antimatter?"

Garos chuckled, shaking his head. "I'm afraid you're still a few moves behind. I *arranged* for them to find out."

Tucker could only stare. "What?"

Devna stepped forward. "I wasn't defying Garos when I came to M'Tezir to rescue you. Rather, I persuaded him to attempt an alternate plan. I went to Maltuvis posing as a messenger from Harrad-Sar. We slave women all look alike to him. I relayed instructions, supposedly from Harrad-Sar, to ship out a quantity of the plant's antimatter reserve before the day of the raid. After all, there was more than enough remaining antimatter and other explosive materials at the factory to devastate the city without letting the entire supply go to waste. Maltuvis was quite happy to salvage some of the antimatter he hopes to use to propel his conquest of the stars, once I assured him that Garos would arrange for the raiders' recon party to be absent at the time scheduled for the move."

"And instead," Garos said, "I simply did the reverse, ensuring that Commander Mullen's team would be *present* when the antimatter was moved. Thus the truth was exposed, the day was saved, and so on."

Tucker was still at sea. "I don't get it. You said

the Sisters were forcing you to cooperate. That they threatened your family."

Garos glared at him as if he were a slow-witted child. "Yes, which is why I couldn't go along with *your* plan without exposing myself and getting my mate and her other husbands killed. I had to betray you before you ruined everything. But Devna's plan had the advantage of keeping me out of it."

"By attributing the order to Harrad-Sar," Devna added, "we will make it look as though he was running a side operation to smuggle out some of the antimatter for himself, and that it was his own greed that led to the exposure of the generators and scuttled the Sisters' plans." She gave a slight, sad smile. "It was easy to persuade his actual slave women in Maltuvis's palace to corroborate my story. They're as happy to get rid of him as we are. He hasn't treated them well."

"One more reason I'm happy to see him suffer," Garos said. "Nothing is as depraved as disrespecting females."

"Nice to see you have some standards," Tucker riposted, though it was halfhearted.

"I'm not a monster, Mister Tucker. I do what I'm forced to do for the good of my family and my people. I was never comfortable with the idea of killing millions of Saurians to achieve that end. I wanted to find a way I could spare them without endangering my family. You didn't offer one. Devna did. And I'm grateful to her for that."

Tucker was dumbstruck. He'd profoundly misjudged

Garos. More—he'd misjudged the whole situation. He'd believed that acting alone and in secret was the only way to prevail, but it had been a simple act of openness and truth that had foiled both the Sisters and Maltuvis. He'd settled on Garos as a target that needed to be destroyed to achieve the mission, yet Garos had been the one whose actions had saved countless lives. Tony Ruiz had tried to talk him into taking the better path, the more open path, but Tucker had convinced him that deceit, intrigue, and violence were the sole, necessary path toward the greater good, and in so doing, he had led Tony to a completely unnecessary death.

Wasn't that just what Section 31 had done to him? Drawn him down the wrong path, blinded him to the better way, led him to do great harm with the excuse that it was for a good cause? And hadn't this whole mission been his attempt to escape from all that?

Maybe there was no escape. Maybe this was all he was now. Even if he succeeded in bringing Section 31 down, it still lived on inside him.

Where could he possibly go from here?

15

Birnam

IN THE WAKE of the events surrounding the forest fire and the discovery of the dryads' funereal practices, Captain Zang had suspended his plans to harvest dryad tissues. Though not completely convinced that the species was self-aware, he was no longer willing to take the risk. He had shifted the *Verne* crew's efforts toward searching for equivalent pharmaceutical compounds in other, less complex species of Birnamite flora. Harvesting the dryads had become a more difficult proposition in any case, since the huge dendriforms had grown wary of humanoids and begun to give them a wide berth. The speed with which the awareness of the tiny animals as a threat had spread through the dryad population was further evidence of their ability to communicate. T'Pol had recommended that the Boomers keep their distance from the dryads as well, so as to minimize the risk of disruption to their culture and way of life.

As for Maya Castellano, there was no clear way to define any crime to charge her with, aside from reckless endangerment. The legal status of the dryads had not been defined at the time of her action, and the authority for penalizing her lay with Zang and the *Verne* crew—but it was hard to imagine a greater punishment than the shame and condemnation she saw in her son's eyes in those few moments when he was even willing to be in the same room with her. Her attempts to explain to Alec that she had done it to protect his future had only made him angrier; he refused to let her use him as the excuse for her actions.

The *Endeavour* crew had stayed on for a few more days to continue their studies, but Hoshi Sato had seen little of Farid Najafi, who had been up on the *Verne* recovering from the burns and smoke inhalation he'd sustained in the fire. He did return to the planet surface when the time came for the Starfleet party to make their final farewells before moving on to their next assignment.

Hoshi greeted him next to the grove of asparagus trees outside the Boomers' camp, offering him a data slate. "This is the best linguistic model I've been able to construct based on the brain scans we got," she said. "A couple of the surviving dryads still had enough tracer in them to let us get some useful data, though we had to do it from a distance and the resolution isn't great. But it's something. Maybe it'll lead to a way to translate their speech, even communicate with them if you decide to try it."

Farid smiled. "Talk to the trees, and have them listen to me? There's a dream come true." He took her hand. "Hoshi, I don't know how to thank you for all you've done for us. Or how to apologize for the liberties I took—"

She placed her other hand atop his. "Don't even think of it. That was all on me." She looked away, grinning nervously. "Please don't take this the wrong way—but I realize now it was never even about you. I mean, yes, you're funny and sweet and sexy, but . . ."

Hoshi let go of his hand. "When I saw you in danger from the fire, I was . . . well, I was concerned, of course. But when I thought it through afterward, I realized it was no more than the concern I'd feel for anyone I saw in danger. I was worried for you, but not . . . not devastated. Not like I was when Takashi was almost killed."

She sighed, folding her hands before her. "That was . . . so terrifying. And ever since then, I've been coping with the price he's had to pay for his heroism . . . the loss of so much of who he was, the struggles every day. I've felt such intense anxiety, such turmoil over my future with him. I turned to you because I wanted to retreat—to hide from that intensity. To take solace in something more fun and carefree.

"But now I see . . . the whole reason my fears are so intense is because my love for him is so intense. It wouldn't be so hard if he didn't mean so much to me. And my concerns for the future wouldn't affect me so much if I weren't truly committed to that future. My fear didn't mean I shouldn't be with him—it meant I *should*. My love for him is strong enough that I'll be there for him no matter how hard it gets. And that's what he needs. It's what *I* need—to know I have that strength in me."

Najafi was quiet for a long moment. "So . . . do you understand?" Hoshi asked.

He cleared his throat. "Um . . . sure. Yes. I'm, I'm glad that your lack of actual caring for me has brought you such clarity. I guess."

"I'm sorry, I didn't mean it that way—"

"No, really, it's all right. It would've been more flattering if you'd been madly in love with me, sure, but I'm glad for you that you have someone you do care about that deeply. And, well, it was fun while it lasted. We'll always have the pitcher plant." They shared an awkward laugh.

He came closer and clasped both her hands this time. "What can I say? Birnam is like some idyllic fairyland. It brings our dreams closer to the surface. We got to share a momentary dream, and I liked it a lot. I got to kiss those lips, which is almost as great an achievement as proving that trees are people too." She blushed and rolled her eyes. "And I'm glad you got something more substantial out of it. It's the least I can do in return for all you did for me and the dryads."

Moving in, Farid kissed her on the forehead. "Thank you, Hoshi Sato. And may the sun never set on your happiness."

March 10, 2166
Starfleet Headquarters

Malcolm Reed strode into Admiral Archer's office with a pleased look on his bearded face. "We finally have a line on Harris, sir."

Archer considered him guardedly, hesitant to get

too excited. Most of the news had tended to be positive in the days since Reed and Marcus Williams had come forward to present their case against Section 31 to the judge advocate general and the Federation Department of Justice. The indictments against Harris and his cadre of unsanctioned spies had come down quickly, and Starfleet's rank and file had been readily cooperating—partly due to Archer's instructions, but largely out of a sense of relief on the part of those officers who had been manipulated or pressured into helping the Section from time to time, only to discover that its hooks were not easy to extract once they were in. Williams had not been the only asset whose conscience had troubled him, and a number of others had agreed to share what they knew once they had learned of the Section's role in the fall of the Partnership. Their cooperation had helped lead to the arrest of over a dozen committed, full-time agents of the cabal so far, and the seizure of the facilities from which they had operated.

Not all consciences had been possible to salve, though. Admiral Parvati Rao, Harris's old Starfleet Intelligence liaison who had been implicated in Section activities by the new testimony, had been found several months dead in her remote home on the plains of Mars. Evidently she had taken her own life not long after the Partnership investigations had begun, perhaps fearing the very chain of events that had led to her exposure. One thing that Rao had been known for, Archer reflected, was her uncannily accurate foresight.

Despite Rao's involvement, the evidence made it reassuringly clear that the core membership of the Section had been a fairly small group of current and former Starfleet officers. T'Pol had been correct in her probabilistic assessment that the conspiracy would need to be relatively small in order to last as long as it had. It also appeared to be limited entirely to the United Earth branch of Starfleet. Evidently the group had been too insular to consider recruiting outside the Earth branch in the five years since the Federation's founding.

As for the use of Article 14, Section 31 of the Starfleet Charter as the group's self-justification and informal name, that fact had been kept out of the press, with Archer's grudging cooperation. It was the judgment of Secretary sh'Mirrin that revealing that information might give the false impression that Starfleet's bylaws actually endorsed such a group, rather than simply being ambiguous enough to be exploited as its excuse—or, even worse, that it might give future officers the idea of following in Harris's footsteps. As far as the news and the history books would record, the organization was simply "the Harris conspiracy."

Indeed, many of its members might remain anonymous as well, for no records of their identities had been found. The operatives now in custody had been identified from their DNA and biometrics, but Harris and his top echelon remained at large—as, of course, did Charles Tucker. Trip would still be officially dead unless he chose to come forward and set the record straight. Archer and Reed were in agreement that they would not reveal his secret without his approval, and they were certain the others who knew of his survival—namely T'Pol, Phlox, Travis Mayweather, and Hoshi Sato— would agree.

Unfortunately, the JAG office's data forensics teams had achieved only limited success at decrypting the Section's computer records or reconstructing those that the agents had attempted to erase prior to their arrest. The JAG assured Archer that enough information had been recovered to shut down the cabal and prosecute most of its members, but certain key categories of information had proved unrecoverable, including data on their secure communication protocols, their top-level organizational structure, the details of their origins, and their long-term plans. The very selectivity of what was lost was suspicious in itself, but it was possible that Harris and his circle had kept that information strictly in their own heads, or in files carried on their persons. Tracking them down had been Malcolm Reed's top priority.

"How much of a 'line' are we talking, Malcolm?" Archer asked.

"It's thin, sir. But we found a trail of ownership leading to a small, private starship with a sophisticated warp drive. We located the hangar, and although the ship was gone, we were able to determine its initial flight plan and range based on hangar records, staff interviews, and in-system traffic scans. It's a given that they've diverged from their filed plan by now, but they only left two days ago, and I've retasked two Andorian Guard ships to track their ion trail. We won't let them get away, sir."

"That's encouraging news, Malcolm. Good work."

"Save it for when we have Harris and all his cronies in a cell, if you don't mind, sir."

Archer rose, came around his desk, and clasped Reed's shoulder. "I think you're more than deserving of a 'good work,' Malcolm. I've been very grateful for your assistance these past few days. With Marcus resigning, it's been . . . well, it would've been a hell of a mess without you helping out."

Reed sighed. "It's a hell of a mess either way, sir. I mean, *Pioneer* is done with its refits. I should be aboard her, taking her back out there. But I need to stay here to testify, to coordinate the search . . . there's no telling how long I'll be out of action, is there?"

"That's actually something I wanted to talk to you about," the admiral said. "Since you'll have to stick around Earth for a while anyway . . . I was wondering if you'd like to take over full-time as my right-hand man."

Reed stared at him, stunned. "It's a very kind offer, Admiral, but I'm not an administrator."

"You're the most disciplined, conscientious, detail-oriented officer I've ever known. You've done a fine job coordinating the investigation." He held Reed's gaze closely. "More importantly, after Marcus's . . . after what happened with him, I need someone I know I can trust absolutely and without reservation. I need you, Malcolm. Will you help me out?"

The captain thought it over for a minute. "When you put it like that, sir, I can't refuse. Yes—I accept."

Archer shook his hand. "Great! Welcome aboard."

"But what about *Pioneer*, sir? They'll need someone to take over as captain. Travis isn't quite ready. But they deserve the best, sir. Who can we find to take over on such short notice?"

The admiral grinned. "As it happens, there's someone I have in mind. A new captain who should've been out there already, but has been prevented by forces beyond her control."

Reed's eyes widened as he realized whom Archer meant.

March 11, 2166
U.S.S. Pioneer

"You're *sure* this wasn't your idea, Malcolm?" Caroline Paris asked as Reed led her through the corridors toward the cargo bay.

"I told you. The admiral had already made the choice when I found out. He wasn't even aware we were involved. It was just a happy convergence of a ship in need of a new captain and a captain in need of a functional ship."

"I'm still not sure whether to be relieved by that or offended that you were too embarrassed to tell your friends about us."

There was humor in her tone, but Reed still fidgeted. "You know how private I am. And the admiral *has* had a great deal on his plate lately."

"I know, I know," she said, squeezing his arm. "I guess I'm just worried they won't accept me. You've all become a pretty close-knit bunch."

"I was a first-time captain when I got *Pioneer*. I needed time to bond with the crew, to win their trust and acceptance. I expect it will go much easier for you." He smiled. "You have a knack for winning people over."

"Well, having a ship that isn't cursed and/or actively out to get me should help too. Although I did feel we were close to cracking *Vesta*'s problems at last. I'm a bit frustrated that I won't get to see it through to the end."

"The nature of the service, I'm afraid. We go where we're posted."

"Yeah, about that . . ." Paris took his arm and stopped him not far from the bay entrance. "I knew our duties would take us apart soon enough, but I figured we'd both be out there. That we'd run into each other from time to time, maybe team up on missions. Now you're gonna be back here on Earth, stuck behind a desk . . . who knows when we'll get together again?"

He replied with a reassuring tone. "On the other hand, being the assistant to a Starfleet chief of staff means I'll be coordinating a lot of the UESPA fleet's operations. Which should give me occasion to speak to the various captains over subspace fairly often."

"Isn't that more the sort of thing you'd usually channel through starbase or sector commanders?"

"Well, yes, as a rule, but there are times when direct contact is more efficient."

"Malcolm . . ."

He took her hand. "Caroline, you have nothing to worry about. No matter how far apart we are . . . we're together. We're connected. I've seen that with other relationships among my friends and crewmates. Having someone they feel connected to brings them a special contentment, even if they're separated by dozens of parsecs for months at a time. I think . . . I'd like to think that what we share will have the same endurance."

Paris clasped his other hand, cradling both of his between hers. "Yeah, I guess I've pretty much lost my taste for casual flings with exotic alien men. I guess you'll have to do."

"You always know how to make a man feel special," he answered wryly. "Now, shall we go in and greet the crew?"

The gathered personnel of *Pioneer* snapped to attention as the two captains entered the cargo bay. Reed paused and took a few moments to drink in the sight of them all, basking in the warmth of the memories their faces evoked. Travis Mayweather, stalwart friend and moral compass. Val Williams, his strong right arm. Rey Sangupta, embodiment of the crew's bold, inquisitive spirit. Bodor chim Grev, the heart of the crew. Kivei Tizahr, still new and hard to get close to, but already indispensable. Tallarico, Liao, Kirk,

Ndiaye, all the rest he'd never gotten to know as well as they deserved to be known.

"Before we begin," Reed announced through a tightened throat, "I just want to say to all of you what an honor it has been to be your captain. It took me time to earn your trust, and in so doing, I became a better officer and a better man. And a happier, less lonely man as well. I trust you know how much you all mean to me even if I don't always express it." Their expressions let him know that they did. "And I know that, if you were able to put up with me, then adjusting to your new captain should be a breeze by comparison." The crew laughed politely, sadly.

Clearing his throat, Reed nodded to Mayweather, who straightened and called, "All hands, attention to orders!"

The crew came to attention as one. Reed raised the data slate in his hand and read from it: "'From Starfleet Headquarters, Office of the Admiralty, to Captain Malcolm Reed, commanding officer *U.S.S. Pioneer*, 11 March 2166. You are hereby requested and required to relinquish command of your vessel to Captain Caroline Paris, commanding officer *U.S.S. Vesta*, as of this date. Signed, Admiral Jonathan Archer, Starfleet Command.'" Turning to Paris, he handed her the encryption key card that would transfer all his command codes and authorizations to her once she inserted it into *Pioneer*'s computer. "I am ready to be relieved."

Paris took the card, then faced the crew and recited

her own, equivalent orders to take command. Finally, she turned to Reed and intoned, "I relieve you, sir."

Reed answered crisply, "I stand relieved."

Turning back to the assembled crew, Paris took a step forward and spoke. "I want to thank you all for welcoming me aboard *Pioneer*, first as a visitor and now as your captain. I can't tell you what a privilege it is to command this ship. Captain Reed has always spoken highly of each and every one of you, and we all know he's not one for giving unearned praise. As for me, I know I'm untried, but I'm determined to prove worthy of you. I'll no doubt be a more easy-going captain than Malcolm was, but that's only because I expect you to live up to his high opinions on your own. And I know you all join me in wishing Captain Reed the very best in his new posting. Of course, all standing orders, regulations, and instructions remain in effect."

Grinning, Paris looked over her new crew. "You're dismissed. Time to get back to work. After all, those new civilizations won't seek themselves!"

Unregistered scout ship
Interstellar space

Tucker sat quietly in the cockpit's pilot seat and brooded, as he had done ever since the subspace news broadcasts announcing Section 31's exposure (though not under that name) had reached his ship. After a while, he started at the realization that Devna's slender hands had begun kneading the tension from his shoulders moments before. Had he been that distracted, or was her approach really that subtle? Most likely, it was a mix of both. "Devna, don't."

"I only wish to help."

"Well, it's not helping."

With a gentle sigh, she glided around him and settled gracefully into the adjacent seat, still dressed in the relatively modest garb she had resumed wearing once Garos's people had smuggled the two of them back out to their scout ship the day before. "If you won't let me ease your tensions with sex like any sensible person would," Devna said, "then at least talk to me. You know I'm a very good listener. And something is clearly disturbing you. I would have thought you'd be happy to learn that your masters had been brought down."

"I am. It's something I feared would never happen. But Harris and his inner circle are still at large."

"Their existence has been exposed, their resources stripped from them. A manhunt is under way. They are badly weakened, at least."

"But they could still come back. This won't be over until they're in prison with the rest."

Her deep green eyes studied him. "But that is not what troubles you so, Trip."

There was something irresistible about her gaze—not in the usual way that Orion women were irresistible, but as a function of something deeper, the strength and sincerity he had sensed within her from the first time they had met. If nothing else, she deserved to know what troubled her colleague and shipmate.

"I'm . . . ashamed," he told her. "I was so convinced that the only way to bring down Section Thirty-one was to play their game. To use lies and tricks and manipulation, to defraud the whole Federation, to gamble with the lives of a whole city's worth of Saurians. I killed people. I got a friend, a good man, tortured and killed. I almost assassinated the person who was actually working to save those Saurians. And all because I convinced myself it was necessary for the 'greater good.' I thought I was rejecting Harris's way of doing things, but I was justifying my actions in exactly the same way."

"We discussed this back on Sauria, Trip. Garos and I used deception too. We made Harrad-Sar the scapegoat for our actions. I have no doubt he'll be killed for it."

"But it wasn't lies and secrecy that made the difference. Yes, Garos used a lie to protect himself, his family—but what saved the Saurians, what scuttled the Sisters' plans, was the one thing I've been hiding from for the past eleven years: an open, public assertion of the truth. It was the Starfleet team detecting the antimatter and *telling* people about it that saved the day, while I was keeping it secret and sneaking around planning to murder someone."

Devna took his hand, her touch warm and soothing. "Hearing the news from Earth has intensified your doubts. Once again, it was an act of openness that succeeded where secrecy and deceit failed."

"Exactly. I thought I was the only one who could bring the Section down. I came up with all these devious schemes to strike from the shadows and cover my own ass . . . and they did no damn good at all. What made the difference was a man of real conscience having the bravery to speak out, no matter the cost to himself. It was someone doing the *right* thing for the right reasons, not the wrong thing for the right reasons."

"Aren't you glad of that, Trip? It means your Federation's ways are vindicated. The ideals you fight for actually work."

"Yes," he said bitterly. "But what worries me is that I couldn't see that. I couldn't see the better way that Marcus Williams saw, that Tony Ruiz saw, that even you and Garos saw." He felt his eyes grow moist. "The man I used to be—the real Trip Tucker—he could've seen that. But I . . . I've lost that. The Section may be gone, but I'll never escape from it. It'll be with me for the rest of my life.

"And that means I can never go back to the life I had."

March 14, 2166
Orion homeworld

The Three Sisters stared at their wall screen in shock and horror as it showed Harrad-Sar being put slowly to death before a massive crowd of Saurians. There was nothing they could do to affect what they saw, for it had taken two days for the subspace signal to reach them across parsecs. Maltuvis had chosen to make the execution of the Sisters' longest-serving, most loyal slave the centerpiece of this propaganda broadcast to his people and to the galaxy at large—and the Sisters were no doubt his primary target audience.

"*Now all may see the truth about the outrageous, false allegations that have been made against this government over the past several days,*" the dictator intoned as Harrad-Sar continued to choke in the transparent-walled gas chamber behind him—itself a propagandistic statement, highlighting the vulnerability of other species to the volcanic gases that Saurians could easily endure. "*Only offworlders would be so callous as to jeopardize countless Saurian lives through the construction of antimatter generation plants so near to populated areas. These Orion creatures managed to infiltrate our shipbuilding facilities—no doubt hoping to steal the secrets of our superior engineering prowess. The antimatter that the Federation-backed resistance claims to have been smuggled* out *of our Veranith factory was, in fact, being smuggled* in *as part of a malicious Orion plot to destroy the plant—just one more act of alien sabotage against our noble people. So foolhardy are these alien interlopers, so divided, that they cannot even avoid disrupting each other's efforts.*

"*But we cannot always rely on their own incompetence to foil their plans,*" Maltuvis went on. "*The offworlders are many, and they all crave the wealth of our homeworld and the products of our inventive genius. So we must remain ever vigilant and ever* strong. We must rededicate ourselves to the enlargement of our planetary defense fleet. To this end, I am ordering a fifty percent increase of our spacecraft factory workforce, which shall be accomplished by lowering the minimum age of employment by an additional four years beyond the previous reduction. I know the strong people of Sauria will rededicate themselves to this arduous task, knowing that they sacrifice for the defense of our world and our future."

Through a remarkable feat of timing, Maltuvis wrapped up his speech just before Harrad-Sar gave off his final death rattle. A massive cheer went up from the assembled crowd, even as Navaar wailed and tore her hair and D'Nesh screamed, cursed, and hurled breakables at the nearest slaves. For her own part, Maras curled up against Navaar's side and shed tears that she did not need to feign. She had known Harrad-Sar for nearly her entire life, and he had served Maras and her sisters well, even back when they were junior operatives in the Syndicate, pretending to the galaxy that he was their master instead of their slave. Their relationship had endured its rough patches over the course of their rise to power, but he had always been unflinchingly loyal, which was why these events were so difficult to comprehend.

Maras let that genuine confusion feed into the naïve persona that came as second nature to her, even—perhaps especially—at times like this. "I don't understand," she keened. "We liked the purple lizard man! We helped him! Why did he kill Sar like that?"

Navaar hugged her closer, something Maras took

comfort in. "I'm so sorry, sweetie. Maltuvis did it to send us a message."

"What message?" Asking the question was Maras's way of offering comfort to her sister in return. Navaar was a skilled problem solver—not on the same level as Maras, but practiced after decades of hard work and scheming to get the Sisters to the top. Guiding her to focus her mind on the problem, and on what to do about it, would help her manage her grief.

Navaar stroked Maras's bare back as she replied. "We were supposed to help him make the Federation look responsible for killing many Saurians, so he could make his people angrier at aliens. That way, when he sent his ships out to conquer other worlds, the people would think he was doing it to protect them, so they'd believe it was the right thing to do. Since Harrad-Sar failed to do that, Maltuvis is punishing him—and punishing us by using the Orions as the target for his people's anger and blame instead of the Federation. So he still gets what he wants, what we spent years helping him achieve, but we get none of what we were promised in return." Her voice grew angrier and her nails dug into Maras's back. Maras indulged her without protest; she'd endured far worse pain in her day, often by choice.

"I can't believe that *gisjacheh* Sar!" D'Nesh snarled as she pushed over an antique end table. "Funneling off antimatter for his own use? What was he thinking? How could he be so stupid?"

"It doesn't make any sense," Navaar said. "But you

know how males are. Irrational creatures, all slaves to their lust and aggression. When they desire something badly enough, their brains shut down. That's why they're so easy to control."

"But they're supposed to desire *us!*"

"Maybe that's it. Maybe Sar was away too long and his conditioning started to weaken." Navaar sighed. "Unfortunately, we'll never know. I wish Maltuvis had at least had the courtesy to let *us* torture him to death, to get the truth out of him. He was ours, after all—it was our right."

"Oh, I would've enjoyed that," D'Nesh moaned with regret. "Remember, I wanted us to kill him years ago, after he bungled the *Enterprise* operation and left us stranded. If you'd let me finish him off then, we wouldn't be in this mess now."

Navaar glared at her more volatile sister. "I'll excuse that because you're upset. You know we never would've regained our status without his loyalty. Whatever mistakes he finally made on Sauria, they shouldn't erase the debt we owe him for all his years of obedience."

D'Nesh folded her arms over her ample bust and glowered at the now-blank viewscreen. "Maybe. But that doesn't help us figure out what to do now. We didn't embarrass the Federation or get them to swear off interference. We've lost Sauria as an ally. We can't count on Garos anymore. So where do we go from here?"

Navaar rose from the couch, glided over to D'Nesh,

and pulled her reluctant sister into a commiserating embrace. "We can talk about that tomorrow, dear. Tonight, we should just process our grief. Find a way to work through it and restore our balance."

D'Nesh nodded, thinking it over. "All-male slave orgy?"

The eldest Sister laughed. "That's your solution to everything. Still—count me in."

Maras jumped up and clapped in excitement, following her sisters from the chamber. But inwardly, her mind was racing. Navaar's dismissive explanation for Harrad-Sar's evident betrayal did not satisfy Maras. He had naturally engaged in the degree of self-enrichment and skimming that was typical and expected in the Orion Syndicate, but he was discreet enough in his personal corruption that it had never come at the detriment of the Sisters' plans. It was also an implausible coincidence that he had smuggled out the antimatter at the exact time that Starfleet had been observing the plant. Maras sensed the hand of Garos behind that—and all the most likely scenarios Maras could model involved the Malurian using Devna as an intermediary.

Devna's failure—and her probable hand in Harrad-Sar's fate—was the most disappointing aspect of this for Maras. She had been genuinely fond of the lithe, pale-skinned slave, impressed by her quiet intelligence and hidden depths and enthralled by her delicate beauty. She and Devna had been magnificent together in bed, and it had been deeply refreshing to have someone with whom she could be herself, someone who could think and discuss and debate on an intellectual level close to her own. Maras had even considered letting Devna earn manumission one day, perhaps promoting her to a full partner, a surrogate Sister to fill the void once D'Nesh was disgraced or executed.

But perhaps Devna's yearning for freedom had been stronger than Maras realized. The human agent Tucker had offered it to her, and perhaps that was why she had betrayed Maras to help him save the Saurians. Or perhaps it was the heightened sense of empathy she had learned from the Deltans, a sentiment that would have made her unable to tolerate an atrocity of the magnitude that Navaar and Maltuvis had plotted. It was easy to deduce that Garos would have been equally unwilling to allow the sacrifice of so many beings that he would have identified with as fellow victims of oppression, no matter how much Maluria would profit from their demise. It seemed most likely that he and Devna had been equally motivated to spare the Saurians and had worked together to find a way. But Maras was content to let Garos keep that secret; punishing his family would do nothing to alter the failure of the plan. And Maras was willing to concede there was merit in Devna's argument that cruelty should not be inflicted needlessly. Indeed, Navaar's plan might have failed precisely because it had relied on excessive cruelty and disregard for life, thereby provoking a stronger counterreaction than a more subtle plan might have done.

But that was all the more reason to be disappointed that Devna had failed to give Maras the means to eliminate D'Nesh. She was the cruelest Sister, always pushing Navaar toward greater excesses of violence and brutality. Perhaps Navaar's repeated failures to tear down the Federation had frustrated her enough to make her receptive to the middle Sister's more extreme approach. As long as D'Nesh was still in play, that pattern was likely to escalate. Maras would have to devise an alternative plan for her elimination—but it was difficult without a confidante like Devna, the most intelligent and capable of the very few slaves to whom Maras had entrusted her secret.

So how do I deal with Devna? Maras wondered. She had never been betrayed before, and she wasn't sure how she felt about it. She could understand Devna's reasons for the act, after all. She even admired the spy for her cunning and independence, her skill at causing such massive disruption through such subtle and undetected action. But at the same time, Maras realized that if Devna was using that skill as a free agent instead of in her mistress's service, then that made her a threat. She knew secrets that could destroy Maras if they were exposed. And Navaar would be devastated by the revelation that her beloved idiot sister had been lying to her all these years. Maras wasn't sure which prospect dismayed her more—losing her life or losing Navaar's love.

Either way, Devna was a threat that would have to be dealt with. In some way, Maras would have to track her down, capture her, and punish her. Whether that punishment entailed ending Devna's life was something she would decide when the time came—but it seemed likely that it would.

After all, Devna was hers, so it was her right.

16

March 16, 2166
Vicinity of Lambda Serpentis

THE ATMOSPHERE aboard Charles Tucker's scout ship had been quiet and uncomfortable for the past several days. Tucker had continued to brood, unsure where to go from here. He longed for T'Pol's comfort and counsel, but he was too ashamed to face her—too afraid that he had lost the last surviving pieces of the man she'd loved. Yet he had rebuffed Devna's efforts to offer him comfort and support, afraid that he would succumb to his current sense of nihilism and take her to bed. If he did that, it would be like admitting that he could never return to T'Pol. The fact that he wasn't quite ready to take that step was the one remaining shred of hope he had—but every day, the temptation of Devna's presence grew stronger. For Devna's part, she had recognized his conflict and thus kept her distance, not wishing to make it harder for him. But Tucker would be grateful when he could finally drop her off at Stameris and go on his way—even though he had no idea where to go.

But as they drew closer to the Lambda Serpentis system, Tucker came to realize that he was not the sole source of anxiety aboard the ship. Devna was troubled too, and eventually his conscience would not let him avoid asking her about it any longer.

"I feel I must return to my mistress," she explained. "I owe that to her."

"To Maras? Are you kidding me? She'll kill you for sure."

"Perhaps not. She is a far more complex woman than she appears. She listens to me. She might understand why I had to betray her."

"You're property to her. She'll never accept your right to make your own decisions, especially not at the expense of her plans."

"You don't know that."

"I have a pretty good idea." He sighed. "Like I told you, some of my ancestors a few centuries back were slave owners. I'm not proud of that part of my heritage, but I've faced it, tried to understand it. Many of them . . . they thought of their slaves like pets, felt something like affection for them and showed them kindness as long as they were obedient and kept to their place. But if those slaves disobeyed or tried to act like equals, their masters would be outraged and they'd be punished severely. Because the masters' whole worldview was built around their right to own other people and have absolute power over their lives. Any fondness they felt for their slaves evaporated if they thought those slaves were challenging that right."

Devna sat quietly for a few moments, absorbing his words. "I do not know what other options I have. You clearly do not want me to remain with you. And if

Maras would not take me back . . . I do not believe I would want another master."

He looked up at that. "Well, now we're getting somewhere. Look . . . maybe we could skip Stameris and keep on to the nearest Federation outpost. I'm sure you could find help there—"

A strident tone from the proximity detector interrupted him. Tucker rushed to the cockpit and took the pilot's seat, with Devna staying close behind him. Examining the readouts, he told her, "There's a ship closing in on us. It just neutralized warp—from these readings, it was going damn fast for a ship that size. Not much bigger than ours, but it's powerful."

"Is it from Stameris?"

"No, it came from . . . from Federation space. But it's not Starfleet. It looks more like . . ." He trailed off in belated recognition. "Oh, no."

"What is it?"

Before he could answer, he felt the all-over tingle of a transporter beam. He saw Devna's lithe form start to shimmer before the beam engulfed them both.

Materializing to find himself and Devna held at gunpoint by two black-suited humans should have been intimidating. Instead, Tucker felt a rush of satisfaction at the sight. Their garb was Section 31 attire, and he recognized the compact, short-haired woman as a high-ranked operative who went by the name Ramirez. The man, an unfamiliar dark-skinned individual with a shaved head, gestured with his phase pistol, prompting the prisoners to descend from the transporter pad. Tucker obliged gladly, looking forward to the meeting about to occur.

As expected, the main room of the scout ship was occupied by several more blacksuits, a few of whom he had encountered over the years and had known or suspected to be core members of the Section 31 conspiracy. At the head of the group was Matthew Harris himself, gazing sternly at Tucker. The erstwhile engineer chuckled. "Well, well, well. Looks like you're all on the run. That must smart. I only wish I could take the credit."

Harris smirked. "Oh, I'm sure you had a hand in it. I appreciate your not wasting our time by pretending to be loyal. Some of the information that Admiral Archer and the JAG office now have in their possession could only have come from you. And from my old friend Malcolm Reed, I take it?"

"Do all the fishing you want, Harris—it isn't gonna do you any good now. You may have given Starfleet the slip, but everyone's hunting for you. They have the Section's protocols, its records, its resources. Any escape routes or hideaways you might have had prepared are burned now. That's something I'll happily take credit for my part in."

Turning his gaze to Devna, Harris asked, "And you, young lady? Are you as determined to bring down your own Syndicate? Or is the fact that our agency is in disarray while yours is still intact exactly what you wanted?"

"What I want," Devna replied, "is a question that

very few people have ever allowed me to consider." She glanced at Tucker. "None so much as this man. All he has wanted is to be free. He thought to offer that freedom to me as well. I do not even know if I want it, but I am thankful to him for wishing me to have it. I wish the same for him in return."

She began to sidle forward as she spoke, but Ramirez stepped in her path and pointed her pistol's emitter at Devna's heart. "No pheromonal tricks, Orion," she advised. "You're expendable."

"No, she's not," Tucker insisted, interposing himself. "That's the whole problem with all of you—thinking you have the right to decide who's expendable."

Harris shook his silvery head. "I thought we saw things the same way, Mister Tucker. We were trying to protect the Federation."

"You were trying to protect your own self-interest. To look for excuses to break the law and do the unconscionable, so you could justify the existence of a conspiracy whose only purpose was to do those things. Give people power like that, and they'll never be willing to give it up. It has to be taken from them." He shook his head. "You all just can't bear to face the fact that you've lost your power. If you were really patriots, you wouldn't have run away. You wouldn't have been ashamed to face the people and tell them what you'd done 'on their behalf.'"

"Some secrets still need to remain secret, Charles. Or were you planning on revealing yourself anytime soon?"

Tucker winced at that. But he felt Devna's warm touch against his arm, and it strengthened his resolve. "I wouldn't hesitate, if it were necessary to make sure your whole conspiracy was destroyed once and for all."

"Oh, Charles." Harris shook his head, looking disappointed. "Do you really imagine this is the end? Section Thirty-one is still in the charter. The Federation will always need the . . . flexibility to cope with the unpredictable. And that contingency has been prepared for." He gestured at the agents around him. "You may have brought down our segment of the operation, but there's a higher echelon that remains untouched. Who do you think recruited us in the first place?"

"Bull. I've seen the evidence. This operation started with you and it'll end with you."

"You've seen what you and Malcolm Reed wanted to believe. I'm happy to let the authorities believe it too, but the truth is that when I left Starfleet, I had to burn so many assets to avoid arrest that I no longer had the resources to accomplish anything like this—until I was enlisted by others of like mind and superior means. Just as all of us were, based on our demonstrated willingness to place what was right above what was legal. And there will always be more . . . volunteers . . . to take our place as the need arises."

Tucker crossed his arms. "*If* this so-called higher echelon exists, I'm sure the judge advocate will be happy to hear all about it once you're in custody."

"Oh, it exists. I know very few specifics, but I know it's there. And it's more pervasive, more deeply woven into the fabric of our society, than you can begin to imagine."

Now the ex-engineer was laughing outright. "Do you think this is some spy movie? You're the one who kept reminding me that we needed to keep our heads down to avoid being discovered. You know as well as I do that if Section Thirty-one were as huge and all-encompassing as you're saying, it couldn't avoid exposure for long."

"That's actually quite true," Harris riposted. "Which is why the organization stays small by periodically casting off anyone proven to be a liability."

Tucker looked around at the weapon emitters pointing his way. "Like me?"

The older man's expression became wistful. Taking in his colleagues with his gaze, he sighed. "Like all of us here, I'm afraid. The sad fact is, you were right about me, Charles. Despite all my smug lectures on the need to stay small and subtle, I fell prey to the very temptation you just described. I intervened too much, too often, in order to justify my role. After the Vertian affair, after Sauria, I should have made sure we laid low for a while. Several of my colleagues here recommended as much. We didn't think we had a choice but to act when the Klingon invasion loomed, and we probably didn't, but I'd already taken too many chances before then." He winced. "And, yes, I went too far. To save our civilization, I knowingly set off the annihilation of another. I won't give you the satisfaction of describing how that's affected my ability to sleep and eat, but I will confess that it was a bad strategic move, an act of overkill that made reactions like yours and Marcus Williams's inevitable. I've made too many bad decisions too close together, and that has made me the greatest liability of all."

"Not you alone, Matt," said the shaven-headed man. "We all shared in the decisions."

Harris looked back at him with gratitude. "I know, Karim. It brings me no pleasure, but we all stand together."

Tucker exchanged a look with Devna. He didn't like the growing sense of grim resolution among the group.

Harris shifted his attention to Tucker once again. "That is the danger of a small, insular cabal. It's necessary for what we must do, but it tends to isolate us from consequences, and that can make us reckless. Which is why it's probably best to close down operations for a while—to trim the excess and regroup before starting over.

"That's why the higher echelon allowed your plan to go forward in the first place, Charles—although they didn't inform me of it until afterward," he added with regret. "Oh, yes, naturally they knew about it from the start. Don't flatter yourself by thinking you could've outsmarted them. In fact, I have to tell you, it was a fairly clumsy undertaking. Far too complicated. Too reliant on factors—and people—you couldn't control. It was bound to go wrong. But the higher echelon calculated that it would help to trigger the events that were needed to purge our greatest liabilities—including all of us."

Karim moved to enter instructions into a console while Harris continued speaking. "The Federation will believe a conspiracy has been exposed and ended forever. I expect the organization will remain dormant for a generation or two, barring extreme emergencies. But sooner or later, someone will recognize the potential implied in Section Thirty-one of Article 14, and will ask the right questions of Starfleet's database. And when the right keywords are entered, they will find the information and resources they need to start again. But for now . . . the board must be cleared. I am sorry, Charles. Ma'am," he added to Devna.

But the Orion woman was gazing at Tucker in alarm, clutching his arm as she realized what he already had: that Karim was shutting down the safeguards on the scout's antimatter containment, one by one.

"I wish there had been a better way," Harris went on as Tucker clenched his teeth hard and pulled Devna against him. "But everything I've ever done is for the greater good of the Federation."

Tucker closed his eyes as a blinding light engulfed him.

Spacecraft *Merlin*
Interstellar space

"Where are we?"

Tucker opened his eyes to find himself and Devna

standing on an unusual-looking transporter platform, the machinery around them sparking and smoking. "Come on," he said, taking the Orion's hand and leading her off the pad. Reaching the console, he activated the ventilation system and shut down power to the unit, though it continued to smolder.

"This was my last-ditch escape route," he explained. "Courtesy of an ally I made last year. A man who's lived a very, very long time and managed to get his hands on some exotic forms of technology. Like a transporter powerful enough to beam us across parsecs—though it could only do it once before burning out. The beacon was implanted in my tooth, and I just triggered it." He took in a gasping breath. "I'm lucky it didn't go off by accident during those torture sessions."

"We both are," Devna said. "Thank you."

He led her from the transporter chamber into the main room beyond. "So we're on a ship?" the Orion asked. "Is anyone else here?"

"No—it was waiting here for my use when I was ready. I needed a way to fake my death and disappear so thoroughly even Harris's people couldn't find me. There's no way any known technology could track the beam here, and the *Merlin*—that's the name of the ship—has no connection to me except through my friend." Akharin had claimed Merlin to be one of the identities he'd adopted during his thousands of years on Earth, but Tucker had suspected he was padding his résumé. "And he's an old hand at making himself disappear."

Devna looked around, impressed at the well-appointed lounge area they had entered. "So this was your escape. Your path to freedom."

He studied her. "You don't look convinced."

"Harris spoke of a higher echelon. What if their resources are greater than you realize?"

"I think he was bluffing. One last mind game so I'd die without being sure I'd really beaten him. If there is anyone higher, why did he say the whole thing would be dormant for a generation or more? It doesn't add up." He shrugged. "Still, just in case, we're probably better off playing dead for a while. Keeping away from the Federation—and from the Syndicate."

She held his gaze intently. "Then you would have me come with you?"

"If you like. As far as anyone knows, we're both dead. Your life as a slave is over, just like my life as a spy. It can be a fresh start for both of us." He fidgeted. "It doesn't *have* to be together. Not in the long run, certainly. But just to start out . . . well, who else do we have?"

Devna continued to contemplate him. "What of the woman you love? The one who gave you reason to hope? Do you not wish to contact her?"

A renewed wave of shame overtook him. How could he face T'Pol again? How could he be worthy of her now? "Maybe in time," he said, hiding in equivocation. "Once I'm sure it's safe. Once I settle on a new identity. Once I . . . figure some things out."

Settling into an armchair, Devna pulled her legs up

and wrapped her arms around them. "To leave one's whole life behind . . . maybe never to return. To become something new. It would be hard. I fear it."

"You can't mean you're nostalgic for the life you had!"

She met his eyes without embarrassment. "It's the only life I've ever known. And it wasn't all bad. I had friends. Sisters, in bondage and in blood. And Orion is a beautiful world. The spectacular mountains . . . the luminous forests . . . the soothing song of the emerald finches. I found peace there . . . when I was permitted to be alone. If I never saw it again . . . never heard the finches sing . . . I would miss it deeply."

She lowered her head, shimmering coils of obsidian hair falling forward to hide her lovely face. Hesitantly, Tucker sat on the arm of the chair and placed a hand on her shoulder. "Sometimes we have to leave the past behind to move forward. We have a new beginning now, Devna. Neither of us knows what that holds, and that's scary.

"But . . . having no idea what to do next . . . having no plans, no program, no path laid out for us by anyone else . . . doesn't it feel . . . free?"

She looked up at him, and watching the wide-eyed smile slowly form on her face as his words sank in was like watching a newborn bird break free of its shell.

Epilogue

March 18, 2166
U.S.S. Endeavour

"So there is still no sign," T'Pol asked with care, "of the anonymous informant?"

On the desk screen in her quarters, Admiral Archer shook his head. She could see in his eyes that he sensed her concern for Trip, but they were both still constrained to be circumspect. Until and unless Tucker emerged on his own, they would respect his wish to remain dead in the eyes of the world.

Although T'Pol's current concern was that his death might no longer be illusory.

"The Andorian cruiser th'Rejjal confirmed that the ion trail of the fugitives' ship terminated at the site of the warp reactor explosion they registered two days ago," Archer told her in a grim tone. *"Their analysis of the debris cloud indicates that the vessel had several living beings aboard. There's wreckage from a smaller scout ship that must have been nearby—probably under tow. It was apparently vacant at the time of the blast, but the radiation and vacuum exposure have destroyed any DNA evidence. There's a possible ion trail that seems to backtrack in the approximate direction of Sauria. But there's no way to be sure."*

"I see," T'Pol replied after a moment. "Thank you, Admiral."

He nodded in silent understanding, though even he could only suspect what she was experiencing now. She had believed Tucker to be dead several times before, but on prior occasions, the awareness of their telepathic bond had remained on at least a subliminal level, so there had never been a complete sense of loss. Now she sensed nothing. The long-range telepathic connection that had been suppressed or broken during her ordeal at Administrator V'Las's orders last year had never recovered. While T'Pol was aware that Trip had planned to falsify his demise once again as a way of eluding any residual Section 31 assets, that did not guarantee that he had succeeded in doing so. The evidence from *th'Rejjal* pointed toward the possibility that Harris had captured Tucker and killed him in the same conflagration through which Section 31's senior echelon had inexplicably sacrificed themselves.

T'Pol schooled herself to calm. Tucker might well have good reason to maintain a low profile until he was confident he could contact her safely. It had been mere days, not even enough time to reach a Federation world or other safe port. It was premature to write off his chances of survival at this point, despite what the evidence said.

Yet the illogical, emotional side that she had always found difficult to contain offered up an unexpectedly logical point: Given her importance to him, surely making some form of contact with her would have been Trip's first priority upon leaving Sauria, or at least upon receiving the news of the Section's exposure. If he were still alive and well, why would he not have let her know in some way?

Perhaps sensing her need for something positive to contemplate, Archer assayed a shift of topic. *"Speaking of Sauria, Maltuvis may have managed to dodge the blame for nearly causing a disaster, but at least he no longer has Orion backing for his conquest plans. If he does intend to expand his empire to other worlds, it'll be slower going without their support. And hopefully the resistance is unified enough now to bring him down before that happens."*

"Yes," T'Pol said. "It is odd, though, that Maltuvis would so decisively terminate his alliance with the Orions. For all his rhetoric of Saurian superiority, he clearly recognizes that he needs outside assistance if he hopes to achieve his ambition of interstellar conquest within his lifetime. It is difficult to believe he has abandoned that ambition."

"He may have had no choice. It was either that or get blamed by the people for risking millions of their lives. They would've turned on him en masse. This way, he still controls Sauria, at least. For now, he'll just have to settle for that."

"Perhaps. But he still has the second-generation warp ships he managed to build previously, and probably a substantial supply of photonic weaponry. Further vigilance will be required. Further intervention may be as well."

Archer sighed. *"Intervention. That leads us right into a whole other can of worms."*

She quirked her brows at the convoluted metaphor. "That requires clarification."

Her stern tone affected the release of tension she had intended, but his laugh was minimal and brief. *"It's just as I feared,"* he went on. *"The investigation into Harris's conspiracy has exposed their knowledge of the Orions' plan to stage the Saurian disaster—and Harris's willingness to let it happen. The knowledge that both those groups wanted us to adopt a nonintervention policy is damning. Shran has seized on it like—well, you know how he gets."*

"Painfully well."

Archer winced at the reminder of their first encounter with Shran as an adversary. His sorrow at their apparent reversion to antagonism was clear on the admiral's face. *"He's painting the support of nonintervention as giving aid and comfort to our enemies, as well as abandoning those in need like the Saurians,"* he went on. *"I've already lost a lot of my backing in Starfleet and the Council. I'm afraid the directive may be dead."*

T'Pol considered. "It could be argued," she said, "that the harmful impact of Section Thirty-one's interventions in other cultures merely reinforces the premise that a prohibition against such unilateral intervention is warranted. Harris will not be the only corrupt or misguided member of Starfleet. Some form of regulatory check on intervention is still necessary."

The admiral nodded without enthusiasm. *"That's basically the case I'm planning to make tonight. There's a debate scheduled before the Council. Shran and I are having it out once and for all. It's probably my last chance to save the directive."* He shook his head. *"I just wish it didn't have to be at the cost of his friendship. I'm dealing with enough loss lately."*

T'Pol held his gaze in understanding. "As are we all, Jonathan."

M'Tezir, Sauria

"Do not concern yourself, Emperor," said the alien on Maltuvis's communication screen. *"As this first shipment demonstrates, I shall be quite capable of satisfying your fleet's need for antimatter without the hazards of surface-based manufacture."*

"You had better," Maltuvis replied. "My offworld alliances have proven undependable in the past." It was a risk to make this contact directly, but the new benefactor had provided encryption protocols even more sophisticated than what the Orions had used, along with a procedure for smuggling antimatter to the fleet under the cover of an asteroid-mining operation, something that had never occurred to Harrad-Sar. Even if the communication were intercepted, it would only be by Starfleet. The rank and file of Saurians knew only what he told them: that aliens were the enemy against whom he would protect them. Any claim that he still colluded with aliens would merely be the propaganda of other aliens, and who would believe them?

"The Orions are nothing but gangsters and pirates," replied the gray-haired mammalian creature on the screen. *"They were unworthy of you. The people of N'Ragolar are strong, ingenious, and driven. What you have built in only a few*

short years is astonishing. I have been searching for allies with a martial spirit like yours. With your ambition and ruthless drive, and with your people's resilience and power, the stars are yours for the taking."

"And are you worthy of us?" the emperor challenged. "You were deposed long ago. Your attempt to retake your world failed. Now you are a renegade, lost and searching for a home. You need me more than I need you, Vulcan."

V'Las, erstwhile Administrator of the Vulcan High Command and current fugitive from Federation justice, seethed at Maltuvis's words, showing far more emotion than the other Vulcans the emperor had met—which was to the man's credit. But he gathered himself and went on with a tight smile. *"All I want, great Maltuvis, is to find a race of beings who prize martial strength and conquest as I do. A people that I can help guide to a great destiny. I believed the Vulcans could be that race, but they failed me. They had been too badly tainted by weakness and pacifism for too long. That is not a problem for you."*

"Not anymore," Maltuvis agreed. "The pacifists did get their grip on this world, but I have driven them out. I succeeded where you failed."

"Yes," V'Las grudgingly conceded through clenched teeth. *"And with my help, you will succeed on a far greater stage. Together, we will build an interstellar empire to surpass the Federation, the Klingons, even the Romulans."*

His wizened features twisted into a cold leer. *"And, in time, to destroy them."*

Starfleet Headquarters

Archer was just wrapping up a revision of his notes for the evening's Council debate when Dani Erickson called. *"It's time,"* she said.

The sadness in her eyes left no doubt what she meant. "Porthos?" he asked, his throat tightening.

She gave a pained nod. *"The vet says . . . there's no point in prolonging his pain any further. Jon, I think he's ready to move on. But he's your . . . your family. You have to be the one to make the call."* A pause. *"I know how busy you are,"* she said. *"If you want . . . you could talk to the doctor now and . . . I'll stay with him for you."*

There was a considerably longer pause before Archer replied. "I'll get back to you." Dani nodded, blinking away tears, and disconnected.

Archer didn't know how much time passed while he sat there, overwhelmed. All the decisions he'd needed to make at this desk paled next to this one. As a Starfleet officer, how could he drop everything, set aside his responsibility to the Council and his allies, in order to say goodbye to his dog? But as a person, as a friend, how could he not?

The sound of Shran's strident voice shocked him out of his reverie. He hadn't even noticed the Andorian admiral storming into his office. "What's the meaning of this delay, Jon? I've been patient. I've put up with your refusal to abandon this absurd proposal even after all the revelations. I agreed to go through the whole blasted debate one more time before the Council. I'm not going to stand for any more delaying . . ." He trailed off, then took a step closer, studying Archer's face. "Jon, what is it? You look like your best friend just died."

Archer couldn't stop the tears from coming, causing Shran to rear back. "You're not far off," the human said in a rough voice. He strove to gather himself, knowing better than to expect sympathy. "I'm sorry. It's just . . . It's Porthos."

The anger instantly drained out of Shran's body, his antennae sagging. "Your animal? The . . . beagle?"

Archer nodded. "He's at the vet. He's . . . in his last hours. Dani called . . . asked if I could come to be with him. To say goodbye." He shook his head, gathering up his notes and preparing to stand. "I know, it's the worst possible time. The Council is waiting, and it's not fair to you—"

Shran was already moving around the desk. He grasped Archer's arm, helping him to his feet. "To hell with the Council, Jon. And to hell with me. Go. Your companion beast should not leave this world alone."

Archer stared at the other admiral in gratitude and shock. "But . . . the directive. The debate . . ."

"The fate of worlds can wait. You have a friend who needs you." His antennae coiled into the equivalent of a shrug. "Maybe this is the wrong time to resolve the debate fairly in any case. The question has been too tainted by Harris and his ilk. We can revisit it at some future time, once we have perspective. I could win easily if I pressed the issue today. But that would not be the right way to win." He lowered his gaze. "It was you who taught me the importance of that."

Archer clasped his old friend's hand, deeply moved. "Thank you, Shran. I don't know what to say."

"Just go be with Porthos." Walking with Archer toward the exit, he spoke again, hesitantly. "I don't suppose . . . that is, I know how hard it can be to say goodbye. If you . . . need me to come with you, lend additional support . . ."

"That . . . would be very much appreciated," Archer said with a bittersweet smile. "Thank you—my friend."

Acknowledgments

Thanks are due as always to my editors Margaret Clark and Ed Schlesinger, who were especially patient with me on this book. Thanks also to Doug Drexler for cluing me in on his cover design and Mark Rademaker for sharing the details of his version of the *Enterprise* XCV-330, based on the Matt Jefferies concept art originally featured in *Star Trek: The Motion Picture*.

Thanks to David Mack for letting me in on the content of his novel *Star Trek—Section 31: Control* and working with me to keep our two independently developed tales consistent with each other. The mathematics T'Pol invokes in her discussion of the probability of a conspiracy's exposure are based on the work of Doctor David Grimes (see Grimes DR [2016] "On the Viability of Conspiratorial Beliefs." PLoS ONE 11[1]: e0147905. doi:10.1371/journal.pone.0147905).

My versions of the Starfleet oaths at Caroline Paris's promotion and change-of-command ceremonies are based on a mix of *Star Trek* precedent and United States military procedure. Any differences from similar oaths and rituals in other *Star Trek* fiction can be attributed to revisions in Starfleet procedure over time.

The discussion of red dwarf habitability is informed by a number of research papers on the subject, including Heath, Doyle, Joshi, and Haberle, "Habitability of planets around red dwarf stars," *Origins of Life and Evolution of the Biosphere*, Vol. 29, No. 4, pp. 405–424 (for heat distribution on a tidally locked planet); Yang, Cowan, and Abbot, "Stabilizing Cloud Feedback Dramatically Expands the Habitable Zone of Tidally Locked Planets," *Astrophysical Journal Letters*, Vol. 771, No. 2, July 10, 2013 (for cloud cover); Kay et al., "Probability of CME Impact on Exoplanets Orbiting M Dwarfs and Solar-Like Stars," *Astrophysical Journal* Vol. 826, No. 2 (for the risk from stellar flares); and Luger et al., "Habitable Evaporated Cores: Transforming Mini-Neptunes into Super-Earths in the Habitable Zones of M Dwarfs," *Astrobiology* Vol. 15, Issue 1 (January 2015), pp. 57–88 (for atmosphere loss and planetary migration). Thanks to Paul Gilster of the *Centauri Dreams* blog for bringing these papers to my attention.

The Saurian shipbuilding factory was largely inspired by the Boeing Everett Factory in Everett, Washington, which I took a tour of during my trip to Seattle in 2011 for my sister Kathleen's wedding. Thanks to the folks at Boeing and to cousin Cynthia for taking me on the tour.

The memory of my beloved cat Natasha informed my treatment of Porthos's final days. It was difficult to dredge up those feelings again, but I feel it serves as a tribute to a dear friend who will always live on in my heart.

About the Author

CHRISTOPHER L. BENNETT is a lifelong resident of Cincinnati, Ohio, with bachelor's degrees in physics and history from the University of Cincinnati. He has written such critically acclaimed *Star Trek* novels as *Ex Machina* and *The Buried Age*; the *Star Trek: Titan* novels *Orion's Hounds* and *Over a Torrent Sea*; the two *Department of Temporal Investigations* novels *Watching the Clock* and *Forgotten History*; and the *Star Trek: Enterprise—Rise of the Federation* series. His shorter works include stories in the anniversary anthologies *Constellations*, *The Sky's the Limit*, *Prophecy and Change*, and *Distant Shores*, as well as the DTI novellas *The Collectors, Time Lock*, and *Shield of the Gods*. Beyond *Star Trek*, he has penned the novels *X-Men: Watchers on the Walls* and *Spider-Man: Drowned in Thunder*. His original work includes the hard science fiction superhero novel *Only Superhuman* and several novelettes in *Analog* and other science fiction magazines, some of which have been compiled in the e-book collection *Hub Space: Tales from the Greater Galaxy*. More information, annotations, and the author's blog can be found at christopherlbennett.wordpress.com.